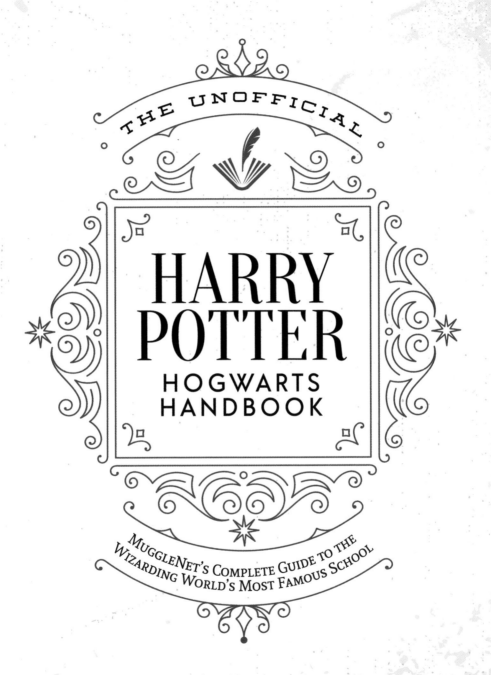

THE UNOFFICIAL

HARRY POTTER

HOGWARTS HANDBOOK

MuggleNet's Complete Guide to the Wizarding World's Most Famous School

A Guide to Britain's Most Well-Known Magical Institution

Although an impressive cast of characters lend their talents to helping Harry Potter defeat the Dark wizard Lord Voldemort, there is one constant anchoring presence in Harry's life, a silent beacon of hope, camaraderie and belonging presenting itself on a near-daily basis (and, well, no, it's not Hedwig, but she's in here, too): Hogwarts School of Witchcraft and Wizardry.

Situated in the remote reaches of the Scottish Highlands, the ancient wizarding institution is the first place the Boy Who Lived truly feels at home after a childhood locked away with his magic-hating aunt, uncle and cousin. It's a place where he can make friends, learn more about his parents and ultimately take his place within the ranks of the wizarding world. It's also a place where he comes face-to-face with the Sorting Hat, gruff gargoyles, gloomy ghosts (and ghost-like memories), maddening mandrakes, nervy Knarls, a flying Ford Anglia that's gone feral, a cursed creature lapping up unicorn blood, a village built by and for wizards and much more. So much of Harry's life revolves around the school that it can be difficult to keep track of exactly how much there is to explore and enjoy, both in the castle and beyond. That's where this book comes in.

If you've ever pondered how house-elves came to be employed in the Hogwarts kitchens, how not to get stuck in a trick step while navigating a shortcut (simple: know when to jump!), what the dungeons might look like to the Slytherins who call them home or how to get to Hogsmeade without coughing up a signed permission slip, this handbook has you covered. Alternatively, anyone wanting to know where they can house their owl in a place that isn't their dormitory, why the most famous wizarding institution in Britain was given a, shall we say, less-than-regal name, how to sign up for Gobstones (just kidding: you won't want to), what the story is behind that foreboding-looking, chained, bloody ghost who keeps lurking around or who that gray, translucent woman is, you're in luck.

Packed with enough history and lore to make Nearly Headless Nick's head spin, this definitive guide pulls no punches when it comes to mapping out everything there is to know about Hogwarts, from its classrooms to its Chamber of Secrets to the communities of creatures living just a short walk from the castle itself. We've also added references to past headmasters and headmistresses, professors' offices, secret passageways, intriguing artworks, school rules and more. Grab your acceptance letter and read on to learn what you can expect to encounter at the place that made Harry the wizard he is today.

Table of Contents

A Note from MuggleNet

As the #1 Wizarding World Resource Since 1999, MuggleNet has devoted more than two decades and counting to learning all there is to know about the inner workings of the *Harry Potter* universe, especially given how J.K. Rowling's internationally popular literary works have spawned a blockbuster film series, world-class theme parks and more. Incredibly, all of this world, in some way, revolves around one singular wizarding institution.

It's safe to say that without a guiding light like Hogwarts School of Witchcraft and Wizardry in his life, Harry Potter would not have turned out the way he did—and we don't just mean he wouldn't have been Sorted into Gryffindor. In fact, he might not have even been born in the first place, simply because his parents, a pair of bright young wizards in their own right, would not have had a school at which to meet. As anyone who's seen the hit play *Harry Potter and the Cursed Child* can attest, a world without the Boy Who Lived, a reality in which Lord Voldemort reigns supreme, is rather bleak indeed, synchronized dance moves aside.

At this ancient school, Harry comes to know who his friends are, as well as who would rather call him an enemy simply due to the lightning bolt-shaped scar on his forehead. Perhaps most importantly, he comes to understand his destiny within the framework of wizarding society: to defeat the most powerful wizard of all time (next to his beloved headmaster, anyway). But before he can vanquish Voldemort, he's got to learn how to ride a broom—which, fortunately, he's a pro at—make it through Potions class with Snape, avoid getting killed while visiting the third-floor corridor and pry himself away from staring at his parents in a mirror that reveals his wildest desires. Did we mention that was just in his first year at Hogwarts? Put simply, there's a lot more where that came from, and

Harry's adventures in Hogwarts's halls, classrooms, grounds and beyond involve confronting any number of threats, from a poltergeist to a three-headed dog to a werewolf to a horde of Voldemort's followers crashing through the castle walls in an epic final battle.

This definitive guide presents the collective knowledge of everything we know about Hogwarts throughout the *Harry Potter* canon, from its sprawling floor plan to its academic calendar to its numerous professors and much more. We've presented this knowledge within a series of chapters that dive into the school's history, the castle itself, the grounds and immediate surroundings, courses and extracurricular activities and those who inhabit this institution full-time, whether human or otherwise. We hope you enjoy poring over Hogwarts's secrets as much as we did uncovering them.

CHAPTER 1

HISTORY & TRADITIONS

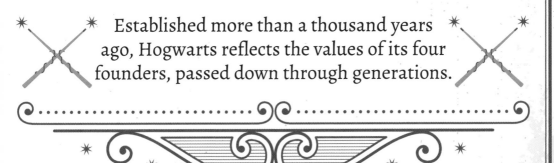

Established more than a thousand years ago, Hogwarts reflects the values of its four founders, passed down through generations.

The Founders

Godric Gryffindor

While Godric Gryffindor's exact birth date is unknown, the founder of Gryffindor House came into the world more than 1,000 years ago in a humble village in southwestern England. Modern witches and wizards know this village as Godric's Hollow.

Described by the Sorting Hat—which should know, given it once belonged to the man himself—as bold and daring, Gryffindor chose only the bravest, most noble students to join his House. Unlike fellow Hogwarts founder Salazar Slytherin, Gryffindor believed any witch or wizard should be welcome at Hogwarts, regardless of blood status, and challenged Slytherin's violent pure-blood supremacist beliefs. Following a serious argument between the two wizards, Slytherin departed Hogwarts forever, leaving Gryffindor and the other founders to continue shaping the school's legacy.

Outside of his school, Gryffindor's most important legacy was the fate of his exquisite goblin-made sword. In the days before the International Statute of Secrecy, witches and wizards were allowed to use magic freely, but many people—Gryffindor among them—believed it "unsporting" to fight Muggles with magic, so this sword became his constant companion. Since Gryffindor's death, it has magically appeared in the Sorting Hat for members of his Hogwarts House in peril, including Harry Potter.

THE SWORD OF GRYFFINDOR

A silver sword featuring a handle inlaid with rubies the "size of eggs," this weapon is engraved with Gryffindor's name just below its hilt. According to legend, only a true Gryffindor can pull it from the Sorting Hat, something

Harry proves during his second year at Hogwarts when he successfully retrieves it and uses it to slay the basilisk in the Chamber of Secrets. Afterward, the sword is kept in Dumbledore's office until Snape removes it during his tenure as headmaster. Ostensibly, he does this to place it in the Lestrange vault in Gringotts and deter attempts to steal it by Dumbledore's Army. In reality, he places a well-made fake in the vault and takes the genuine article to the Forest of Dean, where he uses his doe Patronus to lead Harry to the sword, which has the power to destroy Horcruxes now that it has imbibed basilisk venom. Unfortunately, Harry is also wearing a Horcrux—Slytherin's cursed locket. Sensing its impending demise, the magical item constricts around his neck and begins to strangle him. Ron retrieves the sword and cuts Harry free before destroying the Horcrux himself.

Later, Griphook (a goblin formerly employed at Gringotts) explains to Harry that the ancient sword was forged by goblin king Ragnuk the First. While goblins believe Gryffindor stole the sword from Ragnuk, the truth is quite different—in fact, the sword was made to Gryffindor's specifications. Ragnuk's desire to keep his creation led him to allege the wizard had stolen it. After Gryffindor foiled an attempt by goblins to reclaim the sword, the furious wizard threatened the goblins that if they ever tried to steal the weapon again, he would use it against them. There was no second reclamation attempt. Griphook also holds the view, common among goblins, that whoever makes an item owns it. This means that to goblinkind, any witches and wizards who purchase goblin artifacts are merely leasing them for their lifetime. He asks Harry for the sword in return for his help breaking into the Lestrange vault. As the group breaks into Gringotts, the goblin takes advantage of the chaos to escape with the sword.

However, it quickly becomes evident Gryffindor placed strong enchantments on the sword. Soon after, Neville Longbottom pulls it from the Sorting Hat during the Battle of Hogwarts, using it to behead the snake Nagini, Voldemort's final Horcrux. Aside from the Sorting Hat, the sword is the only known artifact associated with the Hogwarts founders not to be turned into a Horcrux and is used to destroy three: the Gaunt family ring, Slytherin's locket and Nagini.

Helga Hufflepuff

Helga Hufflepuff, who the Sorting Hat says—rather vaguely—comes from "valley broad" (a possible reference to the South Wales Valleys) has perhaps the most practical everyday legacy of the four founders. Skilled at food-related charms, Hufflepuff innovated many of the dishes served in Hogwarts's dining hall to this day.

Known for her considerable work ethic, Hufflepuff stood apart from the other Hogwarts founders in that she felt no obligation to choose students who displayed a particular personality trait. Instead, she pledged to teach any young witch or wizard, taking all students who remained after the other founders made their selections. Aside from dishing out delicious food, Hufflepuff is also noted for bringing house-elves to work in the kitchens at Hogwarts.

HUFFLEPUFF'S CUP

This small golden cup, the only known artifact associated with Hufflepuff, sports two finely wrought handles and is engraved with a badger, the mascot and emblem of Hufflepuff House.

Harry first sees the cup while viewing a memory from Hokey, a house-elf, in Dumbledore's Pensieve. The memory shows young Tom Riddle visiting Hokey's mistress, Hepzibah Smith, an old, rich witch and distant descendant of Helga Hufflepuff. She showed the cup, a prized heirloom, to Riddle in an effort to impress the handsome and charming young man while he was working as an assistant at Borgin and Burkes, purveyors of powerful and often Dark magical items. Hepzibah commented that the cup was alleged to have magical properties but admitted she had never tested them and did not know what they entailed.

Knowing such an artifact was within his grasp, Riddle orchestrated Smith's death just two days later, framing it so that her house-elf would take the blame. He then stole the cup, leaving his position at Borgin and Burkes before its disappearance could be traced back to him. Now styling himself as Lord Voldemort, Riddle used Smith's death as an opportunity to turn the cup into a Horcrux. The storied object fit perfectly with his desire to reject his Muggle father and upbringing and to tie himself to items with great magical history, especially those associated with the Hogwarts founders, in whose school he had found a home and learned about his powers.

Voldemort entrusted the cup to his loyal servant Bellatrix Lestrange, to be safely hidden in the Lestrange family vault at Gringotts Bank, thus connecting it to another ancient magical bloodline. In *Deathly Hallows*, after seeking refuge at Shell Cottage, Harry, Ron and Hermione team up with Griphook to break into the Lestrange vault. Like all the vault's treasure, the cup had the Gemino and Flagrante Curses placed upon it, which respectively cause it to duplicate and burn when touched. Despite this, the trio manage to retrieve the cup, becoming the first people in the bank's recorded history to successfully rob Gringotts. The mayhem of this robbery and their escape, however, finally alerts Voldemort to their hunt for Horcruxes.

Having lost the sword of Gryffindor over the course of their break-in, while others prepare for the Battle of Hogwarts, Hermione and Ron visit the Chamber of Secrets and retrieve basilisk fangs as an alternative means to destroy Horcruxes. There, Hermione uses one of the fangs to stab the cup, leaving it as mere mangled metal. It is the only Horcrux destroyed by Hermione, and, along with the Gaunt ring, it is one of only two Horcruxes that Harry does not see destroyed.

Rowena Ravenclaw

Described by many as "the most brilliant witch of her time," it's no surprise that Rowena Ravenclaw's statue in the Ravenclaw common room depicts her as a beautiful and intimidating woman. Rowena's greatest passion in life was learning, and she welcomed any student who demonstrated wit and intelligence. She is also believed to have come up with the school's name following a dream in which a warty hog led her up a cliff to a clearing with a lake on one side. After finding this location in real life, the founders chose it as the site of their new school.

Though she thrived in her public life, Rowena's family life was tumultuous at best, especially her relationship with her daughter, Helena. Jealous of her famous mother's intellect, Helena stole her mother's prized diadem in an attempt to gain Rowena's mental acuity and fled to Albania.

Soon after, Rowena fell mortally ill. On her deathbed, she requested a baron (who was enamored with Helena) to track Helena down so mother and daughter could reconcile. The baron found Helena in an Albanian forest, confessed his feelings, and urged her to return home, but Helena refused. In a fit of rage, the baron killed Helena before killing himself. Rowena never recovered from the events surrounding her daughter's betrayal and died shortly after, some say of a broken heart. She never revealed to the other founders what became of her diadem.

THE DIADEM OF RAVENCLAW

The only known artifact belonging to Rowena Ravenclaw is her diadem. Said to have been made by the founder herself, the fabled accessory was reportedly her most prized possession. It is engraved with the words "Wit beyond measure is man's greatest treasure." The item is enchanted to increase the wearer's wisdom, and according to lore, it went missing around the time of Rowena's death.

After Helena took off with her mother's diadem, she hid it in a hollow tree in an Albanian forest, where it remained untouched for centuries. While a student at Hogwarts, Tom Riddle ascertained its location by questioning Helena's ghostly form (a.k.a. the Gray Lady). Traveling to Albania, he retrieved the object and later made it into a Horcrux. Back at Hogwarts, Riddle then hid the cursed object in the Room of Requirement. Decades later, when Harry enters the room looking for a place to hide the Half-Blood Prince's copy of *Advanced Potion-Making* during his sixth year, he spots what he believes to be a "discolored old tiara" and uses the legendary diadem to mark the location of the book.

During the Battle of Hogwarts, Harry, Ron and Hermione search for the diadem after Harry learns through his connection to Voldemort's mind that the unknown Horcrux is at Hogwarts. Harry confronts the Gray Lady, who confesses to having told Riddle of its location and reveals her identity. After putting two and two together, Harry bolts off for the Room. But before he can retrieve the Horcrux, Draco Malfoy, Gregory Goyle and Vincent Crabbe arrive, and a fight breaks out. When Crabbe casts Fiendfyre, the room bursts into flames, destroying the Horcrux in the process.

RAVENCLAW'S HOME

According to the Sorting Hat, Rowena is "from glen." A glen is a narrow or deep valley, the word originating in Scottish and Irish Gaelic. It's possible Rowena hails from Scotland, where there are places such as Great Glen, the location of Loch Ness.

DID YOU KNOW?

Xenophilius Lovegood unsuccessfully tried to recreate Ravenclaw's diadem out of Wrackspurt siphons, Billywig propellers, and a Dirigible Plum.

Salazar Slytherin

Salazar Slytherin was one of the first recorded Parselmouths in history, and to this day, it's the ability to speak with snakes that is supposed to set Slytherin's descendants apart. Also an accomplished Legilimens, he used his powers to help create the Sorting Hat and imbued it with the power to sense great cunning and determination, qualities he likewise prized in his students. He is described as having a sinister, monkeyish figure and "a long, thin beard...almost to the bottom of [his] robes."

Slytherin believed students who were not pure-blood wizards should not be permitted at Hogwarts, a sentiment the other founders did not share. Gryffindor, disturbed, took issue with Slytherin's ideals, and with no one on his side, Slytherin left the school.

Before exiting the castle for good, Slytherin created the Chamber of Secrets as a way to ensure his beliefs would remain at Hogwarts—backed up by a deadly basilisk. By speaking Parseltongue at the entrance of the chamber, Slytherin or one of his heirs could unleash the monstrous creature within to purge the school of Muggle-borns.

His last remaining heir, Tom Riddle, later took the name Lord Voldemort and became known as the most powerful Dark wizard of all time.

SLYTHERIN'S LOCKET

This gold locket, a Slytherin family heirloom engraved with an ornate serpentine S made from emeralds, was eventually inherited by Merope Gaunt. She was forced to sell the locket to Borgin and Burkes for 10 Galleons. The locket was then sold to Hepzibah Smith; years later, Merope's only child, Tom Riddle, killed Hepzibah and made off with the item. After styling himself as Lord Voldemort, Riddle turned the locket into a Horcrux, placed it in a sea cave and used Kreacher, the Black family house-elf, to test its defenses. Riddle left him for dead in the cave, but Kreacher escaped and told his master, Regulus Black, about what transpired. Regulus, suspicious of

Voldemort's intentions, took with him a similar locket and returned to the site with Kreacher to exchange the real locket for a fake. Regulus fell victim to the Inferi hidden in the cave, and he ordered Kreacher to destroy the locket, which the house-elf couldn't manage to do.

The summer before Harry's fifth year, the locket is discovered in the drawing room at Grimmauld Place but is overlooked, as no one but Kreacher understands its importance. In 1996, Harry and Dumbledore attempt to acquire the original in the cave, but only find the fake instead. During Harry's Horcrux hunt in 1997, Kreacher reveals Mundungus Fletcher stole the original locket after the Order of the Phoenix abandoned Grimmauld Place. Dolores Umbridge then confiscated it when Mundungus was caught selling magical artifacts in Diagon Alley. Later, Harry, Ron and Hermione break into the Ministry of Magic and steal the locket from Umbridge. Not knowing how to destroy it, the trio hold on to the item for several months, wearing it in turns to keep it safe. Eventually, Ron destroys the Horcrux by using the sword of Gryffindor.

A LINK TO ILVERMORNY

One of Slytherin's distant descendants, Isolt Sayre, went on to found Ilvermorny School of Witchcraft and Wizardry in North America. After Isolt stole her evil aunt Gormlaith Gaunt's wand (which had belonged to Slytherin himself), Gormlaith sought her revenge; she tracked Isolt down and, using Parseltongue, commanded the wand to sleep, rendering it inactive. Since Isolt was not a Parselmouth, she could not reactivate it. After defeating Gormlaith once and for all, she buried the wand on the school grounds—within a year, it sprouted into a tree that contained powerful medicinal properties.

POWERFUL ENCHANTMENTS

The only way to open the locket is to speak to it in Parseltongue. As a Horcrux, the cursed item influences its wearer in numerous ways, similar to how the diary Horcrux affects Ginny Weasley— for example, it can feel burning hot to the touch, create a vision of its wearer's worst fears, and move in such a way that it almost strangles Harry.

The School Crest

The crest of Hogwarts School of Witchcraft and Wizardry is a shield—formally known as an "escutcheon"—that depicts the symbols for each House in their respective colors.

Moving clockwise from the top left, it features the Gryffindor lion in scarlet and gold, the Slytherin snake in green and silver, the Ravenclaw eagle in blue and bronze and the Hufflepuff badger in yellow and black. These four animal mascots encircle the letter "H," which in the case of a crest is called an "escutcheon of pretense." A banner beneath the shield displays the Hogwarts motto: *Draco dormiens nunquam titillandus.* Translated from Latin, it reads, "Never tickle a sleeping dragon."

Each House, for that matter, has an individual crest that derives from the main school crest. While depictions of the crests vary, they all involve the House's symbol and colors.

The symbolism of each crest represents the values of each Hogwarts House. Gryffindor, with its bold colors of scarlet and gold, is known to value bravery, daring, nerve and chivalry. These qualities are often attributed to its symbolic animal, the lion. Gryffindor is also loosely connected to the element of fire.

Slytherin, its chief rival, is known to value ambition, leadership, self-preservation, cunning and resourcefulness. These qualities are often attributed to its symbolic animal, the snake. The House is loosely connected to the element of water, represented in its colors of green and silver.

More than any other House, Ravenclaw is known to value intelligence, knowledge, curiosity, creativity and wit over all else, qualities that are often associated with its symbolic animal, the eagle. Ravenclaw is also loosely connected to the element of air, represented in its colors of blue and bronze.

Last but certainly not least, Hufflepuff is known to value hard work, dedication, patience, loyalty and fair play. These qualities are evocative of its symbolic animal, the badger. Hufflepuff is also loosely connected to the element of earth, represented in its colors of yellow and black.

THE HOGWARTS MOTTO

The etymology is as follows:
Draco = dragon
dormiens = sleeping
nunquam = never
titillandus = tickle
While many British Muggle schools have inspirational or fanciful mottos, the Hogwarts motto is meant to be practical advice.

THE HOGWARTS SCHOOL SONG

The Hogwarts school song is an anthem to the school with no official melody. Each student is encouraged to create a unique tune, tempo and duration when singing. The last time the song was known to be sung was on September 1, 1991, during the welcome feast of Harry's first year. The song appears to have been excluded from feast activities in times of crisis.

The Houses

Gryffindor

Gryffindor House is one of four Houses that first-year students can be Sorted into at Hogwarts School of Witchcraft and Wizardry. Godric Gryffindor, the House's founder, instructed the Sorting Hat to choose students who possess or value courage, daring, nerve and chivalry. Because of this, Gryffindor is also sometimes associated with recklessness and impulsivity. This House has produced many notable wizards, including members of organizations like the Order of the Phoenix and Dumbledore's Army.

QUIDDITCH

The Gryffindor Quidditch team wins the Quidditch Cup during the 1993-1994, 1995-1996 and 1996-1997 seasons. They had previously not won the Cup since at least 1990. Team members wear scarlet robes during matches.

FAST FACTS

- Gryffindor is represented by a lion as well as the colors scarlet and gold.
- In the hourglass that tracks House points, Gryffindor's progress is represented by rubies.
- Gryffindor's House ghost is Sir Nicholas de Mimsy-Porpington, otherwise known as Nearly Headless Nick.

NOTEWORTHY WIZARDS

• Sirius Black
Original member of the Order of the Phoenix, suspected mass murderer, first person to break out of Azkaban unaided

• Hermione Granger
Fights in the Battle of Hogwarts, destroys one of Voldemort's Horcruxes, Minister of Magic

• Lee Jordan
Runs a wartime resistance radio program

• Harry Potter
Defeats Voldemort, Auror, Head of the Department of Magical Law Enforcement

• James & Lily Potter
Original members of the Order of the Phoenix, thrice defy Voldemort, give their lives for their son

• Celestina Warbeck
International singing sensation

• Fred & George Weasley
Start Weasleys' Wizard Wheezes, fight in the Battle of Hogwarts

• Ginny Weasley
Fights in the Battle of Hogwarts, plays for the Holyhead Harpies, Senior Quidditch Correspondent for the Daily Prophet

• Ron Weasley
Destroys one of Voldemort's Horcruxes, Auror, runs Weasleys' Wizard Wheezes

Hufflepuff

Helga Hufflepuff, Hufflepuff's founder, instructed the Sorting Hat to choose students who possess or value the following qualities: hard work, dedication, patience, loyalty and fair play. As a result of Hufflepuff's policy of accepting any student regardless of aptitude, the House is sometimes thought of as producing less talented wizards and witches than the other Houses. This, however, is simply not true. Many successful and influential members of the magical world were Hufflepuffs, including Pomona Sprout, Newt Scamander and Nymphadora Tonks. In fact, throughout its history, Hufflepuff has produced the fewest Dark wizards.

QUIDDITCH

Much to their delight, the Hufflepuff Quidditch Team wins a match against Gryffindor during the 1993-1994 season by a whopping 100 points. Despite several successful matches, the team does not win a Cup between the 1991-1992 season and the 1996-1997 season. Team members wear canary-yellow robes.

FAST FACTS

- Hufflepuff is represented by a badger as well as the colors yellow and black.
- In the hourglass that tracks House points, Hufflepuff's progress is represented by diamonds.
- Hufflepuff's House ghost is the Fat Friar.

NOTEWORTHY WIZARDS

- Hannah Abbott
*Fights in the Battle of Hogwarts,
runs the Leaky Cauldron*
- Cedric Diggory
Triwizard Champion
- Artemisia Lufkin
First female Minister of Magic, 1798-1811
- Eglantine Puffett
Inventor of the Self-Soaping Dishcloth
- Newt Scamander
Notable magizoologist, author of Fantastic
Beasts and Where to Find Them
- Grogan Stump
Minister of Magic, 1811-1819
- Nymphadora Tonks
*Member of the Order of the Phoenix,
Auror, Metamorphmagus*
- Bridget Wenlock
*13th-century arithmancer, famous for her
theories on the number seven*
- Hengist of Woodcroft
Founded Hogsmeade

Ravenclaw

R owena Ravenclaw, the famously clever witch who founded the House, instructed the Sorting Hat to choose students who possess or value the following qualities: intelligence, wit, learning and creativity. But like any other House, Ravenclaw is also sometimes associated with negative qualities—in this case, extreme competitiveness and eccentricity.

QUIDDITCH

During the final match of the 1996–1997 season, the Ravenclaw Quidditch Team loses the Quidditch Cup to Gryffindor by 310 points. Despite pulling off a few solid wins, the team does not win a Cup between the 1991–1992 season and the 1996–1997 season. Team members sport blue robes.

FAST FACTS

- Ravenclaw is represented by an eagle as well as the colors blue and bronze.
- In the hourglass that tracks House points, Ravenclaw's progress is represented by blue sapphires.
- Ravenclaw's House ghost is Helena Ravenclaw, otherwise known as "The Gray Lady." She was the daughter of Ravenclaw House's founder, Rowena Ravenclaw.

NOTEWORTHY WIZARDS

- Millicent Bagnold
Minister of Magic, 1980-1990
- Perpetua Fancourt
Inventor of the Lunascope
- Luna Lovegood
*Fights in the Battle of Hogwarts,
wizarding naturalist*
- Xenophilius Lovegood
Editor of The Quibbler
- Lorcan McLaird
Minister of Magic, 1923-1925
- Laverne de Montmorency
Inventor of love potions
- Uric the Oddball
Famous during the Middle Ages for his strangeness
- Garrick Ollivander
Most renowned wandmaker in Britain
- Ignatia Wildsmith
Inventor of Floo Powder

Slytherin

Salazar Slytherin's instruction for the Sorting Hat was to select students who possess or value cunning, resourcefulness, leadership and ambition. Like any Hogwarts House, there can also be a downside to these values, and Slytherin is often associated with self-preservation that borders on selfishness and a belief that the end always justifies the means.

A pure-blood fanatic, Salazar Slytherin's original vision for Hogwarts was limited only to pure-blood students—that is, students born to magical parents who come from wholly magical families. While valuing blood status is still strongly associated with Slytherin House, Muggle-born Slytherins are not unheard of, if exceedingly rare. This House has produced more Dark wizards than any other House, including Lord Voldemort, who valued blood purity above all else.

QUIDDITCH

The Slytherin Quidditch Team has a (some would say earned) reputation for cheating and unsportsmanlike conduct. Much to their chagrin, the Slytherin Quidditch Team does not win the Quidditch Cup between 1993 and 1997. Team members wear green robes during matches.

FAST FACTS

- Slytherin is represented by a snake as well as the colors green and silver.
- In the hourglass that tracks House points, Slytherin's progress is represented by emeralds.
- Slytherin's House ghost is the Bloody Baron.

NOTEWORTHY WIZARDS

- Regulus Black
*Ex-Death Eater, stole and attempted to destroy
one of Voldemort's Horcruxes*
- Bellatrix Lestrange
Notorious Death Eater, escaped Azkaban
- Draco Malfoy
Master of the Elder Wand, low-level Death Eater
- Narcissa Malfoy
*Lies to Voldemort, affecting the outcome
of the Battle of Hogwarts*
- Scorpius Malfoy
Protects wizarding society from Voldemort's daughter, Delphi
- Merlin
*Member of the Court of King Arthur, founder
of the Order of Merlin, Charms specialist*
- Albus Severus Potter
Protects wizarding society from Voldemort's daughter, Delphi
- Tom Riddle
*Heir of Slytherin, developed an army of followers, took over the
Ministry of Magic and Hogwarts, created seven Horcruxes*
- Rodolphus Lestrange
Notorious Death Eater, escaped Azkaban

Sorting Hat

The four Houses of Hogwarts have at least one thing in common: they don't choose their members. That task falls to the Sorting Hat, which has been used to assign ("Sort") every student to the appropriate House for nearly as long as the school has been in operation. The task originally fell to the school's four founders (see page 8), who each selected the students they wanted in their respective, eponymous Houses. When faced with the question of how this tradition would continue after their deaths, the founders elected to enchant Godric Gryffindor's pointed wizard hat.

Since then, every September before the start-of-year feast, first-year students have been called one by one in alphabetical order to sit in front of the assembled students and faculty in the Great Hall and wear the sentient hat. Having been given the power of Legilimency, the hat can look inside its wearer's mind and formulate which House would be the best fit. During this process, the student can hear the hat's voice inside their head, musing over which House traits they possess. Once the Sorting Hat comes to a decision, it declares that student's House by shouting through the tear in its brim.

While the Sorting Hat quickly obliges Harry's wish not to be Sorted into Slytherin, it sometimes takes a bit longer to work out a suitable answer. If the length of its deliberation exceeds five minutes (as it did with Professor McGonagall and Peter Pettigrew), the student is called a "Hatstall." These events are rare, only occurring about once every 50 years.

The first time Harry sees the ancient, traditional pointed wizard's hat shortly after his arrival at Hogwarts, he describes it as "patched and frayed and extremely dirty." Later, during his second year, Harry encounters the hat in Dumbledore's office, where it is stored when not in use for the Sorting ceremony. Fearing that he belongs in Slytherin, Harry asks it for reassurance—but to his dismay, the stubborn hat stands firmly behind its stance that he would have done well in Slytherin (it has never walked back any of its choices).

When Harry later faces down the basilisk in the Chamber of Secrets, he proves himself a true Gryffindor by drawing the sword of Gryffindor from the hat and slaying the beast. Years later, Neville, who was almost Sorted into Hufflepuff, does the same and promptly beheads Nagini during the Battle of Hogwarts.

THE SONGS OF THE SORTING HAT

The Sorting Hat opens each Hogwarts start-of-year feast by singing a tune about the how the Sorting ceremony works as well as the origins of the school and the traits associated with each House. Incredibly, the Sorting Hat presents a new song every year. Owing to various misadventures on his journeys to Hogwarts, Harry only hears the Sorting Hat's song in his first, fourth and fifth year. In the last song he hears, the hat warns the students that they must stand united to face the troubling times soon to come.

NOTABLE HATSTALLS

Minerva McGonagall, head of Gryffindor House during Harry's time at the school (and a Head Girl of the same during her seventh year as a student at Hogwarts) was nearly Sorted into Ravenclaw. The Sorting Hat took five and a half minutes to determine (correctly it would seem) that Gryffindor was the right fit.

Peter Pettigrew was nearly Sorted into Slytherin, but after a lengthy deliberation, the hat declared Gryffindor was the proper House for the boy who would later sell out his friends in service to the Dark Lord.

Hermione and Neville, though technically not Hatstalls, did slow the Sorting Hat's pace a bit during their respective turns under its brim. It took the hat nearly four minutes to decide between Gryffindor and Ravenclaw for Hermione. Neville, for his part, all but begged the hat to put him in Hufflepuff, somewhat intimidated by Gryffindor's reputation for acts of derring-do. The young man's role in the downfall of Voldemort would suggest the hat, once again, got it right.

Prefects

Every year at Hogwarts, the headmaster or headmistress selects eight upstanding fifth-year students—a young witch and wizard from each House—to be made prefects of the school, a position which grants them authority over their peers. Prefects are required to carry out extra tasks such as guiding new students to their dormitories, patrolling the castle corridors for students breaking the rules and supervising younger students during break times. Prefects can also assign detention. Perks of the job include a carriage dedicated for their exclusive use at the front of the Hogwarts Express (see page 46) and access to the luxurious prefects' bathroom on the fifth floor (see page 84). Students who are chosen to be prefects keep the position for the rest of their time at Hogwarts, which means that at any given time, there are 24 prefects at the school (eight fifth years, eight sixth years and eight seventh years). New prefects receive a letter informing them they have been chosen along with their usual book list in the summer before the school year starts. They also receive a badge emblazoned with the letter "P" on it to wear on their robes as part of their school uniform. Since Ron's badge is described as red and gold and features a lion behind the "P," it can be assumed that prefect badges indicate the House of the wearer.

KNOWN PREFECTS OF HOGWARTS

Hannah Abbott	Robert Hilliard	Padma Patil
Penelope Clearwater	Remus Lupin	Tom Riddle
Cedric Diggory	Teddy Lupin	Gabriel Truman
Albus Dumbledore	Ernie MacMillan	Bill Weasley
Lily Evans	Draco Malfoy	Charlie Weasley
Gemma Farley	Lucius Malfoy	Percy Weasley
Anthony Goldstein	Minerva McGonagall	Ron Weasley
Hermione Granger	Pansy Parkinson	

Head Boy & Girl

The ultimate distinction for any seventh-year Hogwarts student (excluding any special awards such as the one Tom Riddle received for "catching" the culprit behind the attacks on Muggle-borns in his fifth year) is to be made Head Boy or Head Girl by the headmaster or headmistress of the school.

While many Head Boys and Head Girls also serve the school as prefects (e.g., Percy Weasley), this is not always the case. Harry's parents were Head Boy and Head Girl during their final year at Hogwarts, but his father was never a prefect, as he spent too much time in detention (at least according to Sirius Black). Once chosen, these students are in charge of distributing duties to the school prefects and leading the student populace. When the Hogwarts professors search the castle for the escaped convict Sirius Black during Harry's third year, the Head Boy and Girl serve as stand-ins for the staff and assume responsibility for the well-being of all the students gathered in the Great Hall. Like prefects, these students wear a badge on their robes to denote their position. Percy Weasley, for example, is quite proud of (if not slightly obsessed with) his badge—frequently polishing it and wearing it over the school holidays.

A list of former Head Boys is kept in the Trophy Room (which happens to include Tom Riddle's name, as Harry, Ron and Hermione find out) and a similar list is presumably kept for Head Girls.

KNOWN HEAD BOYS AND GIRLS OF HOGWARTS

Albus Dumbledore c. 1898–99
Tom Riddle 1944–45
Minerva McGonagall 1953–54
James Potter 1977–78

Lily Evans 1977–78
Bill Weasley c. 1989–90
Percy Weasley 1993–94
Teddy Lupin 2015–16

The House Cup

At the end of each academic year, the House with the most points for excellent behavior is awarded the House Cup. Throughout the school year, points are awarded or docked based on students' actions, whether submitting quality work in class and performing acts of bravery or engaging in misbehavior and rule-breaking offenses. Houses also gain points when their Quidditch teams win matches. In the entrance hall, enchanted hourglasses filled with gems representing each House keep track of points. At the feast at the end of the year, the Great Hall is decorated in the colors of the winning House. It should be noted the winners of the House Cup after Harry's first three years are unknown.

Teachers and prefects can award or deduct points. During Harry's fifth year, this power is extended to Umbridge's Inquisitorial Squad, who can also deduct points from prefects, which prefects cannot do to their fellows. This contributes to Gryffindor losing all of the points they had accrued over the course of the year, though Professor McGonagall awards 50 each to the students who fought at the Department of Mysteries, including 50 to Ravenclaw for Luna Lovegood's participation, offsetting much of the malevolent point docking by the Slytherins in Umbridge's employ. Even discounting Malfoy's abuse of power as a member of the Inquisitorial Squad, the points system has a few flaws due to favoritism and bias. Professor Snape is quick to deduct points from Gryffindor for minor infractions while ignoring blatant bullying by members of his own House, whereas Professor McGonagall pulls no punches when it comes to disciplining her House. Dumbledore, however, showers Gryffindor with just enough points to win the House Cup at the eleventh hour more than once.

In 1992, Slytherin is poised to win the Cup for the seventh year in a row until Dumbledore awards last-minute points to Gryffindor, launching them from last place into first. Fifty points go to Ron for his impressive game of wizard chess, 50 to Hermione for her use of logic to figure out the potions riddle to get Harry to the Sorcerer's Stone and 60 to Harry for his courage in saving the Stone from Voldemort. Dumbledore then awards Neville 10 points for his bravery in standing up to his friends, clinching the Cup for Gryffindor in a narrow win over Slytherin House.

Gryffindor wins the Cup again in 1993 after Dumbledore gives Harry and Ron 200 points each for rescuing Ginny from the Chamber of Secrets. A third consecutive victory occurs in 1993, in large part thanks to Gryffindor winning the Quidditch Cup.

OTHER REASONS FOR POINTS AWARDED

- Defeating a mountain troll
- Correct answers in class
- Confronting a Boggart in class
- Passing a watering can (to express approval of a *Quibbler* interview)
- Catching Harry escaping from the Room of Requirement
- Alerting the world to the return of Voldemort

REASONS FOR POINTS DOCKED

- Not helping another student in class
- Cheek
- Fighting
- Helping another student in class
- Out of bed at midnight
- Taking a library book out of the castle
- Tackling a troll alone
- Lateness
- Being an insufferable know-it-all
- Throwing a crocodile heart at another student
- Dressing up as Dementors during a Quidditch match to sabotage the Gryffindor Seeker
- Canoodling in a rosebush during the Yule Ball (presumably)
- Discussing social life in class
- Reading magazines under the table in class
- Interrupting in class
- Talking back to a teacher
- Yelling in the Great Hall
- Giving an interview to *The Quibbler*
- Being rude about the new headmistress*
- Contradicting a member of the Inquisitorial Squad*
- Shirt untucked*
- "I don't like you"*
- Being Muggle-born*
- Muggle attire

*Docked by Draco Malfoy as a member of the Inquisitorial Squad

Dining at Hogwarts

Students and faculty at Hogwarts dine together for three meals a day, each served in the school's Great Hall (see page 56). In addition to regular meals, the hall is also the location of a handful of special feasts, one marking the beginning of the school year, one commemorating the end of it and two feasts celebrating Halloween and Christmas, respectively. While the feasts are large-scale spectacles, even day-to-day dining at Hogwarts is a staggering experience, with a generous array of food on offer.

The Great Hall features four long tables (one for the students of each House) and a head table at the end of the hall, which is reserved for Hogwarts staff. In the middle of this table is a special, throne-like chair where the headmaster or headmistress takes their place as head of the school. Floating candles permeate the space, and the ceiling is charmed to resemble the sky (including the weather).

When breakfast, lunch and dinner begin, the serving dishes lining the Great Hall's tables magically fill with delicious, freshly cooked food, courtesy of the house-elves running Hogwarts's kitchens (see page 72). The house-elves who work the kitchens serve a wide variety of appetizing foods featuring ingredients grown on Hogwarts grounds, including but not limited to meats, vegetables, pies, potatoes, pumpkin juice, tea and traditional English dishes such as steak and kidney pie, Yorkshire pudding and treacle tart, all of which are magically sent through the ceiling of the kitchens to the tables above. For special occasions, seasonal or thematic treats—including turkey, bouillabaisse, eggnog and Christmas pudding—are incorporated into unforgettable feasts. Students and staff are free to help themselves to whatever they like for the duration of the meal; afterward, the plates are magically cleared.

HOGWARTS FEASTS

Though it might be possible for a student to become desensitized to the wonder and magic of Hogwarts, the sumptuous feasts hosted in the Great Hall still manage to evoke amazement and awe.

START-OF-TERM

On September 1, Hogwarts has its start-of-term feast. Before the feast begins, first year students are escorted into the Great Hall by one of the teachers and led up to the front of the hall between the House tables and the professors' table to conduct the Sorting ceremony (see page 26). The feast concludes with announcements of new staff members and messages about the school, and each year, the headmaster or headmistress reminds students about the Forbidden Forest (see page 134) being out of bounds. During Harry's time at Hogwarts, the feast is also a time to share Filch's list of banned items.

HALLOWEEN

On October 31, Hogwarts celebrates Halloween with a massive feast in the Great Hall. Thousands of live bats and giant candlelit pumpkins decorate the expansive dining area, and (naturally) sweets and treats of all stripes are part of the spread. A few tricks are also part of the menu, however, as the Hogwarts ghosts typically make an appearance.

CHRISTMAS

The Christmas feast is a sumptuous holiday affair for all students and professors who stay at Hogwarts over the Christmas break. The Great Hall is decorated with giant frost-covered Christmas trees, festoons of holly and mistletoe, snow falling from the ceiling and wizard crackers (which are just like Christmas crackers, except much louder and with more exciting prizes inside).

END-OF-TERM

To celebrate and recognize the successes of the school year, Hogwarts holds its end-of-year feast on the last night of its academic calendar. The feast concludes with the announcement of the winner of the House Cup, beginning with last place. The Great Hall is draped in the winning House's colors. Overall, this feast is seen as an especially happy occasion, with students either returning home for the summer or, for seventh years, leaving Hogwarts to begin the next phase of their lives as witches and wizards.

Holidays

Like most institutions, Hogwarts makes a point of getting its faculty and student body into the spirit of the holidays that fall during the academic year, and the staff pull out all the stops when it comes to creating the right atmosphere for special occasions. These fantastic fetes extend beyond feasts thrown in the Great Hall and are marked by stunning decorations throughout the castle and grounds, casual get-togethers and large-scale themed events. During Harry's time at Hogwarts, many of these events (like nearly everything involving the Boy Who Lived) become memorable for reasons unrelated to the calendar year.

HALLOWEEN

As an ancient place of magical instruction, Hogwarts has more than its share of ghosts (plus a poltergeist), as well as strange, frightening and otherwise noteworthy creatures living on its grounds and beyond. For reasons one can only assume are tied to the nature of Halloween, such beings often make themselves known in dramatic fashion on October 31—and that's to say nothing of the monstrous feast (see page 33) served at the school to celebrate All Hallows' Eve.

It's during Harry's first Halloween feast that Professor Quirrell interrupts the festivities to announce that a troll is in the dungeon. As students are escorted back to their dormitories, Harry and Ron go looking for Hermione, who had reportedly been crying in a girls' bathroom. Even though they manage to accidentally lock the troll in with her, Ron casts *Wingardium Leviosa* on its club and hits it on the head, knocking the creature out cold.

The school dungeons, a moody locale no matter the season, also double as the site of Nearly Headless Nick's deathday party on Halloween the following school year. To commemorate the 500th anniversary of Nick's execution, the Gryffindor ghost requests that Harry, Ron and Hermione attend; also at Nick's request, once at the party, Harry mentions how frightening he finds Nick in order to sway Sir Patrick Delaney-Podmore to admit him into the Headless Hunt, despite the fact that his head is still technically attached due to his botched beheading. Ghosts from across Britain attend—including the Wailing Widow, who travels all the way from Kent—as do other Hogwarts spirits, most notably Peeves (although he's technically a poltergeist) and Moaning Myrtle.

The menu comprises rotting food (including a cake in the shape of a tombstone), and the pungent, rancid flavor makes it almost possible for ghosts to taste it. Entertainment is provided by an orchestra of musical saws. After Harry fails to convince Sir Patrick that Nick is sufficiently frightening, the Hunt begins playing a game of Head Hockey while Nick attempts to give a speech. Upon leaving, Harry hears a voice threatening to "rip and kill" and follows it until he discovers a Petrified Mrs. Norris on a wall that bears a foreboding message: The Chamber of Secrets has been opened.

As a third-year student, Harry and his peers are ushered into the Great Hall following the Halloween feast when Sirius Black, recently escaped from Azkaban, attempts to gain entry to Gryffindor Tower that evening. But when Black fails to give the password, the Fat Lady refuses to allow him in, and he slashes her portrait. Dumbledore conjures sleeping bags for students to spend the night in the Great Hall while the staff search the castle for the fugitive at large.

When Hogwarts hosts the Triwizard Tournament during Harry's fourth year, the Halloween feast coincides with the Goblet of Fire's selection of the tournament champions. Naturally, the goblet causes quite the stir when Harry's name emerges from its flames to indicate he has been chosen as the fourth champion—particularly scary given how dangerous the tournament is known to be.

CHRISTMAS

Students at Hogwarts have the option to remain at school or return home during this especially festive time of year. The staff decorate the Great Hall with mistletoe, holly and a whopping 12 fir trees bearing icicles and candles. To top it off, spells are cast on the ceiling to make it seem like it's snowing indoors and suits of armor around the castle are enchanted to sing carols. A massive traditional turkey dinner with peas, potatoes, gravy and cranberry sauce is presented to all those who remain at Hogwarts, along with flaming Christmas puddings for dessert.

Presents are left at the foot of students' beds on Christmas morning, and a feast is held in the Great Hall. During Harry's first year, he's ecstatic to have a place to stay other than the Dursleys', and even more elated when he finds the presents piled at the foot of his bed. During his second year, Harry, Ron and Hermione follow the Christmas feast in the Great Hall with one of a very different sort when they create and consume Polyjuice Potion during Christmas break. Only a handful of students remain at Hogwarts during Harry's third year, so the students and faculty sit at the same table for the feast. During his fourth year, Harry and many other students remain at Hogwarts for the Triwizard Tournament tradition of the Yule Ball, which is held on Christmas night.

Professor Slughorn hosts an exclusive, invitation-only Christmas party on the last day of classes before Christmas break during Harry's sixth year at the school. The party takes place in Slughorn's office (see page 75), decorated with colored hangings and lit by real fairies. Slug Club members are invited and allowed to bring guests. In addition to Hogwarts students and staff, attendees include former Slug Club members such as author Eldred Worple and his vampire companion Sanguini. That night, Filch catches Draco Malfoy on his way to or from working on the Vanishing Cabinet in the Room of Requirement. As a cover story, Draco claims he was trying to gatecrash the party.

Slughorn is willing to let Draco stay, but Snape, as Malfoy's Head of House, insists on escorting him away.

VALENTINE'S DAY

Although wizards celebrate Valentine's Day (and regard it with just as much excitement or disdain as their Muggle counterparts), Hogwarts does not usually throw a big celebration as it does with other holidays, but Harry sees one cringeworthy exception.

During Harry's second year, Defense Against the Dark Arts professor Gilderoy Lockhart makes a point of celebrating the day in order to boost spirits—much to the displeasure of his fellow teachers—decorating the Great Hall with pink flowers and bewitching the ceiling to release heart-shaped confetti. Lockhart also arranges for dwarves dressed as cupids to deliver singing valentines to students throughout the day. When Ginny sends one to deliver a message to Harry, it forcibly tackles him in a corridor and sits on his ankles to deliver its note, much to Harry's dismay. For his part, Lockhart receives a particularly large number of valentines.

For students able to visit Hogsmeade (see page 139), the intimate (or as Harry calls it, "cramped") Madam Puddifoot's Tea Shop is a popular Valentine's Day destination. Decorated with wall-to-wall romantic decor like cherubs, bows and frills, the cafe makes it a point to cater to couples. During his fifth year, Harry and his love interest, Cho Chang, take part in this unofficial tradition, but when an awkward Harry tactlessly brings up needing to see Hermione in the middle of their date, Cho becomes jealous and storms out.

The Triwizard Tournament

Established about 300 years after Hogwarts's founding, the Triwizard Tournament is a competition designed to test the wizarding prowess of Europe's three most prestigious schools of magic—Hogwarts, Beauxbatons and Durmstrang—while fostering cooperation and friendship between the continent's magical communities. During the year-long event, a champion is named from each school, and whichever fares best in a series of three magical challenges hoists the Triwizard Cup in victory. The schools take turns hosting the event, which is traditionally held once every five years.

These challenges are no mere tests of magical book learning: The Triwizard Tournament is not for the faint of heart, even for those who are participating as mere spectators. In 1792, a cockatrice got loose, and the rogue creature "went on the rampage" (as Hermione puts it), managing to injure the heads of all three wizarding schools. After five centuries of sending teenage students into perilous—and often fatal—battles with beasts, the tournament was discontinued in the face of an ever-mounting death toll. Ever since, generations of wizarding children have grown up hearing about this fabled contest, never expecting it to return.

In 1994, however, thanks to a joint effort of the Ministry of Magic and the three wizarding schools, the Triwizard Tournament is reinstated, with Hogwarts serving as the host school. At first the festivities go as planned: Students from Beauxbatons and Durmstrang arrive and are feted by their Hogwarts hosts, and the air is abuzz with anticipation. As with tournaments past, the selection process to determine which student will represent each school starts with a ceremony involving a large, roughly hewn cup called the Goblet of Fire.

This antiquated artifact is filled to the brim with dancing blue flames that only ignite when a new tournament begins. It is kept in a wooden chest embedded with jewels for safekeeping and is removed by tapping the top of the chest three times with a wand. Students who are interested in competing write their name and school on a piece of parchment, which they then add into the cup, and the Goblet selects the one student from each school it has judged is most worthy of competing in the tournament, expelling each name out of its flames, one by one, to be announced by the head of the host school—in this case, Professor Dumbledore.

Once the Goblet makes its selections, the champions are magically bound to a contract that does not allow them to resign from the event—in other words, whether they're ready or not, they're forced to compete. In an attempt to prevent the kind of bloodshed that marred past tournaments, Dumbledore creates an Age Line to prevent students under the age of 17 from placing their names in the Goblet. On Halloween, the Goblet of Fire selects its champions: Fleur Delacour (Beauxbatons), Viktor Krum (Durmstrang), Cedric Diggory (Hogwarts) and, for the first time in the event's history, a fourth champion (and second Hogwarts student, who is also underage)— Harry. As it turns out, Barty Crouch, Jr., (disguised as Mad-Eye Moody) Confunded the Goblet to convince it that four schools were competing and entered Harry's name under the fourth school. Since the Goblet represents a binding contract, Harry has no choice but to compete.

Before the first task can begin in earnest, the Weighing of the Wands ceremony takes place. Each champion's wand is closely examined and tested in a small classroom to ensure it works properly. During the 1994 tournament, this ceremony is presided over by master wandmaker Garrick Ollivander.

Each Triwizard Tournament consists of three tasks, designed to test each champion's magical prowess, daring, deduction and grace under pressure. It should also be noted that cheating is a traditional, if unofficial, part of the tournament; it is not unheard of for champions to be given help by their school head, even while those individuals serve as tournament judges.

The first task of the 1994 tournament, which takes place on November 24, 1994, sees each champion try to steal a golden egg from a nesting dragon. Each champion is able to retrieve their egg, which contains a clue about the nature of the second task. On February 24, 1995, this second task requires the champions to go into the lake and retrieve a loved one who has been held hostage by merpeople. The only person unable to complete the task is Fleur, who is attacked by grindylows as she navigates the lake's murky waters.

The final task, held on June 24, 1995, has the champions enter a maze filled with beasts, hexes and other dangerous obstacles in an effort to reach the Triwizard Cup at the maze's center. Harry and Cedric arrive at the same time and agree to hoist the Cup together in dual victory. When they touch it, however, they are transported to a graveyard, as the Cup had been transformed into a Portkey. Harry watches in horror as Peter Pettigrew kills Cedric, and Voldemort is resurrected. Voldemort tortures Harry before challenging him to a duel—but when the two fire spells at each other, their twin wand cores connect, causing Priori Incantatem, the Reverse Spell effect, and the ghostly spirits of Voldemort's victims buy Harry enough time to grab the Cup, which transports him back to Hogwarts. Following these horrific events, the tradition of the Triwizard Tournament is once again abandoned.

YULE BALL

Beyond the challenges each competitor must face as part of the Triwizard Tournament, there is another event associated with the tournament that can prove equally difficult to navigate: the Yule Ball, a lavish event that takes place on the evening of Christmas Day. The Triwizard champions are required to attend the ball with a dance partner since they are traditionally the couples who open the festivities with a dance. The dress code for the ball is formal, and all in attendance are required to wear dress robes.

In 1994, the festivities begin promptly at 8:00 p.m. when the champions and their partners are welcomed into the Great Hall (see page 56) to thunderous applause. Attendance to the ball is only for students in fourth year and above, but students in the lower years can attend if an older student invites them. The Great Hall is decorated with garlands of mistletoe, sparkling silver frost covers the walls, and the usual House tables are swapped out for smaller tables laid with gold plates and goblets. Guests are served their dinner by specifically requesting from their plates and goblets what they want from the menu. The food then magically appears in front of them. After dinner is served, the champions and their partners start the ball in earnest with a formal dance followed by entertainment (the wizarding band the Weird Sisters play at the event the year Harry attends). The ball concludes at midnight, though many students wish it would last longer.

The Battle of Hogwarts

On the night of May 1 and into the early hours of May 2, 1998, Harry, along with his classmates, professors and members of the Order of the Phoenix, defends Hogwarts School of Witchcraft and Wizardry from an attack by Lord Voldemort and his Death Eaters. This event is the final showdown between the forces of dark and light in the Second Wizarding War.

Before the battle begins in earnest, Professor Minerva McGonagall duels Headmaster Severus Snape, who then flies out of the castle.

McGonagall casts *Piertotum Locomotor* and commands the suits of armor to rise up and defend the school.

Harry interrogates the Gray Lady about the location of the Ravenclaw's diadem.

Harry, Hermione and Ron head to the Room of Requirement to locate and destroy Ravenclaw's diadem. Draco Malfoy, Vincent Crabbe and Gregory Goyle find them there. A confrontation ensues: Crabbe casts Fiendfyre, incinerating himself and the room while the others escape. The diadem is destroyed in the process.

Voldemort gives instructions to surrender Harry; he promises doing so will prevent anyone from being hurt. In addition to staff, students over the age of 17 are permitted to stay and fight, while underage students are evacuated via a tunnel between the Room of Requirement and the Hog's Head. Some Ravenclaws choose to stay, as well as a few more Hufflepuffs. Half of Gryffindor opts to remain and fight, including underage students who are forced to evacuate. Members of the Order of the Phoenix, alumni, family members of students and other supporters of the cause enter through the Hog's Head tunnel during this time.

Hermione and Ron destroy Hufflepuff's cup, one of the Horcruxes.

The castle's defenses are breached. In addition to witches and wizards, centaurs, Acromantulas, giants, Dementors and eventually house-elves join in the fray.

Casualties include Colin Creevey, Remus Lupin, Nymphadora Tonks, Fred Weasley and Severus Snape, who is killed by Nagini (on Voldemort's orders) in the Shrieking Shack as part of a futile attempt to gain possession of the Elder Wand.

Suddenly back in the Forbidden Forest, Harry listens as Narcissa Malfoy checks to see whether or not he is still alive. When she asks if Draco is alive, Harry covertly answers in the affirmative, and Narcissa announces that Harry is dead. Voldemort forces Hagrid, who had been captured, to carry Harry's body back to the castle.

Harry is revealed to have miraculously survived the Killing Curse again, much as he did as a baby. In the Great Hall, Harry faces off against Voldemort, explaining how the Elder Wand is loyal to him rather than Voldemort.

Ceasefire. Putting on his Invisibility Cloak, Harry heads to the Forbidden Forest, where he surrenders himself to Voldemort. Along the way, he uses the Resurrection Stone, and the spirits of his parents as well as Sirius and Lupin embolden him on his journey.

Molly Weasley kills Bellatrix Lestrange in a duel.

The fighting resumes.

Voldemort casts *Avada Kedavra*, sending Harry into a sort of limbo that resembles King's Cross station. Here, he speaks with Dumbledore, who says he can return to the living, and observes a deformed version of Voldemort's damaged soul. As it turns out, Harry himself was an unintended Horcrux.

Voldemort declares victory and urges his opponents to join his cause. Neville Longbottom refuses, so Voldemort places the Sorting Hat on his head and sets it on fire. Fortunately, Neville pulls the sword of Gryffindor from the hat and uses it to kill Voldemort's snake, Nagini, the final Horcrux to be destroyed.

Voldemort casts *Avada Kedavra* at the same moment Harry casts *Expelliarmus*— when the spells collide, Voldemort is killed by his own rebounding curse.

Planning Your Arrival

Though every student at Hogwarts is different, the ways in which they are admitted to and arrive at the school are the same for all. Well, almost all.

THE BOOK OF ADMITTANCE

In a small, locked tower at Hogwarts School of Witchcraft and Wizardry, there is an ancient book bound in peeling black dragon hide that has not been touched since the four founders placed it there. At its side, there is a small silver inkpot from which protrudes a long, faded quill. At the first sign of magic in a British child, the Quill of Acceptance—made from a feather thought to have been taken from an Augurey—inscribes the child's name in the Book of Admittance. The Book and Quill's mutual decision is final, and Hogwarts does not admit anyone whose name has not first been written inside the book. Supposedly, the Quill appears to be more lenient than the Book, satisfied to mark a child's name at a mere suggestion of magic. The Book, however, refuses to be written in until there is dramatic evidence of magical ability. Non-magic children born to witches and wizards—also known as Squibs—are sometimes born with an aura of magic around them, but this fades and does not seem to confuse the Book and Quill. Together, these magical items have never made a mistake since their inception.

ADMISSION

Once a student's name has been inscribed into the Book of Admittance, they can expect to receive a letter of acceptance slightly before their eleventh birthday. The letter is written in green ink by the deputy headmaster or headmistress of Hogwarts and includes a list of required textbooks and materials for the upcoming year. When a student is Muggle-born, the letter is delivered in person by a member of Hogwarts faculty. Harry is a special case. His aunt and uncle try to keep his acceptance letter from him, resulting in more letters being delivered in increasingly elaborate magical ways: first by regular mail, then by being rolled up and hidden inside each of two dozen eggs, then by an onslaught of letters bursting through the fireplace, and finally by Rubeus Hagrid, visiting in person and beginning a lifelong friendship.

FUNDING
Hogwarts tuition is free for all students; costs are covered by the Ministry of Magic. Items such as robes, books, wands and classroom supplies need to be purchased, but Hogwarts has a special fund to help financially challenged students afford what they need. This fund was notably made available to Tom Riddle, who was accepted to Hogwarts from a Muggle orphanage and had no funds of his own.

TRANSPORTATION
From early historical accounts, we know Hogwarts students used to arrive at school in various ways arranged by their parents: broomstick, enchanted carts or carriages, Apparition or by riding a variety of magical creatures. This caused several instances in which wizards traveling to Hogwarts were spotted by Muggles. After the imposition of the International Statute of Secrecy in 1692, Portkeys—enchanted objects, typically something a Muggle would consider trash, that transport a person to a prespecified location at a specific time— were arranged. Unfortunately, as much as a third of the student body would either miss their Portkey time slot or be unable to find the object altogether. Despite Portkeys being less than ideal, it wasn't until a Minister of Magic's special interest in Muggle technology inspired an alternative solution that the problem of safe and secret transportation was solved for good.

KING'S CROSS STATION, PLATFORM NINE AND THREE-QUARTERS
Ottaline Gambol—British Minister of Magic from 1827 to 1835—used her fascination with Muggle technology as inspiration for the Hogwarts Express. Wizards needed a discreet way to transport hundreds of students to Hogwarts School of Witchcraft and Wizardry, so Gambol commandeered a Muggle train of unknown origins. According to classified files at the Ministry of Magic, there is evidence of a large-scale operation involving 167

Memory Charms as well as the biggest Concealment Charm ever performed in Britain. Reportedly, the morning after this operation, Hogsmeade residents awoke to find a railway station that had not been there previously. Meanwhile, Muggle railway workers in Crewe, England, all shared the feeling they had misplaced something. Hogsmeade was presumably chosen for the station's location because it is a small, entirely wizarding village that sits just outside the Hogwarts grounds, and would eliminate any security risk to the castle itself by virtue of its location outside Hogwarts's protective spells.

With the destination sorted, there was still the predicament of a departure station. The Ministry of Magic felt strongly that despite Muggles' determination not to notice magic even when it was right in front of them, constructing a magical train station in London would be irresponsible, if it was even possible. During this initial period, there is no record of where students boarded the Hogwarts Express. Evangeline Orpington—British Minister of Magic from 1849 to 1855—proposed an elegant solution: adding a concealed platform to the newly built King's Cross station situated in north London, England.

Platform nine and three-quarters is accessible only to witches and wizards and is entered by walking through the barrier between platforms nine and ten. To prevent Muggles from potentially catching a glimpse of the magical travelers in their midst and causing a scene, the Ministry of Magic sends a plainclothes team of employees to alter memories along the platform at the beginning and end of every Hogwarts school year.

Because of the train's Muggle origin, many pure-blood parents disapproved of the train at first. However, little could be done about this because the Ministry of Magic soon forbade any other method of traveling to Hogwarts.

HOGWARTS EXPRESS

On September 1 of each year, the entrance to platform nine and three-quarters opens up onto a platform housing the Hogwarts Express. Looking back at the entrance from the platform side, one can see a wrought-iron archway with the words, "Platform Nine and Three-Quarters." The train, a scarlet steam-powered locomotive, billows smoke, and a sign announces that the Hogwarts Express will depart at eleven o'clock.

The Hogwarts Express typically only runs six days per year (round trips for the beginning and end of term, as well as the Christmas and Easter holidays), but on those days its platform at King's Cross is bustling with activity. Hordes of students and parents move through the steam as cats weave between legs and owls hoot to one another.

At eleven o'clock, a whistle sounds, announcing the train's departure; the hiss of pistons fills the platform as the train begins to move. Family members stand on the platform and wave as their children set off for school. The platform then stays empty until the scheduled return journey from Hogsmeade station.

A typical beginning-of-term journey on the Hogwarts Express begins upon departure from King's Cross station promptly at 11:00 a.m. and ends at Hogsmeade station in the early evening. The train itself consists of several cars, the first of which is reserved for Hogwarts prefects. Each car holds compartments set off a corridor for groups of students to sit. A witch, often referred to as the Trolley Witch, pushes a tea trolley through the train during the trip selling various food and drink.

When Harry's son Albus is on board the train to attend his fourth year at Hogwarts, he encounters the Trolley Witch, who is revealed to have been hired by Ottaline Gambol herself to make sure students were transported safely. This would make the witch more than 190 years old, possibly explaining why she doesn't remember her own name. The witch claims to have caught a few students trying to escape the train, but when Albus and Scorpius Malfoy escape the train, she is unsuccessful in stopping them.

Upon arrival at Hogsmeade station, students disembark from the Hogwarts Express and begin the second leg of their journey to the castle itself.

BOATS ACROSS THE LAKE
A large freshwater lake—also known as a "loch" in Scotland, where the school is located—sits to the south of Hogwarts Castle, which perches

atop a cliff overlooking the water. After arriving at Hogsmeade station via the Hogwarts Express, first-year students board small boats in groups of no more than four. These boats are propelled by magic in a fleet across the lake toward the cliff where there is an underground harbor. The boats also ferry first-year students back to Hogsmeade station at the end of term.

CARRIAGES

Along a rough, muddy road near Hogsmeade station, roughly one hundred carriages sit waiting for students to arrive each September 1. The carriages smell of mold and straw. During good weather the tops are left open, but there are hoods attached during inclement weather. The carriages transport second- through seventh-year students at the beginning and end of each term and holiday break and are pulled by Thestrals, winged horses with skeletal bodies and—despite their bat-like wings—reptilian features. These Thestrals are a herd that belongs to the school, and they are trained to pull the carriages unassisted from the station, around the lake and to the castle. Thestrals are only visible to those who have witnessed death, meaning many students believe the carriages are enchanted to operate autonomously. If students arrive after the carriages have left the station, they will be forced to walk to the castle, as Harry does at the start of his sixth year.

OTHER METHODS OF ARRIVAL

While there are very few sanctioned methods for Hogwarts students to arrive at the castle, visiting students are less limited.

During the 1994 Triwizard Tournament, students from French school Beauxbatons Academy of Magic arrive at Hogwarts in a powder-blue flying carriage as large as a house. The carriage is pulled by 12 Abraxans, a magical breed of powerful, winged Palomino horses, each the size of an elephant. These horses are bred by Headmistress Madame Maxime, who asserts that they only drink single malt whisky and require "forceful handling." Students from Durmstrang Institute—thought to be located somewhere in the far north of Europe—arrive that same year. They surface from the center of the lake (see page 123) in a magical ship. The ship has a skeletal look about it, as though it has been resurrected from wreckage. Its portholes shine with dim, misty lights. The ship travels underwater through magical means and is capable of traveling between bodies of water that are presumed to be disconnected from one another.

After missing the Hogwarts Express in September 1992, Harry and Ron fly an enchanted Ford Anglia from King's Cross to Hogwarts. The turquoise car was bought by Ron's father, Arthur Weasley, for what he claimed to be an opportunity to take it apart and indulge his curiosity of Muggle technology. Instead of simply exploring the vehicle, Mr. Weasley enchanted it to fly, installed an Invisibility Booster, and enchanted the car's inner spaces to fit large amounts of luggage and several more people than expected. Near school grounds, the car begins to break down and crashes into the Whomping Willow (see page 125). The car dumps its passengers and their items onto the ground and flees into the Forbidden Forest (see page 134).

As danger mounts in the wizarding world, Hogwarts and the Ministry of Magic begin allowing alternative modes of travel to the school. The second term of Harry's fifth year, he returns on the Knight Bus, and by the following Christmas, students can travel via the Floo Network directly into the Deputy Headmistress's office.

HOGSMEADE WEEKENDS

While boats and carriages are used to transport students at the beginning and end of each term and holiday break, they do not serve as a mode of transport for student visits to Hogsmeade. On select weekends throughout the year, students from third year onwards are allowed to visit Hogsmeade; however, they must walk there and back. For those in the know, some of Hogwarts's secret passages provide a shortcut to the village.

CHAPTER 2

THE CASTLE

Steeped in lore, this ancient, sprawling
building has plenty of secrets and surprises
for those who know where to look.

The Marauder's Map

In the 1970s, four talented young Gryffindors—Remus Lupin, Peter Pettigrew, Sirius Black and James Potter—forged a unique friendship at Hogwarts. When it became clear to the other three members of the group that Lupin was a werewolf, they undertook an almost impossibly advanced bit of magic so they could keep their friend company when the full moon turned him into a monster: They became Animagi, learning to transform into animals (a rat, a dog and a stag), thus keeping themselves safe from the werewolf's bite but still allowing them to be there for Lupin. Together, they adopted the nicknames Moony, Wormtail, Padfoot and Prongs, respectively, in reference to the animal forms they took to accompany Lupin during his monthly transformations.

Through exploring the Hogwarts grounds as Animagi, these mischief-prone friends created the Marauder's Map. Enchanted with a Homonculous Charm, this parchment outlines every room within the castle and its immediate grounds and also reveals the names of every person in each location via a labeled ink dot. The charm works on everyone, even if they are employing magical camouflage such as an invisibility cloak, Polyjuice Potion or self-Transfiguration. It can even recognize ghosts, Peeves the poltergeist and Mrs. Norris. The map also includes the secret passageways and shortcuts the Marauders discovered during their extensive exploration of Hogwarts.

Although it may look like an ordinary blank piece of parchment to anyone who comes across it, to access the map, a user must touch a wand to it while saying the words, "I solemnly swear that I am up to no good." To hide the map, the user again touches their wand to the parchment and says, "Mischief managed!" Should the map fall into the wrong hands, it is charmed to repel all attempts to access its secrets in the most insulting way possible.

Locations

The Castle

To ensure their school of magic would remain protected and apart from Muggle society, the founders of Hogwarts chose to construct the castle on a remote mountain in Scotland, placing concealment enchantments for added security. At that time, the International Statute of Secrecy had not yet been passed, meaning medieval Muggles were keenly aware that magic existed—they also persecuted those who possessed a talent for it. Young witches and wizards in particular were vulnerable, as they had not yet learned to control their magic and couldn't be reasonably expected to hide their gifts under pressure. Hence the safe haven of Hogwarts School of Witchcraft and Wizardry was born.

The floor plan of this illustrious school is labyrinthine, sprawling across seven main floors, as well as the ground floor (where the entrance hall and Great Hall are found) and the lower underground level (where the dungeons and kitchens are found). When Harry sees Hogwarts for the very first time as he walks from the Hogwarts Express to the boats that take first years across the Great Lake, it is described as "a vast castle with many turrets and towers." Harry is known to have visited five towers during his time at the school—Gryffindor Tower, Ravenclaw Tower, Astronomy Tower, North Tower and West Tower.

Armed with the Marauder's Map, given to him by Fred and George Weasley, Harry discovers secret passageways and shortcuts he likely would not have otherwise found and uses them for various purposes. There are other quirks to the castle, including walls that open like doors, doors that are walls, and doors that require tickling or asking nicely to open. Of the castle's 142 staircases, some lead to different places depending on the day of the week while others feature trick steps that cause unsuspecting students to sink into the floorboards. As Dumbledore once said to Igor Karkaroff, we should "never dream of assuming [we] know all Hogwarts's secrets."

Courtyard

A large, open area on the Hogwarts grounds, the courtyard is where students head for a bit of fresh air and sunshine during breaks between classes and after lunch. In fact, they're required to go outside by school rules, even during colder months, and are only allowed to stay inside the castle during periods of heavy rain. Students can access the courtyard through a door on the ground floor off the entrance hall. It's the perfect spot to collect one's thoughts, discuss Quidditch or purchase some illicit goods from the Weasley twins.

KEEPING THE COLD OUT

During one of the colder days in their first year at the school, Hermione casts Bluebell Flames in a jam jar to keep the trio warm as they brace themselves against the frigid air of the courtyard. The three friends have to hide the blue fire from a passing Snape, as he would likely consider this against the school rules.

Entrance Hall

Illuminated by torchlight, the high-ceilinged entrance hall makes a grand impression as the main entrance into the castle. Students enter the ground-floor space through two huge oak doors. Next to these doors are suits of armor.

To the right of the entrance doors is the Great Hall and a broom closet, in which Harry and Hermione hide themselves in 1994 while using a Time-Turner. Opposite the oak doors is the marble staircase that leads to the upper floors of the castle. On either side of the staircase is a set of stairs that go down to the lower floors of Hogwarts—the right staircase leads down to the kitchens and the Hufflepuff common room, while the left leads to the dungeons and the Slytherin common room. In one of the corners opposite the main entrance are the hourglasses that record the House points awarded and deducted over the course of the school year.

To the left of the marble staircase is an empty chamber where first years gather prior to the Sorting ceremony. A corridor next to the chamber leads down to the ground-floor classrooms, which are not in regular use. However, the centaur Firenze holds Divination lessons here in classroom 11 in 1996 after he is hired to replace Professor Trelawney. Further along is a staffroom with two gargoyles on either side of the door, as well as a door that provides access to the courtyard.

CHOOSING THE TRIWIZARD CHAMPIONS

During the Triwizard Tournament in 1994, the Goblet of Fire is placed in the center of the entrance hall for 24 hours to allow eligible students to submit their names. The Goblet of Fire sits on the three-legged stool that is usually used for the Sorting ceremony, and Dumbledore draws an Age Line around it to prohibit underage students from entering the tournament (and possibly meeting a ghastly demise).

The Great Hall

Like all students at Hogwarts, Harry pays his first visit to the Great Hall on his first night in the school, when first years are led into the hall to be Sorted in front of the assembled student populace and staff. Still new to the wizarding world, he describes the hall as a "strange and splendid place," one that surely leaves an impression on all who enter.

As the hub for all activity at Hogwarts, the Great Hall functions as a gathering space for daily meals, exams, owl post deliveries and extracurricular activities, as well as annual functions, such as the Sorting ceremony for first years, after which all students and staff dig in to the traditional start-of-term feast (see page 33). Several of the Great Hall's most notable events include an amateur production of "The Fountain of Fair Fortune"; Professor Lockhart's dueling club (where Harry learns he's a Parselmouth); and Halloween 1993, when escaped convict Sirius Black breaks into Hogwarts and every student spends the night in sleeping bags on the Hall floor. The Great Hall also hosts the Yule Ball in 1994 and is the setting for Apparition lessons attended by Harry, Hermione and Ron during their sixth year. Most importantly, it's where the final showdown between Harry and Lord Voldemort takes place, in which the powerful Dark wizard is laid low by his own rebounding curse.

Located off the school entrance hall (see page 55), this large room can be accessed through a pair of enormous double doors. There are five long tables in the hall, one for each House and one for staff. The headmaster or headmistress of the school can be found seated in the middle of the latter. Students sit at their respective tables, which are magically cleared at the end of each meal, for breakfast, lunch and dinner. These tables are lit at night by thousands of floating candles hovering overhead, and the entire hall is festooned with elaborate decor during special feasts (see page 33). The order of the House tables changes during Harry's first few years at the school. As Harry is being Sorted, he notes the tables are arranged from left to right as Gryffindor, Ravenclaw, Slytherin, Hufflepuff, but later notes their order as Slytherin, Ravenclaw, Hufflepuff, Gryffindor.

The most striking feature in the Great Hall by far is its enchanted ceiling, which is bewitched to replicate a live projection of the sky above. It's such convincing spellwork, in fact, that Harry thinks it looks like the room opens directly into the heavens, which can range from a clear starry night to a gray stormy day (complete with lightning bolts). Memorably, the end of the Second Wizarding War is heralded by the red-gold glow of the sunrise bursting across the enchanted ceiling as Harry and Lord Voldemort face off just before Voldemort's death.

THE PLAY THAT ALMOST BURNED DOWN THE HALL

During Armando Dippet's term as headmaster, theatrically inclined Herbology professor Herbert Beery proposed having the students put on a production of "The Fountain of Fair Fortune," adapted from the fairy tale of the same name in *The Tales of Beedle the Bard*. Beery enlisted the help of Dumbledore, then a Transfiguration professor, to produce special effects for the show, as well as Professor Silvanus Kettleburn, the Care of Magical Creatures instructor, to provide a suitable creature stand-in for the white worm that the three witches encounter on their journey to the Fountain. Dumbledore's contributions went off without a hitch, but when Kettleburn placed an Engorgement Charm on an Ashwinder to portray the worm, the snake burst, covering the hall in a cloud of burning embers and smoke. The Ashwinder also managed to lay several fiery hot eggs, which caused the stage to erupt into flames, prompting the staff to evacuate the hall. Although there were no fatalities (not counting the Ashwinder), Dippet issued a ban on theatrical productions at Hogwarts.

Classrooms

Hogwarts students have the option to enroll in an expansive curriculum with classes held all around the castle as well as across the grounds. Care of Magical Creatures, for example, takes them to locations as varied as the Forbidden Forest and Hagrid's hut, while Herbology takes place in massive greenhouse complexes.

First- and second-year students have classes selected for them (see page 155), but older students are allowed to choose their electives and specialties according to their tastes. Especially hard-working students may be given the opportunity to use a Time-Turner, like Hermione does in 1993, to fit more classes into their schedule than would normally be possible.

FIRST AND SECOND YEAR

Seven core subjects are taken in the first and second years: Astronomy, Charms, Defense Against the Dark Arts, Herbology (see page 129), History of Magic, Potions and Transfiguration. First-year students are also required to partake in basic broom-flying lessons.

ASTRONOMY

Astronomy classes take place in the highest level of the Astronomy Tower, the tallest tower in the castle. Typically considered out-of-bounds except during class time, this location boasts an unobstructed view of the sky, making it an ideal location for observing celestial objects. Practical portions of Astronomy exams take place inside the tower as well.

The Astronomy Tower is situated almost directly above the front doors of the castle and is surrounded by a parapet. A steep spiral staircase leads to an iron-handled door, through which the top of the tower can be accessed.

During Harry's first year at Hogwarts, he and Hermione meet with Charlie Weasley's friends at the top of the Astronomy Tower to hand off Norbert(a), Hagrid's baby dragon, into Charlie's care.

In 1997, during the Battle of the Astronomy Tower, Death Eaters deploy the Dark Mark from the tower. That same night, Severus Snape casts a Killing Curse at Dumbledore, throwing the headmaster from the tower.

CHARMS

Charms classes take place in a classroom down the aptly named Charms corridor, which can be found on the third floor of the castle near the off-limits third-floor corridor. Just outside, there is an opening to a secret passageway that leads to a gallery containing suits of armor and the trophy room, as well as a portrait depicting several drunken monks.

Though there is little description of the classroom besides having one window that overlooks the front entrance to Hogwarts, Professor Flitwick—described as a "tiny little wizard"—has to stand on a stack of books to see over his desk.

During the winter season, Professor Flitwick decorates the Charms classroom with fluttering fairies that look like shimmering lights.

DEFENSE AGAINST THE DARK ARTS

The location of the Defense Against the Dark Arts classroom is slightly contested. It is widely believed to be located on the first floor, while the professor's office is located on the second floor. Contrary to this, Dolores Umbridge's office during her time as Defense Against the Dark Arts professor is noted as being the same as previous professors yet on the third floor. This conflicting information has never been clarified.

During Quirinus Quirrell's time as professor, the classroom is reported to smell strongly of garlic. A rumor circulates that this is to ward off a vampire Quirrell had encountered while traveling in Romania.

During Gilderoy Lockhart's tenure, a lesson with Cornish pixies goes disastrously awry. The pixies shatter a classroom window, spray ink from bottles and hang Harry's classmate Neville Longbottom from the iron chandelier.

When Severus Snape teaches the subject, the classroom takes on a similarly gloomy look to match its newest professor's personality. Snape takes the liberty of redecorating it with pictures of people who appear to be contorted in pain or with grotesque injuries (although it's unclear whether this is meant to inspire his students or spur them into paying attention).

This classroom where Snape teaches N.E.W.T.-level students is on the third floor. (Note: It is unknown whether N.E.W.T.-level students actually use a different classroom, or if the author simply forgot where she placed the original, or perhaps classrooms simply move at their whim. The castle is magic, after all.)

HISTORY OF MAGIC

Students learn about the history of magic in a classroom on the first floor. There is a blackboard through which the ghostly Professor Binns enters and exits at the beginning and end of each lesson, as well as a thick glass window with a narrow ledge.

During Harry's third year, Professor Remus Lupin makes use of this classroom after hours to teach Harry how to cast a Patronus Charm.

POTIONS

Potions classes are held in a classroom in the Hogwarts dungeons. The room is large enough to hold at least 20 students with cauldrons and worktables. Due to its location, the classroom is usually quite cold, especially in the winter, when students can sometimes see their breath hanging in the air during lessons.

Shelves dotted with jars of pickled animals line the walls. In the corner, there is a basin into which water pours from a gargoyle's mouth. This room also features a blackboard and a student supply cupboard for ingredient storage.

When Severus Snape is Potions professor, his office and personal ingredient store are adjacent to the classroom.

TRANSFIGURATION

The Transfiguration classroom features a professor's desk as well as separate desks for each student, giving them enough room to practice their spells comfortably. The location of the classroom is unknown, but it is very far away from the Defense Against the Dark Arts teacher's office, making it an ideal place to cause trouble to draw Umbridge away.

During the 1994 Triwizard Tournament, Harry uses the classroom during lunch break to practice spells.

THIRD YEAR AND ABOVE

Third-year students are required to choose a minimum of two additional subjects to study in addition to the seven core subjects carried over from their first and second years. They may choose from Ancient Runes, Arithmancy, Care of Magical Creatures (see page 129), Divination and Muggle Studies. Alchemy and other specialized subjects may be offered for N.E.W.T.-level students if there is enough demand.

ALCHEMY

The location of this classroom is unknown.

ANCIENT RUNES

The location of this classroom is unknown.

ARITHMANCY

The location of this classroom is unknown.

DIVINATION

Students attend Divination lessons in a classroom at the top of the North Tower. It can be accessed through a circular trapdoor marked with a brass plaque. The trapdoor releases a silver ladder. Ostentatiously decorated in an eclectic style, this round room is described as looking like a cross between "someone's attic and an old-fashioned tea shop" and contains about 20 small, circular tables surrounded by armchairs and poufs, creating an intimate atmosphere.

During classes, the window curtains are drawn and red scarves are draped over the lamps, casting a dim, crimson light throughout the space. The shelves along the walls hold feathers, candles, cards, crystal balls and teacups. Due to the fireplace, the room feels oppressively warm, and a large copper kettle over the open flames emits a sickly perfume smell.

Although Professor Sybill Trelawney teaches most of Harry's Divination sessions, classes that are taught by the centaur Firenze beginning in 1996 are moved from the North Tower to classroom 11 on the ground floor, presumably so that Firenze can more easily access it. During this time, the classroom resembles his natural habitat, the Forbidden Forest, and is magically decorated with a mossy floor, boulders and trees. Students sit on the ground. Firenze also makes stars appear on the ceiling for students to observe as part of his teaching.

MUGGLE STUDIES
Muggle Studies classes are located in a classroom on the first floor.

EMPTY CLASSROOMS
Due to this ancient wizarding institution's sheer size, numerous classroom spaces are left unoccupied or are used as storerooms. Hogwarts's resident poltergeist, Peeves, often busies himself by causing trouble in these spaces.

It is in one of these empty classrooms that Professor Minerva McGonagall recruits Harry to be the youngest player on a Hogwarts Quidditch team in a century (making him a notable exception to the convention that first-year students do not play on House teams).

Many conversations between Harry, Hermione and Ron happen in stolen moments inside empty classrooms. During their second year, the trio slip into an empty classroom on the floor above Professor Lockhart's office to discuss Harry's ability to understand Parseltongue. During the trio's third year, Fred and George Weasley pull Harry into an empty classroom to discreetly gift him with the Marauder's Map.

Empty classrooms are also a popular spot for young couples to sneak into for some alone time. Percy Weasley is caught kissing Penelope Clearwater inside of one by his little sister, Ginny Weasley. Empty classrooms also serve as a location for students to gather inside during breaks when inclement weather prevents them from going outside.

UNUSUAL CLASSROOMS

At the onset of the Second Wizarding War, Apparition classes are offered at the school for students who will be at least 17 by the end of the following August. They cost 12 Galleons and are held in the Great Hall when poor weather forces their relocation from the grounds.

In Harry's fifth year, Professor Dolores Umbridge refuses to teach what Harry considers to be adequate Defense Against the Dark Arts classes. In response, Harry uses the Room of Requirement (see page 92) as a classroom for a secret group of students called Dumbledore's Army to practice defensive spells in secret.

Common Rooms

Each Hogwarts House has its own common room and dormitories where its students sleep, study and socialize between classes.

GRYFFINDOR
For much of his time at Hogwarts, Harry spends many hours enjoying the warm, friendly confines of the Gryffindor common room.

ENTRANCE
Gryffindor Tower is located on the seventh floor of Hogwarts Castle. The entrance is guarded by a portrait known as the Fat Lady, who is briefly replaced by the knight Sir Cadogan after her painting is damaged by Sirius Black during Harry's third year. When the correct password is provided, the portrait swings forward to reveal the entrance to the common room.

INTERIOR
The common room is round and cozy with plush armchairs, tables, a fireplace and a noticeboard for announcements about Hogsmeade trips, Apparition lessons, Quidditch training schedules and lost-and-found notices. The fireplace can be connected to the Floo Network, allowing Harry and Sirius Black to communicate (but not travel) through it. Two spiral staircases lead to the boys' and girls' dormitories, one for each year, and students sleep in four-poster beds with red velvet curtains. If a boy attempts to go up the girls' staircase, an alarm sounds and the steps turn into a slide. According to *Hogwarts: A History*, the founders considered boys less trustworthy than girls and thus only found this precaution necessary for the girls' dormitory. Parties are held in the Gryffindor common room after House victories, including Quidditch matches and Harry's performance in the first task of the Triwizard Tournament. Harry and Ginny share their first kiss in the common room after

Gryffindor wins the Quidditch Cup.

HUFFLEPUFF

The Hufflepuff common room is the one House living space Harry never sees in person. Harry sees Cedric Diggory go down a staircase to the right of the marble stairs in the entrance hall after the Triwizard champions are selected by the Goblet of Fire, presumably to his House common room.

ENTRANCE

The Hufflepuff common room is conveniently located along the same corridor as the kitchens, one level below the entrance hall, behind a stack of large barrels in a nook on the right side of the corridor. Entry is gained by tapping on the barrel in the middle of the second row to the rhythm of the name of the House founder, "Helga Hufflepuff," causing the lid to swing open for the entrant to crawl inside along a passageway to the common room. Intruders should beware: This is the only common room entrance that does not merely refuse entry to those without the correct password or response but employs a repelling device that sprays vinegar at anyone who taps the wrong barrel or the incorrect rhythm. For more than 1,000 years, no outsiders have infiltrated the common room. This powerful countermeasure is not without its downsides, however, as one can imagine a tired or forgetful Hufflepuff making a mistake in their tapping and getting soaked with vinegar as well.

INTERIOR

The cozy Hufflepuff common room is round and earthy with a low ceiling, a perpetually sunny feeling no matter the weather and circular windows offering views of grass and dandelions. Its location keeps it well protected from storms and wind. Furniture includes tables made of polished, honey-colored wood and overstuffed chairs and sofas with yellow and black upholstery. There are large amounts of burnished copper and plants decorating the room, on circular shelves and hanging from the ceiling. Plants range from flowers and cacti to talking and dancing plants provided by Head of House and Herbology Professor Pomona Sprout. There is a portrait of Helga Hufflepuff holding her signature golden cup above the mantelpiece, which has carvings of dancing badgers. Four-poster beds in the dormitories, which are reached through round doors in the walls, have patchwork quilts. The space is complete with copper lamps and copper bed warmers hanging on the walls for added warmth and light.

RAVENCLAW

Harry visits the Ravenclaw common room when Luna Lovegood takes him there to see Rowena Ravenclaw's statue and get a closer glimpse at what Ravenclaw's diadem looks like.

ENTRANCE

Ravenclaw Tower is located at the top of a spiral staircase, accessible from the fifth floor of the castle, behind an old wooden door with no handle or keyhole—only a bronze knocker shaped like an eagle. Once knocked, the eagle's beak opens and asks a question in a soft, musical voice. These queries tend to be riddles or puzzles rather than straightforward trivia. When an acceptable answer is provided, the eagle may compliment the entrant for their cleverness, and the door swings open. If the potential entrant is unable to answer the question, they must wait for someone who can in order to gain access. It's not unheard of for a crowd of Ravenclaws to form outside the door as students struggle to work out an answer. Due to the difficulty associated with its doorway, the entrance to Ravenclaw's common room is not concealed. This protocol is not entirely secure, however, as Professor McGonagall is able to successfully answer a question and gain entry despite her being a Gryffindor.

INTERIOR

The Ravenclaw common room is a wide, circular, airy space featuring blue and bronze silks hanging on the walls and arched windows that provide a stunning view of the Hogwarts grounds and surrounding mountains. The domed ceiling and midnight-blue carpet are decorated with stars, and there are tables, chairs and—appropriately for the most studious House—numerous bookcases. A white marble statue of Rowena Ravenclaw wearing her diadem stands in an alcove opposite the entrance, beside a door that leads to the dormitories. The marble diadem has the words "Wit beyond measure is man's greatest treasure" etched into it. The dormitories are located in turrets off the main tower and contain four-poster beds with sky-blue silk eiderdowns. Given the room's high altitude, forceful wind can be heard whistling around the windows.

SLYTHERIN

During their second year, Harry and Ron drink Polyjuice Potion to disguise themselves as Vincent Crabbe and Gregory Goyle; none the wiser, Malfoy leads them into the Slytherin common room, where the Gryffindor students get a rare look at their opposing House's living quarters.

ENTRANCE

The Slytherin common room is located in the Hogwarts dungeons behind a stone door concealed within a damp stone wall. When Harry and Ron enter with Malfoy, the password is "pure-blood." This password changes every fortnight and is posted on the noticeboard for ease of reference. Slytherins are trusted to never share the password or bring outsiders into the common room. Before Harry and Ron, no non-Slytherin student had entered the common room in more than seven centuries.

INTERIOR

The underground common room is situated within the school's lake, giving it the atmosphere of a mysterious shipwreck. It is a long, low room with rough stone walls and windows that frequently offer a view of the giant squid swimming by. Round, greenish lanterns hang from the ceiling by chains, while the lanterns in the dormitories are silver. Students sleep in four-poster beds with green silk hangings and bedspreads with silver embroidery. Medieval tapestries on the walls portray the adventures of famous Slytherins.

Library

The Hogwarts library is home to tens of thousands of books on thousands of shelves and is an incomparable resource for any student whether they're searching for an obscure spell or the specifics surrounding the most recent goblin rebellion. Students and teachers from all Houses study, write essays and pore over books in this part of the castle throughout the school year. Many students, however, are too scared to ask the strict and possessive Madam Pince for any help finding one of her precious books, making research an extremely challenging process.

The library closes promptly at 8:00 p.m., but Madam Pince will kick out any student before that time if she suspects them of writing in her books or eating in their immediate vicinity. Hogwarts library books contain a warning in them from the fierce librarian: "If you rip, tear, shred, bend, fold, deface, disfigure, smear, smudge, throw, drop, or in any other manner damage, mistreat, or show lack of respect towards this book, the consequences will be as awful as it is within my power to make them." According to Dumbledore, although there are spells placed on every library book, Madam Pince also adds unusual jinxes to certain books. Once, for example, he doodled on a copy of *Theories of Transubstantial Transfiguration*, at which point the book beat him about the head. Hermione, however, manages to rip out a page about basilisks from a library book without being attacked by either the book or Madam Pince.

On the front page of each library book is a list of every student who has taken out the book and the date it's due back. The library has a waiting list for particularly popular books, but this appears to be rare since Hermione is horrified by the possibility of waiting two weeks for *Hogwarts: A History* in her second year. Students are expected to bring their own textbooks to school, and there is no indication that Hogwarts has reserved copies in the library for students who lose them or forget their books. Individual classrooms, however, sometimes hold extra copies of old textbooks. Students are allowed to bring library books back to their dormitories, but bringing them outside onto school grounds is forbidden—or so Snape would have Harry believe.

HERMIONE IN THE LIBRARY

Hermione may be one of the most frequent users of the library, and she employs its services for far more than just casual reading and essays on goblin rebellions. Library books allow Hermione to brew Polyjuice Potion, discover the basilisk in the Chamber of Secrets and determine that Rita Skeeter is an unregistered Animagus. She uses her preternatural research skills to help other people and creatures too, making a case for Buckbeak's trial, preparing Harry for the Triwizard Tournament tasks and familiarizing herself with the sordid history of house-elf enslavement. While it's true that Harry, Ron and Hermione each become accomplished practitioners of the arcane during their time at the school, it's Hermione's research that saves the day more often than not.

HARRY THE RULEBREAKER

Hermione might be the one student who uses the library more than any other, but even she isn't desperate or daring enough to sneak into the library after hours. Twice, Harry uses his Invisibility Cloak to visit the library at night, once to look for books about Nicolas Flamel and a second time to search for a solution to the second task of the Triwizard Tournament. He may even be the only student to sleep in the library overnight (though admittedly not on purpose). Although Harry doesn't get caught during either of these visits, he does get kicked out of the library for breaking other rules, like eating Easter chocolate near the books and reading his (highly annotated) copy of *Advanced Potion-Making*.

RESTRICTED SECTION

The library is split into sections, each devoted to subjects like invisibility and dragons. At the back of the library, separated from the rest by a rope, is the Restricted Section. These books can only be accessed through a signed permission slip from a teacher and are primarily used by older students as resources for their advanced Defense Against the Dark Arts classes. The books here are old and faded, and many have titles in other languages—one even has a dark stain on it that looks like blood. Even the Restricted Section, however, has its limitations. Dumbledore is strict about keeping books about Horcruxes out of student hands and confiscates any that have existed in the past—including a book titled *Secrets of the Darkest Art*, which gives explicit instructions on how to make and destroy Horcruxes. Hermione only finds one paragraph mentioning Horcruxes in the entirety of the library, appearing in a foreboding book appropriately named *Magick Moste Evile*. Harry, likewise, struggles extensively to find a spell that will allow him to breathe underwater, despite asking Madam Pince for help and getting permission from Professor McGonagall to search in the Restricted Section.

A humble rope may not seem like effective protection against curious students with magical capabilities, but the books in the Restricted Section also boast their own protective enchantments. When Harry first goes there to find a book on Nicolas Flamel, he gets the impression the books are whispering about him because they can sense he isn't allowed in the area. The first book he opens screams loudly, possibly as an alarm to show that an unapproved student is trying to access the books. Similarly, when Hermione takes out *Magick Moste Evile* to see if she can find information about Horcruxes, it wails when she slams it shut.

THE BENEFITS OF WATCHING AND EAVESDROPPING

When it comes to gaining valuable information, the library is one of the few places in the castle where students from all Houses gather together, and as such, it makes a prime location for characters to watch each other, run into allies or antagonists and eavesdrop. Its copious shelves of books are perfect for hiding behind, and the general quietude allows for conversations to easily carry. In Harry's second year, he eavesdrops on Hufflepuff students talking about their suspicions that he is the heir of Slytherin. In his sixth year, Draco Malfoy overhears Hermione saying that Filch can't recognize potions that are in the wrong bottle, which inspires him to attempt to poison Dumbledore with a bottle of Madame Rosmerta's oak-matured mead. Ron is able to deduce that Hagrid is doing something suspicious with dragons by watching where he stands among the shelves, and Viktor Krum uses the pretense of studying to gather more intel about Hermione and work up the courage to ask her to the Yule Ball. The library may be a place of strict rules, but students still find plenty of ways to cross boundaries.

The Kitchens at Hogwarts

In order to provide satisfying meals for all Hogwarts students, staff and (on rare occasions) international guests, the castle relies on its magnificent kitchens to get the job done right. Though the exact whereabouts of the Hogwarts kitchens are known to relatively few students, the area can be accessed via the staircase on the right of the main marble stairs in the entrance hall (see page 55), which descends toward the Hufflepuff common room (see page 65). Paintings of food line the corridor at the base of the stairs, including a large still-life of a silver bowl of fruit which conceals the door to the kitchens. The trick to gaining entry is a well-placed tickle—in this case, users must tickle the pear in the fruit bowl, which will squirm and giggle before transforming into a large green door handle.

The kitchens lie directly beneath the Great Hall (see page 56) and mirror the castle's grand gathering space both in size and layout. Every dish, plate and utensil is laid out on these tables and then magicked up to their matching House or staff table above, giving the impression that the food appears out of nowhere. The walls and floor of the kitchens are made of stone, and a main focal point of the space is its giant brick fireplace at the far end of the room.

When it comes to dining at the school (see page 32), Hogwarts feasts such as those at the start of the year or on Halloween include many dishes that were originally created by school founder Helga Hufflepuff (see page 10). The feasts are served with gold plates and goblets, and since such lavish utensils are never mentioned as being used during everyday meals, it's presumed they are reserved for special occasions. Cold drinks, however, are usually served in goblets regardless of the occasion, as befits the slightly medieval tastes of the wizarding world.

Students who dare to sneak a bite between meals can venture downstairs for a free snack. According to Dumbledore, Harry's father,

James, used to don his Invisibility Cloak in order to steal down to the kitchens and grab food undetected. Many years later, Fred and George Weasley always find willing accomplices among the house-elves who work in the kitchens when it comes to procuring food for parties in the Gryffindor common room (usually to celebrate Quidditch victories).

The kitchens are staffed entirely by house-elves who (apart from the odd freed elf) wear the standard uniform of a tea towel bearing the Hogwarts crest. It is the Hogwarts kitchens where Harry is reunited with Dobby, almost two years after managing to survive the house-elf's attempts to save his life during Harry's second year at the school, and Winky, who arrives to take a job at Hogwarts after her master, Barty Crouch, Sr., frees her after the disastrous 1994 Quidditch World Cup.

Perhaps owing to the fact that Harry is not a Hufflepuff student (meaning he wouldn't go out of his way to explore this corridor), Harry only learns how to access the kitchens during his fourth year at the school, when Hermione conducts an investigation into Hogwarts's house-elves and their well-being. Visiting the kitchens and meeting the house-elves who cook and clean at the school is a key moment in Hermione's development of the Society for the Promotion of Elfish Welfare (S.P.E.W.). However, far from inspiring insurrection on her visits, she ends up making herself unwelcome amongst the house-elves, who are content serving the school's headmaster.

It is Kreacher, the Black family house-elf, who eventually incites a rebellion among the Hogwarts elves. After inheriting the elf along with number twelve, Grimmauld Place after Sirius Black's death, Harry takes Dumbledore's advice to send Kreacher to work in the Hogwarts kitchens. The house-elf returns to this role during what would've been Harry's seventh year at the school when Harry, Hermione and Ron fail to make it back to the Black ancestral home following their infiltration of the Ministry of Magic. Later, during the Battle of Hogwarts, Kreacher leads a charge of house-elves armed with carving knives and cleavers from the kitchens to attack Death Eaters and help end the Second Wizarding War.

Offices

Though Harry only visits a handful of them during his years of study at Hogwarts, it's safe to assume most members of staff at the school are provided with their own respective offices. For instance, while it is never explicitly mentioned whether or not Madam Hooch or Madam Pince have an office, considering how other support staff like Argus Filch and Madam Pomfrey have their own spaces, it follows that Hooch and Pince would as well. After all, a venue would be needed for Oliver Wood and Madam Hooch to delve into the deeper points of Quidditch when the Scottish weather inevitably turns foul or for Madam Pince to raise her voice at idle doodlers and chatters. Perhaps, though, with the library as her base of operations, Madam Pince can do all her work (including prowling the shelves for potential despoilers of books) from there and doesn't need her own office.

It is also unclear whether or not other staff are assigned offices. Hagrid's gamekeeper's cottage effectively doubles as his office while he teaches Care of Magical Creatures. But because the humble hut is Hagrid's dwelling, it is likely not available for Professor Grubbly-Plank to use when she covers lessons for him while he is "indisposed" (avoiding people) following Rita Skeeter's article that reveals him to be a half-giant. Likewise, Hagrid's hut is likely kept closed while he is on assignment recruiting giants in 1995 on Dumbledore's behalf.

The nurse's office, occupied by Madam Pomfrey, is found in the hospital wing (see page 79) just off the main ward. This means she is close at hand to dispense care—and chocolate—to her patients, but it does necessitate Harry casting *Muffliato* over her door during his sixth year to keep her from overhearing Dobby and Kreacher brawling.

Harry visits **the Defense Against the Dark Arts teacher's office** under a number of different professors' tenures during his time at Hogwarts. Gilderoy Lockhart, the professor during Harry's second year, limits his office decor to pictures of himself. During Harry's fourth year at the school, Barty Crouch, Jr., who had been living under the guise of Professor Moody, fills the office with objects for Dark Arts detection. The following year, when Dolores Umbridge holds the post, the sadistic professor opts to decorate her office with kitten plates. This room also serves as the location where Harry helps Lockhart sign autographs as part of detention, has tea with Lupin (and a grindylow) as a third-year student and confronts Barty Crouch, Jr., following the third task of the Triwizard Tournament. While Harry's time spent with Lockhart is less than pleasant, it pales in comparison to Umbridge's particularly brutal take on having Harry write lines in her office night after night as punishment for his speaking out about the truth of Voldemort's return.

Professor McGonagall's office, where she delivers such iconic lines as "Have a biscuit, Potter," can be found on Hogwarts's first floor. McGonagall's penchant for tartan (as part of her Scottish heritage) extends to the patterned tin in which she keeps her Ginger Newt cookies. The office offers a view of the Quidditch pitch, and it is likely it's from this prime vantage point that McGonagall first observes Harry's talent on a broom. During Harry's sixth year at the school, when increasingly dangerous times call for additional security measures, McGonagall's office is temporarily connected to the Floo Network to offer students a safe means of returning to Hogwarts following the Christmas holidays. Behind a concealed door in the office is a bedroom described as "sparse [and] stone-floored."

Slughorn's office is comfortably furnished to better host his Slug Club gatherings, such as the Christmas party Harry attends with Luna Lovegood during his sixth year at the school. Despite the cozy surroundings, Slughorn's office is both the scene of Ron's almost-lethal poisoning (on his 17th birthday) and where, decades prior, the professor gave a young Tom Riddle important information regarding the creation of Horcruxes.

Other offices include **Filch's office**, where the school's caretaker keeps chains well-oiled just in case he is given permission to use them on a student (and where, unbeknownst to Filch, the Marauder's Map was stored for a solid decade). **Professor Flitwick's office**, meanwhile, is only briefly mentioned as the seventh-floor location where Sirius is locked up after his capture to await the Dementor's Kiss.

THE HEADMASTER'S OFFICE

The Hogwarts headmaster or headmistress's office is located in one of the castle's towers and can be entered on the seventh floor (although in 1994, it's on the second floor; the author has admitted to making mistakes about the floor locations). It is guarded by a large (and, in Harry's opinion, "very ugly") gargoyle, which only moves out of the way once the correct password has been given. Notably, the gargoyle refuses entry to Dolores Umbridge when she seizes the position of headmistress by staging something of a coup; somehow, it refuses to consider her claim valid.

Once the gargoyle opts to jump aside, the wall behind it splits open to reveal a moving stone spiral staircase. This staircase carries people up the tower and deposits them in front of a polished oak door with a griffin-shaped brass knocker.

Inside, the office is large and circular, with windows overlooking the Quidditch pitch on the grounds and the surrounding mountains. The Sorting Hat, when not in use during the Sorting ceremony, is kept here. Portraits of the school's previous headmasters and headmistresses line the walls, their occupants either "sleeping" (see page 108) or waiting to weigh in on their current successor's plans for the school.

During Dumbledore's time as headmaster, the room also houses Fawkes the phoenix and is filled with various artifacts, from a Pensieve to Lunascopes to delicate silver items emitting puffs of smoke that Harry never identifies. Harry destroys a great number of these unknown objects in his grief after Sirius's death.

It is in this office that Harry learns a great deal about his destiny in terms of his fight against Lord Voldemort, including the contents of the prophecy, the Dark wizard's use of Horcruxes and the final revelation that Harry must sacrifice himself to destroy Voldemort.

Decades later, after Hermione becomes Minister of Magic, she returns to this room to visit Headmistress McGonagall, who promptly chews out her former student for being in possession of an illegal Time-Turner.

PASSWORDS TO THE HEADMASTER'S OFFICE

"lemon drop" (or "sherbet lemon" in
original UK version) - 1992
"Cockroach Cluster" - 1995
"Fizzing Whizzbee" - 1995-1996

"Acid Pop" - 1996
"toffee éclairs" - 1997
"Dumbledore" - 1998

STAFFROOM

When Hogwarts staff need a place to relax, gather, discuss and support each other throughout the school year, they visit the staffroom, a long, wood-paneled space furnished with dark wooden chairs and other mismatched seats. Reserved for staff only, this space is guarded by two stone gargoyles, one on either side of the entrance. During Harry's first year at the school, it is in this room that Professor Snape receives medical treatment from Argus Filch after tangling with Fluffy, a giant three-headed dog, on Halloween. It should be noted, however, that Harry accesses the room unchecked—hoping to retrieve his copy of *Quidditch Through the Ages*, he walks in and sees a serious bite wound on Snape's leg, courtesy of his visit with Fluffy. Harry and Ron likewise access the room during their second year at the school, when the friends race to warn Professor McGonagall about the Chamber of Secrets. But when McGonagall calls for all students to return to their dormitories, the Gryffindors dart into a wardrobe, only to later hear their Head of House announce Ron's sister, Ginny, has been taken into the chamber.

This wardrobe later plays a key role in Professor Lupin's first Defense Against the Dark Arts lesson for his class of third-year students, which takes place the following school year. He takes the whole class into the staffroom to practice confronting and expelling a boggart which has taken up residence in the wardrobe. Two years later, during Dolores Umbridge's tenure as headmistress of Hogwarts, teachers are no longer permitted to speak freely in the staffroom and must resort to whispering in corridors.

On a more macabre note, the staffroom is also where the ghostly Professor Binns died. After having taught at Hogwarts for many years, the History of Magic teacher expired from natural causes in front of the staffroom's fireplace, but instead of passing on, he elected to get up from his spot in front of the hearth and continue teaching his subject as if nothing had changed.

During the Battle of Hogwarts, Harry sees the moaning remains of the gargoyles guarding the staffroom, which have been smashed apart by a stray jinx.

Hospital Wing

Students or staff requiring medical attention are sent to the hospital wing on the first floor of the castle behind a set of double doors (although during Harry's fifth year, he runs up multiple flights of stairs to get there, which may have been a mistake on the author's part). Inside, visitors will find rows of beds fitted with white linen sheets, separated by privacy screens. Madam Pomfrey heals all who seek aid, but if an ailment is beyond her ability, the patient is transferred to St. Mungo's Hospital for Magical Maladies and Injuries.

TRIPS TO THE HOSPITAL WING

Harry takes several trips to the infirmary, as do many of his friends and classmates (and even a few professors) as detailed here:

HANNAH ABBOTT Receives Calming Draught for exam stress.

KATIE BELL Hit in the face with a Quaffle during Quidditch practice and accidentally given a Blood Blisterpod by Fred; touches a cursed silver and opal necklace and is later transferred to St. Mungo's.

MARIETTA EDGECOMBE Pimples spell out "SNEAK" across her face after she betrays Dumbledore's Army, a result of Hermione's jinx.

FILIUS FLITWICK Stunned by Professor Snape.

GREGORY GOYLE Grows boils after getting hit with Harry's *Furnunculus* spell (or Pimple Jinx) that was intended for Malfoy.

HERMIONE GRANGER Spends several weeks recovering in the hospital wing after ingesting Polyjuice Potion that was accidentally made with cat hair; brought to the hospital wing by Snape after she and Harry are attacked by Dementors (Madam Pomfrey prescribes chocolate); front teeth grow alarmingly fast after being hit by Malfoy's *Densaugeo* curse meant for Harry, and she allows Madam Pomfrey to make them slightly smaller than they originally were; receives large yellow boils on her hands after coming into contact with undiluted Bubotuber pus in hate mail sent by Rita Skeeter's readers; cursed by Dolohov and put on a regimen of 10 different potions.

LEANNE Treated for shock after witnessing Katie Bell getting cursed by touching a necklace.

NEVILLE LONGBOTTOM Breaks wrist after falling off broomstick during first flying lesson; gets covered in boils due to having made an error while brewing Cure for Boils; knocked unconscious in fight with Crabbe and Goyle; nose broken by Dolohov; injured running at Death Eater's curse blocking stairs.

DRACO MALFOY Arm injured in hippogriff attack after insulting Buckbeak in Care of Magical Creatures class; wounded by Harry casting *Sectumsempra*.

MINERVA MCGONAGALL Takes four Stunning Spells to the chest, transferred to St. Mungo's.

CORMAC MCLAGGEN Eats a pound of Doxy eggs for a bet and misses Quidditch tryouts.

ELOISE MIDGEN Attempts to curse her acne off but accidentally removes her nose in the process, which Madam Pomfrey reattaches.

MONTAGUE Apparates into a toilet after being trapped in a Vanishing Cabinet for a day and a half.

ALASTOR MOODY Rescued after months of imprisonment in a magical trunk.

ALBUS SEVERUS POTTER Broken arm from staying in the past too long while using a Time-Turner.

HARRY POTTER Wakes up three days after his confrontation with Quirrell and Voldemort—friends and admirers have sent gifts, although Madam Pomfrey does not allow a toilet seat from Fred and George Weasley; spends a night regrowing the bones in his right arm with the help of Skele-Gro after a rogue Bludger breaks his arm during a Quidditch match and Lockhart removes the bones; wakes up in the hospital wing after falling from his broom during a Quidditch match against Hufflepuff due to Dementors on the pitch; brought to the hospital wing by Snape after he and Hermione are attacked by Dementors (Madam Pomfrey prescribes chocolate, and Dumbledore locks the friends in so they can use the Time-Turner to save Sirius and Buckbeak); given a Sleeping Potion after the third task of the Triwizard Tournament (Sirius is allowed to stay with him in dog form); wakes up with a cracked skull after being knocked out by a Bludger hit by substitute Gryffindor Keeper Cormac McLaggen and later summons Kreacher (joined by Dobby) and asks them to spy on Draco.

JACK SLOPER Knocked out, possibly by his own Beater bat.

ALICIA SPINNET Hit with a jinx by Slytherin Keeper Miles Bletchley that causes her eyebrows to grow so thick and fast that they cover her eyes and mouth.

DOLORES UMBRIDGE Catatonic after being carried off by centaurs in the Forbidden Forest, frightened by the sound of hooves.

WARRINGTON Skin develops the texture of cornflakes (targeted as a member of the Inquisitorial Squad).

BILL WEASLEY Mauled by werewolf Fenrir Greyback in human form.

GINNY WEASLEY Bed rest after being taken into the Chamber of Secrets; broken ankle mended by Madam Pomfrey.

RON WEASLEY Hand swollen and green after being bitten by Norbert(a) the Norwegian Ridgeback dragon; cleans bedpans without magic for detention; leg broken by Sirius in dog form dragging him into the Whomping Willow; hexed by Peter Pettigrew; arms scarred by brains in Department of Mysteries, Madam Pomfrey applies Dr. Ubbly's Oblivious Unction; drinks oak-matured mead that Slughorn planned to give Dumbledore for Christmas and which Malfoy had poisoned (saved by Harry's use of a bezoar and treated with essence of rue).

NOTABLE MENTIONS
• Colin Creevey, Justin Finch-Fletchley, Nearly Headless Nick, Hermione Granger and Penelope Clearwater: Petrified by basilisk, visitors barred after final attack, revived with mandrake draught in the spring.

• Nameless Gryffindor fourth-year and nameless Slytherin sixth-year: Leeks sprouting out of their ears after a scuffle in the corridors before the Quidditch final.

• Miss Fawcett (Ravenclaw), Mr. Summers (Hufflepuff) and Fred and George Weasley: Beard removal after attempting to magically age themselves to get past the Age Line around the Goblet of Fire in an attempt to participate in the Triwizard Tournament.

Owlery

A cold, drafty, circular stone room with glassless windows, Hogwarts's owlery is located at the top of the West Tower and houses hundreds of owls of various breeds that are owned by the school and its students. Owing to its numerous animal occupants, it is covered in straw and owl droppings. Mouse and vole skeletons litter the floor, and its walls are lined with perches for the many birds that call it home.

Harry is first seen visiting the owlery during his fourth year to covertly send a letter to Sirius and keep up their secret correspondence. On one occasion, Fred and George Weasley arrive, acting suspicious and secretive about a letter they intend to send; it's later revealed to be for Ludo Bagman, who paid their winning Quidditch World Cup bet in vanishing leprechaun gold.

Later, on a random Saturday morning during the following school year, Cho Chang encounters Harry there while on an errand to send a birthday present to her mother. The two discuss Quidditch, and Cho uses the moment to applaud Harry for his bravery in standing up to Umbridge and telling the truth about Cedric Diggory's untimely death.

At that moment, Filch bursts in with Mrs. Norris, claiming he heard Harry was placing an order for Dungbombs. To his dismay, he's too late to see for himself—Harry has already sent Hedwig off with a letter to Sirius. Cho corroborates Harry's story, saying she witnessed Harry sending his letter even though she arrived afterward.

Many years later, Scorpius Malfoy, Albus Potter and Delphi use the room as a meeting place to talk through how to dismantle a confiscated experimental Time-Turner.

Prefects' Bathroom

Hogwarts prefects have access to a private bathroom located on the fifth floor of the castle behind the fourth door to the left of a statue of Boris the Bewildered, a wizard who appears lost and has his gloves on the wrong hands. Despite the room's name, Quidditch captains are also allowed inside. The Hufflepuff Captain during Harry's fourth year at the school, Cedric Diggory (also a prefect), advises Harry to "take a bath" with his golden egg there before the second task of the Triwizard Tournament. Harry sneaks in with the help of the Marauder's Map and his Invisibility Cloak; Cedric advises that the password is "pine fresh."

The walls and floor are made of white marble, while overhead, a chandelier bathes the room in candlelight. Long white linen curtains decorate the windows, and a painting in a gold frame on the wall depicts a blonde mermaid on a rock. The bathtub, also made of white marble, is quite large and looks more like a swimming pool—it's deep enough to tread water and also features a diving board. Around the edges of the pool are about 100 golden taps with different colored jewels in each handle. Each tap carries water with a unique bubble bath of a more magical nature than one might find in a Muggle spa. These include pink and blue bubbles as large as footballs, extremely dense ice-white foam that Harry suspects could support his weight, aromatic purple clouds that hover just above the water's surface and a jet that bounces off the water in arcs. The pool fills up surprisingly quickly for its size. Fluffy white towels are provided for any who wish to take a dip.

Moaning Myrtle, a ghost who haunts the girls' bathroom on the second floor, will occasionally leave her space to spy on prefects taking baths. When she encounters Harry in the bathtub struggling to make sense of his golden egg for the Triwizard Tournament, she suggests opening the egg underwater just as Cedric did. Ultimately, her advice allows Harry to hear the merpeople's song, by which he deduces that the second task will involve recovering a stolen treasure from the lake.

Moaning Myrtle's Bathroom

Many students prefer to avoid this bathroom that is variously identified as being on the first or second floor. However, the second floor location is more commonly accepted, and the initial mention of it being on the first floor is likely an error. This out-of-order room is more commonly known as Moaning Myrtle's bathroom, after its moody spectral inhabitant (see page 219). Candles flood the bathroom with dim light, giving the room a depressing and gloomy feel.

Decades after her death, the ghost of Myrtle Warren will occasionally make her presence known by flooding the toilets, causing any nearby students to flee in panic. Its wooden stalls are ill-maintained, and the room features a row of chipped sinks.

In 1992, Harry, Ron and Hermione brew Polyjuice Potion here as part of a plot to gain access to the Slytherin common room. Unfortunately, Hermione discovers she accidentally picked up a cat's hair rather than Millicent Bullstrode's, and she hides in one of the rundown stalls after turning into a humanoid cat. That school year, Ginny Weasley uses the bathroom to access the Chamber of Secrets; while in her right mind, she attempts to destroy the cursed diary that's possessed her by flushing it down a toilet. Harry and Ron conclude that the entrance to the Chamber of Secrets can be accessed via a broken sink with a small snake scratched into its tap. When someone utters the word "open" in Parseltongue, the sink descends into the floor, revealing a large pipe.

Many years later, in an attempt to alter the past, Albus Potter and Scorpius Malfoy use the room while on a mission to change Cedric Diggory's fate during the events of the Triwizard Tournament.

Hogwarts's Staircases

A whopping 142 staircases can be found throughout Hogwarts. These come in a variety of shapes and sizes—wide, narrow, rickety or spiral-shaped—and are predominantly made of stone or marble. Some lead to a different location on a particular day of the week, while others might feature a vanishing step that students have to remember to jump over—which certainly helps keep first years on their toes.

A grand marble staircase is located in the entrance hall of Hogwarts Castle, opposite the main doors on the ground floor. It provides direct access to the upper seven floors of Hogwarts. Meanwhile, the staircase to the right of this grand one leads down to the kitchen and the Hufflepuff common room, while the staircase on the left allows for access to the Slytherin common room and the dungeons. Another popular staircase, the most well-traveled route to the Gryffindor common room, takes students from the second floor to the fourth floor. The entrance is hidden behind a tapestry, and this staircase in particular is notorious for its vanishing step halfway up, which frequently catches Neville off guard, often necessitating the help of his fellow Gryffindors to get him out. Harry also finds himself stuck in the stair while wandering around the castle in 1995.

Spiral staircases are common at Hogwarts. For instance, the tallest tower at the school, the Astronomy Tower, boasts a steep spiral staircase that leads up to the ramparts for access during Astronomy lessons. Similar stairs can be found in the Ravenclaw Tower (which takes students to the Ravenclaw common room, see page 66) as well as the North Tower (which takes students to the Divination classroom, see page 61). Hogwarts also boasts at least two moving staircases: One leads to the headmaster's/headmistress's office, and the other is a swiveling staircase near the Defense Against the Dark Arts professor's office.

Hogwarts's Corridors

Although the use of magic is forbidden in the many corridors at Hogwarts, these busy, communal spaces appear to be magnets for exciting incidents. Very few descriptions of the exact layout of corridors on each floor exist.

DUNGEONS
The dungeons (see page 98) are said to have many corridors leading to different chambers, including the Potions classroom, the Slytherin common room (see page 67) and Severus Snape's office.

GROUND FLOOR
The entrance hall (see page 55) contains entrances to the Great Hall, staff room, caretaker's office, classrooms, courtyard and other levels of the castle.

FIRST FLOOR
Accessible via the large marble staircase in the entrance hall, the first floor houses several main classrooms and offices, including the Defense Against the Dark Arts and Muggle Studies classrooms (see page 59 and page 62), as well as Professor McGonagall's office (see page 75). It includes a balcony overlooking the entrance hall.

SECOND FLOOR
The corridors that run throughout the second floor provide entrances to an out-of-order girls' bathroom (see page 85) as well as a shortcut to Gryffindor Tower (see page 64), which can be found tucked behind a tapestry. A map of Argyllshire also hangs in a corridor on the second floor.

THIRD FLOOR
Various third-floor corridors allow for access to the trophy room (see page

90) and an armor gallery (see page 116). The statue of a humpbacked witch (through which is a secret passage) is located in a corridor on this floor, as is the Charms classroom (see page 59). There is also a statue depicting the "ugly stone head of a medieval wizard" which can be found in an alcove along a corridor. Other items of note on this floor include a swiveling staircase and a window overlooking the front drive. During Harry's first year at Hogwarts, one of the third-floor corridors also holds the trapdoor to where the Sorcerer's Stone is hidden.

FOURTH FLOOR
The fourth-floor corridors include a bathroom, a painting of a landscape, a secret passage to Hogsmeade (found behind a large mirror; see page 139) and a narrow staircase (concealed behind a tapestry) with a trick step.

FIFTH FLOOR
A bathroom reserved specifically for prefects is located off a corridor on the fifth floor (see page 84), the fourth door to the left of a statue of Boris the Bewildered.

SIXTH FLOOR
A corridor on the sixth floor provides an entrance to a boys' bathroom as well as, in Harry's fourth year, the trophy room.

SEVENTH FLOOR
The seventh floor contains corridors that lead to Professor Flitwick's office (see page 76) and the headmaster's office (in 1996, at any rate—in 1994, it's on the second floor; see page 76). Other items of note include the Fat Lady's portrait (see page 106) and Sir Cadogan's portrait (see page 106). The Room of Requirement (see page 92) is accessible on this floor opposite a tapestry of Barnabas the Barmy that depicts a scene in which he attempts to teach trolls to dance ballet.

The Third-Floor Corridor

The third-floor corridor can be accessed through a door at the end of the Charms corridor.

During the 1991–1992 academic year's start-of-term feast, Dumbledore announces that the "third-floor corridor on the right-hand side" is strictly out of bounds, not just for all students but staff as well, and that exploring the area would almost certainly prove fatal. Unfortunately, the next day, Harry and Ron become lost on their way to class and are caught by Argus Filch trying to access the locked door guarding the corridor.

Later that year, Harry, Ron, Hermione and Neville hide in the corridor from Filch after Malfoy tells the castle's caretaker that students have been hanging out in the trophy room past curfew. They access the corridor through the door at the end of the Charms corridor, which Hermione unlocks with a simple *Alohomora* charm. Inside the corridor, the group finds a giant three-headed dog, who they later discover has been named "Fluffy" by Hagrid.

During the 1991 Halloween feast, Professor Quirrell unleashes a troll on the school in an attempt to buy time to access the trapdoor in this corridor.

Professor Quirrell also attempts to reaccess the chamber at the end of the school year, this time succeeding. However, the trio follows him after discovering what Fluffy is doing at Hogwarts and what he's guarding under the trapdoor: the Sorcerer's Stone.

A SECRET PASSAGEWAY

After Sirius's attack on the Fat Lady's portrait in 1993, Snape searches the third-floor corridor and patrols the scene. The vigilant Potions professor makes it difficult for Harry to access one of the hidden passageways out of Hogwarts that can be found behind the statue of Gunhilda of Gorsemoor (see page 113).

Trophy Room

Situated on the third floor of Hogwarts Castle, the trophy room can be accessed by the main marble staircase or a secret passageway in the armor gallery. However, the room has also been known to appear in a different location: In 1995, Harry spots it on the sixth floor of the castle while using the Marauder's Map. (The author has admitted to making mistakes regarding the locations of certain rooms.)

That said, the trophy room is (usually) adjacent to the armor gallery and has windows throughout the room. This windowed room showcases a host of awards, plates, statues, medals, cups, shields and, of course, trophies, which are kept in crystal glass display cabinets. Some of these prizes date back to the founders' era.

During the 1991–1992 academic year, Harry agrees to a wizard's duel with Malfoy after completing his first broomstick lesson. The terms: wands only, no contact, to be conducted at midnight in the trophy room (because, as Draco mentions, the room is always left unlocked after curfew). Harry's second is Ron Weasley, while Malfoy's second is Vincent Crabbe. Harry and Ron are joined by Hermione and Neville, who agree to go along simply because they can't get back into Gryffindor Tower. The group enters the trophy room at midnight. While waiting for their opponents to show up, the four students hear Filch just outside the door, telling Mrs. Norris to sniff around for them. The Gryffindors carefully exit the trophy room before sprinting down the armor gallery toward a secret passageway behind a tapestry near the Charms classroom. Moments later, the friends discover just why the third-floor corridor is out of bounds: a three-headed dog.

In 1992, Ron serves detention with Argus Filch in the trophy room after crashing his father's flying Ford Anglia into the Whomping Willow. His punishment: cleaning all the trophies without using magic.

While polishing prizes, Ron comes across an interesting bit of intel: Tom Riddle's Special Award for Services to the School (which he promptly vomits slugs all over and must clean repeatedly). He relays this discovery to Harry and Hermione, who are looking for information on the student whose diary they found in the girls' bathroom on the second floor. Unfortunately, Ron is forced to buff the Quidditch Cup 14 times before Filch is satisfied with his handiwork.

Tom Riddle's Special Award for Services to the School, a prize given to students whose outstanding accomplishments benefited Hogwarts in a great way, is tucked away in a corner cabinet. He received the award in 1943 for finding the person who opened the Chamber of Secrets, although it was later discovered that Riddle himself had opened the chamber in 1943. The trio also find Tom Riddle's name on a Medal for Magical Merit and a list of Hogwarts Head Boys. Harry and Ron also receive Special Awards for Services to the School at the end of the 1992-1993 academic year for saving Ron's sister, Ginny, and slaying the basilisk in the Chamber of Secrets.

The Triwizard Cup likely ends up in the trophy room after Harry wins the Tournament in 1995.

PEEVES

Peeves, Hogwarts's infamous poltergeist, is known to bounce around the trophy room from time to time. Harry first notices him taking a visit to the trophy room in December of 1993 while checking the Marauder's Map in order to leave the school unnoticed to visit Hogsmeade. Harry later observes Peeves in the trophy room just before the second task of the Triwizard Tournament while exiting the prefects' bathroom with his golden egg.

Room of Requirement

Over the centuries, many students have stumbled across the Room of Requirement, though few know how to use the charmed chamber to their full advantage. Also known as the Come and Go Room, this magical space is situated on the seventh floor across from a tapestry that depicts Barnabas the Barmy teaching trolls to do ballet. Incredibly, it can alter its proportions in keeping with whatever the user most needs it to be, whether a closet for storing a collection of chamber pots or a sanctuary in which to hide forbidden treasures, by reading the mind of the user as they walk back and forth in front of the space three times. On the third pass, a stretch of blank wall transforms, revealing a polished door with a brass handle. The room can also change and grow while in use depending on the developing needs of its users.

THE ROOM AND RESISTANCE

As Voldemort's forces grow stronger during Harry's time at Hogwarts, students call upon the Room of Requirement as a place of resistance. Based on a helpful tip from Dobby the house-elf, Harry uses the room as the headquarters for Dumbledore's Army. When accessed by members of the D.A., the room transforms into a large space, and its torch-lit walls are lined with bookcases. Silk cushions line the floor for people to sit on or fall onto when Stunned, and its numerous shelves are filled with books as well as handy gadgets such as Sneakoscopes, Secrecy Sensors and a Foe-Glass.

Two years later, when Voldemort takes over Hogwarts, Neville escapes from Amycus and Alecto Carrow, the Death Eater sibling duo, by returning to the Room of Requirement. To accommodate him, the room contains a hammock and Gryffindor House-themed wall hangings. As time goes on and more and more members of the D.A. need a place to hide, the space grows; it boasts multicolored hammocks, tapestries featuring House crests, bookcases, broomsticks, a wireless radio and, once girls begin seeking shelter at the hideout, a nice bathroom. The walls of this safe haven are made of dark wood and have no windows, and a balcony runs around the edges of the room. Within the friendly confines of this safe haven, Hogwarts students plan and launch a resistance to Voldemort's regime.

Since the room is not able to provide food for hungry students (an exception to Gamp's Law of Elemental Transfiguration), it instead offers a secret passageway to the Hog's Head Inn. This route connects to a portrait of Ariana Dumbledore, who moves between the Hogsmeade pub and the Room of Requirement to communicate messages. Strangely, people who travel through the passageway also show up in her portrait. Aside from reading the needs of its users, the semi-sentient room senses their motivations: For instance, it somehow deduces that Aberforth Dumbledore, Albus's brother, is aligned with the anti-Voldemort students and chooses to reveal this passageway to him. Before the Battle of Hogwarts, Harry, Ron, Hermione and many other members of the Order of the Phoenix and the D.A. use this passageway to enter the castle and participate in the final showdown against Voldemort.

THE ROOM OF HIDDEN THINGS

The room can clearly be instrumentalized for noble purposes, but when it takes the form of the Room of Hidden Things, it is most often used to secret away dark and dangerous objects. The Room of Hidden Things seems to represent a basic need in generations of Hogwarts students, teachers and staff: to conceal or guard shameful items. It appears in the same form to everyone who uses it for this purpose and simply increases in size as the objects within it pile up. These real objects (as opposed to ones created by the room) continue to age, break down and die as they are left abandoned in this space. The room keeps its curious collection of hidden items in a sort of limbo space, in case their owners (or anyone else) would like to retrieve them. It never disposes of these objects.

Since Hogwarts students and staff have long needed to hide a mind-boggling variety of things, the room has grown to be the size of a cathedral. Its vast landscape of stacked objects looks almost like a city to visitors, lit up from the natural light pouring through its towering windows. This room contains thousands of books and a number of Fanged Frisbees, winged catapults, potions, hats, jewels, bottles, swords, broomsticks, bats, crates, broken trunks, robes, cups, shields, a sparkling necklace, broken furniture, a chipped bust of a warlock, an acid-blistered cupboard, a blood-stained ax, dragon eggshells, a stuffed troll and, to Harry's eyes, a skeleton of a five-legged creature (which has since been identified as a Quintaped).

The room also contains the Vanishing Cabinet that is broken by Peeves in Harry's second year (which Montague gets shoved into by Fred and George in Harry's fifth year). Malfoy spends most of his sixth year at the school in this room trying to fix the cabinet. He eventually succeeds, using it as a means to bring Death Eaters into Hogwarts.

Sybill Trelawney, for her part, uses the room in order to hide the numerous empty sherry bottles that would otherwise reveal her drinking habit. During one such visit, she stumbles upon Malfoy having just completed his work on the Vanishing Cabinet. A pinch of Peruvian Instant Darkness Powder allows him to conceal his identity as he pushes her from the room.

Worried that Snape will discover the Half-Blood Prince's copy of *Advanced Potion-Making*, Harry stows the book in the Room of Hidden Things. To mark its spot, he places it inside an acid-burned cabinet topped with a bust, a wig and a discolored tiara. Little does he know that this tiara is actually Ravenclaw's diadem, which Voldemort has turned into a Horcrux.

Having found the room as a student, Voldemort—then known as Tom Riddle—arrogantly believed he was the only one who knew how to access the space. After graduating, he returned to Hogwarts to ask

Dumbledore for the Defense Against the Dark Arts job. He used this opportunity to hide the diadem in the Room of Hidden Things. The Dark wizard did not place any curses or protective enchantments on it, unlike with his other Horcruxes, perhaps because he assumed that in a room that large and cluttered, it would take any one person years to find it, and because he believed no one else knew about the room.

Harry, Ron and Hermione enter the Room of Hidden Things during the Battle of Hogwarts to search for the diadem of Ravenclaw. Draco, Crabbe and Goyle follow them in and a battle ensues. During the fighting, Crabbe casts Fiendfyre. In moments, a magical blaze tears through the room, destroying the diadem in the process.

THE ROOM'S PROTECTIONS
Since the Room of Requirement's purpose is to give the user what they want, it can provide near-total protection and privacy if utilized properly. The room appears on no known map and may be enchanted to be Unplottable. This extends to people accessing the room as well, so that anyone inside appears to have disappeared entirely from the Marauder's Map.

Much to Harry's chagrin, the room will not allow users to simply ask to see the version of the room someone else is using. Curious individuals must know exactly what the room is being used for in order to be able to access it. The Inquisitorial Squad, however, knows enough about why Harry and the D.A. are using the room to ask it for evidence of the group's existence—in return, the room gives them the sheet on which all members signed their names.

Loopholes like this can be closed, however, if the user is explicit about not allowing certain groups of people into the room. Neville is particularly skilled at this, and when the D.A. uses the room as a base to hide from Amycus and Alecto Carrow, he gives the room instructions to not let any Carrow supporters in. As long as one person remains inside the room, nobody else can change the use of the room for their own purposes. Other members of the D.A. are then able to come and go as they please while still keeping those inside safe from intruders.

Due to its frequent use, the Room of Hidden Things appears to allow for the least protection and privacy. Despite what is surely Draco's strong and explicit desire to be left alone while repairing the Vanishing Cabinet, Trelawney is still able to enter the room while he is using it. This version of the room seems to consider its ultimate purpose— providing a safe haven—of a higher importance than the individual needs of its user, and on some level, Draco appears to realize this. He prepares himself for the possibility of intruders by setting up Crabbe and Goyle as Polyjuiced guards and brings Peruvian Instant Darkness Powder with him on the off chance he is interrupted.

DEALING WITH MULTIPLE DESIRES

At its core, the Room of Requirement is designed to fulfill the needs of its users. Sometimes, these needs are easy to understand, such as when Harry realizes he needs a whistle for D.A. lessons and immediately finds one. The room has more subtle capabilities in mind reading, however, and can also listen to multiple people at once. When the room turns into the D.A. headquarters, it transmutes itself according to the collective needs of Ron, Harry and Hermione. As such, it forms itself to be an amalgamation of all of their desires, whether conscious or unconscious. Hermione is delighted when she finds shelves of books, including *A Compendium of Common Curses and Their Counter-Actions, The Dark Arts Outsmarted, Self-Defensive Spellwork* and *Jinxes for the Jinxed*. Ron, who unfortunately had been Stunned by Harry multiple times during Triwizard Tournament practice, is excited to see that the room has provided cushions with which to break their fall. The Dark Detectors in the room seem likely to have been inspired by Harry's forays into the impostor Moody's office the year before.

The more users who occupy the space, the more potentially complicated it could be for the room to accommodate all of their desires, especially if those desires are conflicting. The room seems to prioritize previous users' desires over those of newcomers. For example, when Harry is in the Room of Hidden Things during what would've been his final year at Hogwarts, his desire to find the diadem is superseded by Voldemort's desire for the diadem to stay hidden. Since the room honors its original purpose (to hide things) over the users' current purpose (to find them), the Summoning Charm cannot be used in this version of the room.

Another example of this concept is when Dobby decorates the D.A. headquarters for Christmas with mistletoe and golden balls with Harry's face on them and the slogan "Have a Very Harry Christmas." Despite how badly Harry wants for these decorations to disappear immediately before anyone else sees them, the room does not comply. He is forced to take them all down by hand.

OTHER KNOWN FORMS OF THE ROOM

The Room of Requirement has undoubtedly taken on countless forms across its storied existence. Many of its uses are so benign that the users in question don't recognize the enchanted nature of the room. Filch finds cleaning supplies there when he is running low, and, in turn, Fred and George use it to hide from Filch in a broom cupboard version of the room. Others know about the room and use it for their own purposes. In 1927, Dumbledore visited the Mirror of Erised in the room and gazed at a vision of himself with Grindelwald. In later years, when Dumbledore was wandering the corridors at night in need of a bathroom, the room filled itself with chamber pots. Dobby uses the room as a safe place for Winky to sleep off the effects of butterbeer, and it provides a small bed and alcohol antidotes. The room is well known among house-elves as the Come and Go Room, and they presumably use it for other needs in their tending of the castle.

Dungeons

Beneath Hogwarts lie several torch-lit dungeons and stone chambers connected by passages. Some of these dreary, gloomy spaces are easily accessible, while others can only be reached by magical means.

POTIONS CLASSROOM AND SNAPE'S OFFICE

Potions classes are held in a dungeon that can be reached by a staircase that's accessible via a door in the entrance hall (see page 55). The classroom itself is large enough to hold at least 20 students with room for cauldrons and worktables.

Also in the dungeons is the office of Severus Snape, Potions master from 1981 to 1996. The walls of this dimly-lit room are lined with shelves of glass jars that contain bits of animals and plants suspended in different potions. The office also contains a fireplace and a cupboard with Snape's private stock of ingredients. In January 1996, Harry begins attending Occlumency lessons with Snape in this office, where he notes there are hundreds of such jars. Snape eventually vacates the office after being appointed headmaster of the school.

HAPPY DEATHDAY, NICK

On October 31, 1992, Sir Nicholas de Mimsy-Porpington's 500th deathday party is held in "one of the roomier dungeons" at the castle. In keeping with the macabre theme, the space is decorated with black velvet draperies, as well as a chandelier fitted with black candles that emit blue flames. Nearly Headless Nick invites Harry, Hermione and Ron to join the festivities. Rotted, moldy food is served (because the ghosts are almost able to taste it), and musical saws are played for entertainment.

Several other noteworthy non-living guests are in attendance at Nick's spectral soirée, including Sir Patrick Delaney-Podmore, the leader of the Headless Hunt (a ghostly clique who refuse to admit Nick into their ranks, based on the fact that Nick's head was not completely severed from his body), who steals the spotlight from Nick by cracking jokes about the gloomy atmosphere. The other Hogwarts House ghosts are also present, along with the ghost of a knight with an arrow sticking out of his forehead. Some speculate this is the ghost of Harold II, the last Anglo-Saxon king of England, who died when William the Conqueror invaded and whose eye was shot through with an arrow.

HONORABLE MENTIONS

Because Hogwarts boasts such an intricate layout, several spaces are also underground and close to the dungeons. The Hogwarts kitchens (see page 72) aren't located in the dungeons, but they are located directly beneath the Great Hall (see page 56), making them technically underground. Despite this, the space is described as a high-ceilinged room.

Located on the same floor as the kitchens, the Hufflepuff common room also counts as an underground room. Hufflepuffs and Slytherins are the only two Houses with underground common rooms, a dramatic difference from Gryffindor and Ravenclaw's tower-based rooms.

The Chamber of Secrets, much like the hiding place of the Sorcerer's Stone, can be accessed via an entrance on an upper floor of the castle. Despite its second-floor entrance, the chamber is actually situated underneath the castle, likely somewhere under the lake and beneath the dungeons.

It certainly begs the question: What other secrets are hiding in the Hogwarts dungeons?

Chamber of Secrets

Deep below the main structure of Hogwarts Castle lies the Chamber of Secrets, a hidden room that for centuries held the terrifying key to Salazar Slytherin's plans for Hogwarts.

After constructing Hogwarts Castle about 1,000 years ago, the founders of Hogwarts disagreed over which sorts of students they would accept into their school. Initially, they attempted to resolve the ensuing differences of opinion by creating four Houses, in which each founder could select the students they would most like to teach. As time went on, it became clear that the pure-blood supremacist beliefs of Salazar Slytherin meant he wouldn't accept Muggle-born students at the school. Godric Gryffindor took issue with this prejudice, and with tensions rising, Slytherin left Hogwarts. Before he did, however, he created a subterranean space that would come to be known as the Chamber of Secrets.

It should be noted that this chamber may have originally been built as a private headquarters for Slytherin to teach his students spells classified as Dark Arts (another topic of dissension among the founders). By the time Slytherin took his leave of the school, however, he intended for the space to house a terrifying monster—the basilisk—which, when unleashed by one of his Parseltongue-speaking descendants, would eradicate Hogwarts's Muggle-born populace.

While it would be inaccurate to paraphrase Dumbledore and say that the Chamber of Secrets was "a complete secret, so, naturally, the whole school knows," legends of its existence had widely circulated among those who attended Hogwarts. Yet, by the time Harry attends the school, countless generations of magical historians along with Hogwarts headmasters and headmistresses had searched in vain for evidence of the Chamber's existence; after centuries of dead ends, it came to be regarded as mere legend.

Prior to Harry's descent into the Chamber, the nature of Slytherin's monster remained largely unknown. Perhaps Slytherin and his descendants preferred the mystery surrounding the legendary "horror within" and so were less forthcoming about describing their "pet" basilisk below the basement, lest any wizard seek it out in an attempt to destroy the creature. A giant magical snake that can kill people with its stare, the basilisk was trained by Slytherin to listen exclusively to Slytherin and his heirs, as opposed to any random Parselmouth (a witch or wizard gifted with the ability to speak Parseltongue, the language of snakes). Basilisks can live for "many hundreds of years"—the basilisk Harry slays is most likely the same one Slytherin placed in the Chamber almost 1,000 years before. In that time, the monster must have found an ample food supply of small animals in the Chamber's tunnels and grew to be at least 20 feet long.

By the 18th century, in keeping with evolving hygiene standards, the time had come for Hogwarts to have a plumbing system. Prior to toilets being installed in the castle, the Chamber could be accessed through a concealed trapdoor leading to a series of magical underground tunnels that in turn led to the entrance of the Chamber (and allowed the basilisk to slither beneath the castle floors). During this time in the school's history, Slytherin's heir, Corvinus Gaunt, a distant ancestor of Tom Riddle, was in attendance at Hogwarts. Knowing the Chamber needed to remain secret in order to ensure its future success, Gaunt intervened in the construction plans to secretly re-conceal the trapdoor as the site of a bathroom.

By the 20th century, the basilisk had taken advantage of Hogwarts's extensive plumbing system and used it to move unseen throughout the castle. While Harry is scared to hear a voice coming from inside the castle walls as a second-year student, any non-Parselmouth at Hogwarts would only hear hissing—an assuredly unremarkable occurrence for 200-year-old magical plumbing. The basilisk has easy access to the pipes via the second-floor girls' bathroom where the Chamber's secret entrance is hidden (see page 85). One of the taps on the bathroom's sinks has a small snake scratched into its side. If the snake is commanded to open in Parseltongue, the tap spins and glows bright white, and the sink in question descends out of the way, revealing a large pipe down which a person can slide toward the Chamber. While visiting the Chamber, Harry estimates that it's located miles beneath the school. Meanwhile, Ron deduces from the damp and slimy walls of the tunnels leading to the Chamber that it likely lies beneath the lake at Hogwarts (see page 123).

As the two friends and Professor Lockhart trudge onward in search of Ron's sister, Ginny Weasley, they discover the tunnels surrounding the Chamber are made of stone and are large enough to stand in. The space's probable location beneath the lake means the floors are wet, but apart from the skeletons of the basilisk's meals and the occasional giant shedded snakeskin, these tunnels are fairly empty. Eventually, Harry reaches a stone wall featuring two carved serpents—the creatures appear to be entwined, their eyes set with emeralds.

Only speaking Parseltongue can open this wall, and while Slytherin intended this to mean only Parselmouths like himself and his family could open the Chamber, in 1998, Ron proves that mimicry of Parseltongue (even after several failed attempts) is also sufficient. On successfully commanding the entwined serpents to open, they separate as the wall parts into two, revealing the main chamber.

The ceiling of this long, tall space is supported by stone pillars. It is so poorly lit, however, that Harry can hardly make out the ceiling. Adding to the forbidding gloom of this dark, green-hued, dungeon-like area is a noticeable chill in the air. Not one for understatement in interior decorating, Slytherin had another series of carved serpents winding and twisting around every pillar as a symbol of his family's House and rare special ability. As a final touch, he placed a gigantic full-body statue of himself against the Chamber's far wall that reaches to the ceiling; it depicts him as an aged, robed wizard with a thin beard that cascades nearly to the floor. With a third Parseltongue command from the heir of Slytherin, the statue's mouth opens, releasing the basilisk within.

It's unclear how many of Slytherin's descendants used the space over the years. Corvinus Gaunt certainly maintained access to the Chamber, and during Harry's time at the school, Harry overhears how the Chamber had been opened decades prior, supposedly by then student Rubeus Hagrid. In reality, fifth-year Slytherin student (and heir of Slytherin) Tom Riddle—who would later come to be known as Lord Voldemort—accessed the Chamber and unleashed the beast. The basilisk eventually killed Muggle-born Myrtle Warren, who would go on to haunt the bathroom entrance to the Chamber as the ghost known as Moaning Myrtle.

Riddle brought his potential murder spree to a swift end when he realized it would lead to the closure of the school and his permanent return to the orphanage in which he grew up. He successfully pinned the murder on Rubeus Hagrid and claimed the monster in question had been Hagrid's pet Acromantula, Aragog. Viewed as a hero, Riddle received an award for special services to the school; meanwhile, Aragog fled to the Forbidden Forest to live out the rest of his days, and Hagrid was expelled. Tragically, Hagrid would also briefly spend time in Azkaban prison when the basilisk attacks begin anew during Harry's second year at Hogwarts.

Harry and his friends spend most of their second year solving the mystery of the Chamber's location and monster, only to discover that the Tom Marvolo Riddle of the possessed diary Ginny had been writing in was the birth name of the Dark wizard known as Lord Voldemort. The ghost-like memory of Riddle releases the basilisk, and thanks to a bit of help from Fawkes the phoenix and the Sorting Hat, Harry pulls the sword of Gryffindor from the hat and uses it to slay the monster before plunging a basilisk fang into the diary, unknowingly destroying the first of Voldemort's seven Horcruxes.

About five years after these events, during the run-up to the Battle of Hogwarts that precedes Harry's final struggle against Lord Voldemort, Ron and Hermione return to the space to procure basilisk fangs, which they then use to destroy another Horcrux, the cup of Helga Hufflepuff.

Given that Fawkes was not present to lift Ron and Hermione out of the Chamber as he once did for Ginny, Harry, Ron and Gilderoy Lockhart, the two friends make use of a broomstick to ascend from the space's subterranean depths.

Enchantments & Protections

A number of complex enchantments conceal and protect Hogwarts Castle from intruders both Muggle and magical. Muggles who wander in the immediate vicinity of the castle, for instance, will see only ruins and signs telling them to turn back. Wizards and witches, on the other hand, will encounter defenses that prevent unauthorized entrance by magical means, which are much stricter in times of war. According to Hermione, *Hogwarts: A History* details how Muggle technology fails to work at Hogwarts in that the concentrated abundance of magic causes too much interference.

As Hermione frequently reminds Harry and Ron, it is impossible to Apparate into, out of or within the Hogwarts castle and grounds. However, this rule does not apply to house-elves, whose magical abilities wizards never seem to take into consideration when casting protective enchantments. Similarly, Fawkes the phoenix is able to disappear and reappear elsewhere in a flash of flame, which Professor Dumbledore uses to bypass the enchantments when he escapes Cornelius Fudge's attempt to arrest him by grabbing Fawkes's tail feathers and vanishing with the bird. The Apparition prohibition is lifted only in the Great Hall for students to take Apparition lessons the following school year.

In terms of other magical means of deterring intruders, when Harry is a third-year student at Hogwarts, the Ministry of Magic stations Dementors around the school for protection against Azkaban escapee Sirius Black. Security is further tightened after Black manages to infiltrate the castle—in one memorable example, Professor Flitwick even goes so far as to teach the school's front doors to recognize a picture of the fugitive.

Three years later, after Voldemort's return has been publicly acknowledged and Rufus Scrimgeour takes over as Minister of Magic following Cornelius Fudge's dishonorable departure, the Ministry deploys a task force of Aurors to the wizarding institution. The castle's existing protections are strengthened and additional security measures are added, including defensive spells and charms and a series of countercurses. Dumbledore bewitches the gates himself, and the walls are equipped with anti-intruder jinxes. Filch uses a Secrecy Sensor, which can detect jinxes, curses and concealment charms, to check students for banned items or Dark objects coming into and out of the castle. Dumbledore later undoes his own enchantments while flying back to the school from Hogsmeade with Harry after their journey to the cave.

Prior to the Battle of Hogwarts, Professor McGonagall instructs the staff to put in place every protection possible. Professor Flitwick casts complex incantations, including *Protego Horribilis*, that cause a peculiar rushing noise like wind across the grounds.

Art & Artifacts

The walls and corridors of Hogwarts Castle are adorned with decorations, including oil paintings, tapestries, statues, suits of armor and busts. These often depict famous wizards or scenes in wizarding history and have magical properties, such as the ability to move and speak. Subjects of paintings can leave their frames and visit other pictures either within the castle or in another location where the subject has a portrait. The people, characters and other beings depicted in these works aren't quite as sentient as living beings, however—the extent of the personality and interactivity of a portrait is based on the power of the subject and how much time they spent with the painting to teach it to act like them and pass on their own qualities and wisdom. Caretaker Argus Filch appears to be responsible for the maintenance and restoration of these items.

The castle is also home to a number of significant magical objects. As a historic magical landmark itself, founded by the greatest magical minds of their time and attended by every luminary in the British wizarding world since, it makes sense that Hogwarts would have developed quite a collection over the centuries. As one of the safest places in the wizarding world, it is also a logical choice to house artifacts for safekeeping, preservation and study.

THE FAT LADY

The portrait of a large woman wearing a pink silk dress, known as the Fat Lady, stands guard to the entrance to Gryffindor Tower. She resents being awoken for late entry to the common room so much that she will lie about the password changing out of pure annoyance. She once gave Molly Weasley a telling-off for returning to the dormitory at four o'clock in the morning after a nighttime stroll with her future husband, Arthur. The Fat Lady sometimes leaves her portrait at night, as when Harry and Ron sneak out to duel Malfoy during their first year at Hogwarts; when Hermione follows them, she finds herself unable to get back into the common room with the Fat Lady gone.

In 1993, recently escaped convict Sirius Black slashes the Fat Lady's painting after she refuses him admittance to Gryffindor Tower without the password on Halloween. She flees in terror and shame, and Peeves spots her running through a landscape on the fourth floor. She is later found hiding in a map of Argyllshire on the second floor (see page 87). After being restored by Filch, she demands additional protection and is given security trolls.

The following school year, a wizened witch from another painting named Violet tells the Fat Lady that Harry has been selected as Triwizard champion before he can make it back to the dormitory. At Christmas, Violet and the Fat Lady get tipsy from downing chocolate liqueurs together. Two years later, they overindulge again at Christmas by drinking all the wine in a painting of drunk monks by the Charms corridor; while recovering from her wicked hangover, the Fat Lady appears pale and is sensitive to noise (the password that day is "abstinence"). After Dumbledore's death, while grieving his passing, she allows Harry into the common room without the password.

SIR CADOGAN

Located on the seventh floor of the castle, Sir Cadogan's portrait depicts a short, squat knight in a suit of armor with an oversized sword and a fat gray pony. He is first seen in Harry's third year at Hogwarts when he leads Harry, Ron and Hermione to the Divination classroom by traveling through various paintings. Chivalrous to a fault, the knight is desperate to demonstrate his prowess, but he proves helpful if presented with a quest.

Long ago, Sir Cadogan was a wizard and a knight during a time when wizards lived and worked among Muggles. Through his friendship with Merlin, he became a member of King Arthur's Knights of the Round Table. Noticeably absent from Muggle Arthurian tales, Sir Cadogan is portrayed in the wizarding versions as "hot-headed and peppery" and excessively brave. His chief triumph is having slain the Wyvern of Wye, a dragon-like creature that bit his wand in half, ate his horse and melted his sword and visor. After stumbling upon a fat pony idling in a nearby meadow that fateful day, the fearless knight charged back into danger, fully expecting to die in glorious battle. When he pierced the beast's tongue with his broken wand, the wyvern exploded. This story gave rise to the common wizarding phrase "take Cadogan's pony," meaning to make the best of a difficult situation.

After the Fat Lady is attacked by Sirius (see page 106), Sir Cadogan is the only painting who volunteers to be her replacement. Due to his insistence on challenging people to duels and coming up with new passwords twice a day, he is not popular among students. On Christmas, he hosts a party in his painting with monks and former Hogwarts headmasters. Sir Cadogan is later removed from his post after he allows Sirius into Gryffindor Tower when the fugitive provides a list of all the passwords for the week (the same list Neville Longbottom wrote after convincing the knight to tell him the passwords in advance). About four years later, the knight cheers Harry on to victory during the Battle of Hogwarts.

Sir Cadogan bears some resemblance to Miguel de Cervantes's Don Quixote—a bumbling, deluded man who believes he is a knight and invents quests and battles where there are none. Another potential influence could be King Pellinore—a well-meaning but overeager, clumsy knight obsessed with hunting the Questing Beast—from T.H. White's *The Sword in the Stone*, the first part of his Arthurian retelling *The Once and Future King*, a source of inspiration for the author.

The Portraits of Hogwarts's Headmasters & Headmistresses

Honor-bound to serve the current headmaster or headmistress of the school, the portraits of previous head staff of Hogwarts hang in the head's office and are painted before the death of their subjects. The author stated in an interview, perhaps jokingly, that headmasters are expected to die in office; abdication or abandonment are unacceptable. The portraits are kept under lock and key and can only be visited by their subjects, who then imbue them with memories and wisdom to create "a faint imprint of themselves."

The subjects of these portraits typically appear to be asleep in their frames, a ruse they employ to eavesdrop on conversations. Aside from providing counsel, their duties might include traveling to their other portraits to either deliver a message or report on specific individuals or events, acting as a trusted go-between when the current headmaster is indisposed.

PHINEAS NIGELLUS BLACK

Black, the least popular headmaster, is depicted with black hair, dark eyes and a pointed beard and often visits his other portrait at number twelve, Grimmauld Place to report on events or deliver messages to the Order of the Phoenix. In 1995, he relays the news that Voldemort's snake, Nagini, attacked Arthur Weasley at the Ministry of Magic. During the trio's Horcrux hunt from 1997 to 1998, his portrait at number twelve, Grimmauld Place is placed in Hermione's beaded bag when the trio goes on the run; he reluctantly provides them information on what's going on at Hogwarts and passes intel about their locations to Headmaster Severus Snape, enabling the latter to give them Gryffindor's sword when the friends need it most.

DILYS DERWENT

A Healer who once worked at St. Mungo's Hospital, Derwent's portrait has hung in the headmaster's office since 1768. In 1995, she returns to her portrait at St. Mungo's to report back on Arthur Weasley's condition.

ARMANDO DIPPET

Dumbledore's predecessor is depicted as a frail-looking old wizard. He takes his responsibility to the current headmaster seriously and scolds Phineas Nigellus Black for failing to do so.

ALBUS DUMBLEDORE

Hanging behind the headmaster's chair is Dumbledore's portrait, which appears shortly after his funeral in 1997. He is usually seen sleeping in his frame but notably advises Headmaster Snape on how to give the sword of Gryffindor to Harry. Following the Battle of Hogwarts, Harry speaks briefly with Dumbledore about what to do with the Elder Wand and Resurrection Stone. On October 31, 2020, Dumbledore's portrait visits Harry, now a middle-aged Auror at the Ministry of Magic, at Harry's office at the Department of Magical Law Enforcement and speaks about old times.

EVERARD

Everard is sent to his other portrait at the Ministry of Magic to warn others about the attack on Arthur Weasley; later, he relays what he saw to Headmaster Dumbledore.

DEXTER FORTESCUE

In 1995, Fortescue announces his disapproval of Cornelius Fudge and Dolores Umbridge after Professor McGonagall comments on how Willy Widdershins got off lightly following the "regurgitating toilets" incident. Dexter says that in his day, he did not "cut deals with petty criminals." He occasionally uses an ear trumpet and is distantly related to Florean Fortescue, who runs an ice cream parlor in Diagon Alley.

The Mirror of Erised

The true origins of the Mirror of Erised, an ancient magical artifact, and how it came to reside at Hogwarts are shrouded in mystery. As tall as a classroom ceiling, the item's ornate gold frame rests on two clawed feet and is inscribed with the words "Erised stra ehru oyt ube cafru oyt on wohsi." When read backward, the message becomes "I show not your face but your heart's desire" and explains the item's true purpose: to reflect the user's deepest and most desperate desires.

In 1927, Professor Dumbledore went looking for the Mirror in the Room of Requirement, which he discovered under a black velvet curtain. In it, he saw the image of his past lover, Gellert Grindelwald. Many years later, he uses the mirror again and sees his family whole: his long-deceased father, mother and sister returned to good health, and his brother reconciled with him.

During the 1991–1992 academic year, the Mirror is relocated from the Room of Requirement to a disused classroom, which is where Harry first finds it during the Christmas break. Harry sees his family in the Mirror—most notably, his mother and father, along with several other family members. He takes Ron to see the Mirror the following night, expecting to show Ron the Potters Harry never knew, but instead, Ron sees himself as Head Boy and Quidditch Captain. Obsessed, Harry continues to visit the Mirror throughout the Christmas break until Dumbledore finds Harry staring before the object one night. He warns the young student to not "dwell on dreams," that the Mirror would be moved to a different location and to not go looking for it. He also tells Harry that he sees himself with a pair of socks.

After the Christmas break ends and classes resume, Professor Dumbledore moves the Mirror of Erised through the trapdoor in the third-floor corridor, where it is used as the final puzzle to protect the Sorcerer's Stone from Professor Quirrell and Lord Voldemort. Designed to present the Stone to someone who would like to find it but would not use it, the Mirror shows Harry an image of himself reaching into his pocket and pulling out the Stone—at which point Harry feels a sudden weight in his pocket.

Harry largely takes Dumbledore's advice and doesn't dwell on the Mirror, although he does recall the mysterious object after his godfather, Sirius, dies near the end of the 1995-1996 academic year, hoping that his two-way mirror would work similarly and that he could use it to see Sirius. Unfortunately, this proves not to be the case. The Mirror crosses Harry's mind earlier the same school year during his Occlumency lessons with Severus Snape—in one lesson, Snape watches Harry's memory of seeing his parents waving at him in the Mirror.

According to *Hogwarts: An Incomplete and Unreliable Guide*, Dumbledore returns the Mirror to the Room of Requirement, where it is presumably destroyed during the Battle of Hogwarts when Vincent Crabbe casts Fiendfyre.

SEEING LOVE

According to Dumbledore, seeing love in the Mirror of Erised is a rare occurrence, and most people either see themselves as rich or immortal. It follows, then, that Lord Voldemort would see himself ruling the wizarding world for eternity. Dumbledore, of course, is an exception in that during his youth, he saw an image of Gellert Grindelwald (whom the author has stated Dumbledore loved) gazing back at him.

Tapestries

The tapestries lining Hogwarts's halls are often left unnamed, presented without context and conceal secret passageways. One memorable tapestry depicts Barnabas the Barmy's futile attempt to train a group of trolls in the art of ballet (they club him instead). It hangs in the seventh-floor corridor opposite an entrance to the Room of Requirement. The Slytherin dormitories also house several medieval tapestries depicting adventures of famous Slytherins.

UNSPECIFIED TAPESTRIES

In 1991, Percy Weasley leads the Gryffindor first years through two doors hidden by tapestries to the Gryffindor common room. Later, Harry, Ron and Hermione find a hidden passageway behind a tapestry while running from Argus Filch.

The following school year, Filch bursts through a tapestry to chastise students about tracking mud into the castle.

In Harry's fourth year, the trio accesses a door behind a tapestry leading to a staircase (with a trick step) often used as a shortcut.

As a fifth-year student, Harry slips behind a tapestry only to find Fred and George Weasley eavesdropping behind the door it conceals.

The following school year, a Fanged Frisbee—confiscated by Hermione from a fourth year— attempts to take a bite out of a tapestry in the Gryffindor common room.

During the 1996–1997 academic year, when Death Eaters take over Hogwarts, bright tapestries depicting House symbols adorn the walls of the Room of Requirement, where the remaining members of Dumbledore's Army live in hiding. A tapestry representing Slytherin House is noticeably absent.

During the Battle of Hogwarts, the trio resorts to hiding behind tapestries in order to catch their breath.

Statues

S tatues at Hogwarts depict notable witches and wizards as well as animals, such as the two winged boars flanking the front gates. A statue of Gregory the Smarmy conceals the entrance to a secret passageway (see page 118) Fred and George Weasley claim they discovered in their first week at the castle. Harry and Ron hide behind a large stone griffin while trying to warn Hermione about a rogue troll. A stone gargoyle guards the entrance to the headmaster's office (see page 76) and leaps aside if given the correct password.

In 1993, in a third-floor corridor, Harry finds a statue of a humpbacked witch believed to be Gunhilda of Gorsemoor. It conceals the entrance to a secret passageway that leads to Honeydukes's cellar.

While en route to the prefects' bathroom in 1994, Harry spots a statue of Boris the Bewildered, a confused-looking wizard wearing gloves on the wrong hands.

During the 1995–1996 academic year, in order to avoid being teased by his brothers, Ron hides behind a statue of Lachlan the Lanky on the seventh floor near the head of the stairs that lead to the sixth floor. That year, Harry encounters two stone gargoyles guarding the entrance to the staffroom (see page 78). He also hears from Nearly Headless Nick about how Peeves is planning a prank that involves a bust of Paracelsus, which can be found in the corridor leading from the Gryffindor common room (see page 64) to the owlery (see page 83). Harry spots Mrs. Norris, Argus Filch's cat, prowling this corridor before she disappears behind a statue of Wilfred the Wistful.

In 1998, Harry encounters Rowena Ravenclaw's life-sized white marble statue in her House's common room (see page 66); she is depicted wearing her infamous diadem. During the Battle of Hogwarts, Minerva McGonagall uses the spell *Piertotum Locomotor* to animate the school's statues and suits of armor to protect the school by fighting Voldemort's forces.

Pensieve

Pensieves are rare and powerful magical items that wizards use to sift through their memories. Harry encounters a Pensieve in Headmaster Dumbledore's office while studying at Hogwarts and uses it to understand how a number of people and events influenced the rise of Lord Voldemort.

APPEARANCE

These objects are wide, shallow basins made of stone or metal and are often elaborately decorated with precious stones. The Pensieve at Hogwarts is made of stone with ancient Saxon runes and symbols carved in its sides. When a Pensieve is in use, it emits a silvery light from its depths. Thoughts that have been poured into the basin appear as a bright, cloud-like, whitish-silver substance that is constantly in motion. Harry remarks they look like "light made liquid—or like wind made solid."

HOW IT WORKS

Difficult to use, Pensieves are usually only mastered by powerful witches and wizards. Such items are, in essence, private archives of their owners, so much so that they are typically buried with the associated witch or wizard upon death. Since it is the property of the school, the Pensieve at Hogwarts does not belong to anyone and is used as a magical reference source for headmasters to access the wisdom of their predecessors.

Memories stored in a Pensieve are accurate and not based on the user's specific memory of a situation; in other words, they preserve memories of events as those events occurred, untainted by bias or emotion. Memories can be altered, but such tampering is evident to the user.

When viewing a memory within the Pensieve, the user appears to have to touch the contents to begin the process, an action that incorporeally transports them into the memory to live it as it happened.

HARRY POTTER AND THE PENSIEVE

Dumbledore keeps the Hogwarts Pensieve in a cabinet in his office. He explains to Harry that when he has too many thoughts and memories crowding his mind, he "siphons" them into the Pensieve using his wand to better "spot patterns and links."

The first two times Harry reviews memories in the Pensieve, he does so without permission; intrigued by the thoughts swirling in the basin, he feels compelled to touch them and finds himself occupying Dumbledore's memories. The following school year, when Dumbledore instructs Severus Snape to teach Harry Occlumency, Snape borrows the Pensieve to store some of his most embarrassing memories in an effort to keep them hidden. Unfortunately, Snape leaves the Pensieve unattended and Harry winds up visiting one of them.

During the 1996–1997 academic year, Dumbledore uses memories gathered from other people stored in small crystal bottles to show Harry information regarding Tom Riddle's progression into Lord Voldemort. One of these memories is from Potions professor Horace Slughorn, which looks as if it has "congealed" or "gone bad," and a strange fog clouds the scene. Dumbledore explains this is evidence that Slughorn doctored the memory. Harry later obtains the unedited memory from Slughorn, in which the teacher instructs Riddle about how Horcruxes are made.

The next year, Harry uses the Pensieve to view the memories a fatally wounded Snape gives him in the Shrieking Shack. As Snape dies, a silvery blue substance, "neither gas nor liquid" gushes from his mouth, ears, and eyes. Harry uses his wand to collect and bottle it in a flask. Ultimately, these memories reveal to Harry that he is, in fact, a Horcrux.

ACCORDING TO LEGEND...

The Hogwarts Pensieve was originally found half-buried in the ground on the spot where the founders decided to build the school.

Suits of Armor

Hogwarts's numerous suits of armor possess some degree of magical sentience and often move of their own accord. They will laugh at clumsy students (e.g., Neville Longbottom) who fall through the trick step in a staircase and will turn to watch students hiding behind them or whom they spot sneaking down the corridor at night. On many occasions, Peeves has amused himself by locking up Mrs. Norris inside of one.

Despite their capacity to roam, these suits in this enchanted medieval panoply have been spotted in a few recognizable locations in the castle. Some appear to guard the front doors, while others can be found near such locations as the kitchens, the Defense Against the Dark Arts classroom, and at the top of the staircase with the trick stair. A suit of armor is also seen near the room containing the Mirror of Erised, around the corner from the History of Magic classroom, and at the top of the marble staircase, respectively. Students and staff visiting the trophy room (see page 90) are likely to stroll past the long gallery lined with many suits of armor.

On rare occasions, these prized sets of metal garments are given special treatment. Prior to the Triwizard Tournament, the armor is oiled before Beauxbatons and Durmstrang students arrive so that the suits move quietly around the castle. During the Christmas season, lights or everlasting candles are placed inside the suits of armor to create a lantern effect. The armor is also enchanted to sing Christmas carols. They don't seem to know all the words, however, prompting Peeves to hide inside them and add his own rude lyrics. Beauxbatons's champion, Fleur Delacour, finds the suits of armor neither impressive nor charming and calls them "ugly."

During the Battle of Hogwarts, Professor McGonagall uses the *Piertotum Locomotor* spell to bring them to life. Armed with swords and spiked balls on chains to help protect the castle, the suits of armor jump into action. When McGonagall duels Snape, one suit of armor shields Snape from daggers and is bewitched by Flitwick to attempt to crush Snape under its weight.

Vanishing Cabinet

Vanishing Cabinets are extremely valuable magical artifacts that allow their users to slip inside and be magically transported into a partner cabinet. Not much is known about the history of the large black-and-gold Vanishing Cabinet at Hogwarts, but its twin was at some point acquired by Borgin and Burkes. In Harry's second year, Nearly Headless Nick persuades Peeves to drop the Vanishing Cabinet in a classroom directly above Filch's office in order to provide a diversion for Harry. The broken cabinet is then kept on the first floor until Harry's fifth year, when Fred and George push Montague into it to stop him from taking points from Gryffindor. Montague is stuck there for a day and a half, alternating between being able to hear conversations in Hogwarts and Borgin and Burkes. Nobody on either side is able to hear him, however. When he finally attempts to Apparate out, he gets stuck in a toilet on the fourth floor. The experience affects Montague severely, leaving him confused for days afterward until his parents decide to collect him from the school.

After this unfortunate incident, the Vanishing Cabinet is removed from the first floor and placed in the Room of Requirement. Malfoy, upon hearing Montague's story, realizes that the cabinet has a twin in Borgin and Burkes that would allow him to lead people into Hogwarts unsupervised after repairing the one in the Room of Requirement (see page 92). He instructs Borgin to keep the partner cabinet safe and to not sell it. Draco then spends his sixth year locked away in the Room of Requirement attempting to repair the cabinet and finally succeeds at his task at the end of the school year. He uses the cabinet to bring Death Eaters into the castle to help him murder Dumbledore.

Following Dumbledore's untimely death, the repaired cabinet remains in the Room of Hidden Things and is presumably destroyed along with the rest of the objects in the room after Crabbe conjures Fiendfyre during the Battle of Hogwarts.

Secret Passages Within the School

An ancient school of magic like Hogwarts is bound to have its share of secrets, including these hidden passageways.

SECOND FLOOR

During the 1995–1996 academic year, when Fred and George Weasley set off fireworks to annoy Headmistress Dolores Umbridge, the twins hide on the other side of a door concealed behind a tapestry (see page 112). This tapestry is most likely on the second floor since the fireworks are described as being set off a floor below Umbridge's office, which appears to be on the third floor. The entrance to the Chamber of Secrets is located in the second-floor girls' bathroom (see page 85) and can be accessed through a sink with a tiny snake on the copper tap. When the user says "Open up" in Parseltongue, the tap turns white and spins and the sink lowers into the floor to reveal a large pipe. Another tapestry on this floor hides a staircase to the fourth floor, while a further unnamed tapestry conceals a staircase to the seventh floor.

THIRD FLOOR

A concealed passageway can be found on the right-hand side of the third floor, in a corridor near the first-year Charms classroom. Harry, Ron, Hermione and Neville use this to escape from Argus Filch. When trying to avoid Peeves while out of bed at night with a draught of Felix Felicis during the 1996–1997 school year, Harry slips through a shortcut on this floor.

FOURTH FLOOR

On the fourth floor, a secret stairway can be accessed behind a tapestry. This stair is narrow and goes down two floors instead of one, leading to an exit behind another tapestry. This shortcut is commonly used by Gryffindors as a quicker way to reach their common room (but has a disappearing trick step).

Harry gets stuck there once and almost gets caught by Filch and Snape. He also uses this shortcut when chasing Snape and the other Death Eaters in the immediate aftermath of Dumbledore's death.

FIFTH FLOOR
When Dumbledore's Army uses the Room of Requirement during Death Eater rule in 1998, the room lets students out somewhere different every day. When Harry and Luna use it, they are let out on the fifth floor.

SEVENTH FLOOR
During the Battle of Hogwarts, Harry, Ron and Hermione hide at the top of a staircase behind a tapestry on the seventh floor near the Room of Requirement. When Death Eaters find them, Hermione casts a spell that turns the staircase into a slide. The trio then exits out of a tapestry before Hermione turns the exit into a solid wall (which appears to be on the second floor). This shortcut is likely the same one Ron and Harry use to get to Gryffindor Tower after Quidditch practice during their sixth year. They likely enter on the second floor, where they stumble upon Ginny and Dean kissing, then continue up the stairs until they are let out near the Room of Requirement.

SECRET PASSAGES ON UNKNOWN FLOORS
- Hogwarts has walls that appear to be doors and doors that do not open unless "asked politely" or when tickled in the correct place. In 1996, Harry tries to avoid Cormac McLaggen and Lavender Brown by accessing a door that appears to be a wall that leads to the Potions classroom (see page 60).
- As first-year students, Harry and Hermione take a shortcut to the Astronomy Tower with Norbert(a) in the dead of night.
- When Harry tracks mud up to the Gryffindor common room (see page 64) in 1992, Filch appears from behind a tapestry and leads Harry to his office.
- In 1994, Mrs. Norris disappears behind a statue of Wilfred the Wistful in order to reach Filch (see page 113). This suggests there may be a passageway behind this statue, which is located somewhere between Gryffindor Tower (see page 64) and the owlery (see page 83).

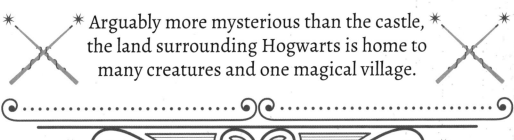

CHAPTER 3

THE GROUNDS & BEYOND

Arguably more mysterious than the castle, the land surrounding Hogwarts is home to many creatures and one magical village.

Hogwarts Castle is set in extensive grounds, which, much like the school, are protected by various magical enchantments. The clearest description of the relative positions of things around Hogwarts Castle comes from a map of the school grounds hand-drawn by the series's author, which is included in the *Harry Potter: A History of Magic* exhibition.

Located just south of the castle, the Great Lake runs up to the base of the cliff on which the school is perched. In every year except their first, Hogwarts students journey from Hogsmeade station (where they have arrived via the Hogwarts Express) to the castle by riding in Thestral-drawn carriages which take them past the lake and Hogsmeade village to enter the Hogwarts grounds north of the castle. The wrought-iron gates here have a stone pillar on either side, each topped with a winged boar. The carriages continue up a sweeping drive to the entrance hall doors. As they travel up the drive, the carriages pass the school Quidditch pitch on their right and the gamekeeper's cabin (a.k.a. Hagrid's hut) on their left. Behind the cabin and its accompanying pumpkin patch lies the dark and massive expanse of the Forbidden Forest.

Not far from the gamekeeper's cabin is the Whomping Willow, a violent tree that attacks anyone who comes near it.

Close to the castle, on its east side, lies the Hogwarts vegetable patch that supplies the Hogwarts kitchens as well as the greenhouses containing a variety of magical plants for use in Herbology classes. The lawns between the Quidditch pitch and the castle are where Madam Hooch conducts flying lessons for first-year students.

Great Lake

Four-person rowboats (magically propelled without oars) convey first-year students from the lake's eastern shore toward the school—a Hogwarts tradition. The boats pass through an ivy-covered opening in the cliff on which Hogwarts Castle sits before reaching a rocky underground harbor beneath the school. From there, a passageway leads to the lawns in front of the main entrance.

The surface of Hogwarts's massive freshwater lake is regularly described as smooth like glass and can freeze over in winter. The waters are not always calm, however—torrential rains cause the water level to rise, and at the start of Harry Potter's fourth year, the lake becomes so storm-tossed that first year Dennis Creevey is thrown from his boat, though he is ultimately rescued by Hogwarts's largest resident—the docile giant squid. This squid carries on a friendly rapport with Hogwarts's students, who frequently feed it toast or tickle its tentacles, and has even been known to enjoy swimming alongside students from time to time.

During the 1994-1995 academic year, in which Hogwarts hosts the Triwizard Tournament, a whirlpool appears in the center of the lake as a watery portal to convey the visiting Durmstrang ship. This is the only time the lake is seen to be used as a portal to other places, but it is suggested on Wizarding World Digital that magical watercraft might be able to travel from one body of water to another in this manner.

The dark black surface of the lake hides a rich world below, which is readily on view to Slytherins through their common room windows. Harry sees it for the first time during his fourth year at Hogwarts, when he dives into the lake's waters to complete the second task of the Triwizard Tournament. Among the other creatures that dwell in the lake, apart from the giant squid, are grindylows—horned water demons that force Beauxbatons champion Fleur Delacour to retire from the task—and merpeople. The merpeople Harry meets during the second task of the

Triwizard Tournament wear pebble necklaces and are armed with spears. There's a whole village on the lake's floor where merpeople live in stone houses tending their gardens and pet grindylows. It is decorated with art, including paintings and a large statue of a merperson in the village square. Merchieftainess Murcus appears to be the leader of this community. About two years after the end of the Triwizard Tournament, merpeople sing at Dumbledore's funeral from just below the surface of the lake before rising to listen to the memorial service.

Harry experiences two critical moments on the shore of the lake. He produces his first corporeal Patronus, a stag (like his father's), to save Sirius, Hermione and himself from a swarm of Dementors. It also serves as the location of "Snape's Worst Memory," which causes Harry to rethink how he sees his parents and their peers after he views it in the Pensieve.

Whomping Willow

One of the more memorable features of the Hogwarts grounds, the Whomping Willow is a tree unlike any other that stands ready to pummel trespassers at a moment's notice.

As second-year students, Harry and Ron encounter Hogwarts's infamous Whomping Willow by crashing into it while flying Arthur Weasley's Ford Anglia to the school. Unlike its mundane Muggle counterparts, this magical tree possesses a degree of sentience and a capacity for unleashed aggression. It does not like to let anything into its immediate vicinity, and when Harry and Ron ram it with their car, it lives up to its name and pummels them. Shortly after, the Ford Anglia saves the students by reversing them out of reach (the Willow tries to give chase, only to find itself restrained by its roots). The Whomping Willow sustains quite a bit of damage from the crash and has to be tended by Professor Sprout; when Harry spots it the next day with its boughs done up in slings, he feels a twinge of guilt. The Whomping Willow (unknowingly) gets its revenge against Harry for the car crash the following school year, however. After Dementors cause Harry to fall off his broom during Gryffindor's Quidditch match against Hufflepuff, Harry's beloved Nimbus Two Thousand is blown into the Willow, and the tree proceeds to smash it into splinters.

According to Professor Snape, the Whomping Willow is a very valuable tree, but this was not why it was planted at Hogwarts; that happened to conceal one student's terrible secret. In Harry's third year at the school, Professor Remus Lupin explains to Harry that the tree was planted the year Lupin began his studies at Hogwarts. While it had initially seemed doubtful as to whether or not Lupin, a werewolf, could (or should) attend the school, Albus Dumbledore insisted he should and made various accommodations to that end. He set aside the Shrieking Shack in Hogsmeade as an isolated safe space for Lupin to transform each full moon, and to mitigate the chances of anyone encountering Lupin during his werewolf phase, the incredibly violent tree was placed over the entrance to deter people from wandering near.

When Fred and George Weasley first give Harry the Marauder's Map (see page 52), they point out that the entrance to one of the secret passageways leading from the school grounds to Hogsmeade is obstructed by the Whomping Willow. Little does he realize at that moment that the tree is not merely blocking the passage by chance but rather purposefully planted to conceal and guard it.

Getting past the Willow is easy enough for those in the know: Simply press a knot on its trunk. This temporarily immobilizes the Willow, allowing enough time for someone to enter the passage via a hole between the tree's roots. This is usually achieved by either prodding the knot with a stick (easily done using that handy charm *Wingardium Leviosa*) or by training a cat/Kneazle crossbreed to do it (enter Crookshanks).

During Lupin's time at the school, Harry's godfather, Sirius Black, once attempted to play a vicious "trick" on Snape by telling him how to disarm the tree and enter the tunnel during a full moon. Snape, who had been curious about where Lupin went every month and why, had already disarmed the tree and entered the tunnel before James Potter managed to pull him to safety, but not before Snape glimpsed Lupin in his werewolf form.

Unfortunately, telling a bunch of teenagers to stay away from a dangerous tree only works so well. A game developed soon after it was planted where students would try to get close enough to touch the Willow's trunk. This continued until a student named Davey Gudgeon almost had an eye taken out by the tree; from that point on, students were forbidden to go near it.

The Quidditch Pitch

Quidditch tryouts, practices and matches take place on an outdoor field on the school grounds, down the sloping lawns leading from the castle. Three golden poles with hoops stand at each end of the pitch. The stands contain hundreds of seats high in the air to give spectators a view of the airborne action, but some still bring binoculars to observe every detail of the match. The commentator is stationed at a podium and speaks into a magical megaphone that amplifies their voice. Behind a barrier is a section of lower seats, which students may sit in to watch practices. During Harry's third year at the school, it is mentioned that three-quarters of the crowd are wearing scarlet for Gryffindor, while 200 people are sporting green in support of Slytherin, which indicates the stands hold at least 800 spectators in total.

Teams must reserve the pitch for practice in advance, but a note from their head of House can grant special permission in rare circumstances. During the 1992–1993 academic year, Snape takes advantage of this exception in order to allow the Slytherin team room to use the pitch to train their new Seeker, Draco Malfoy, much to the dismay of the Gryffindor team, which had already booked the field for that time. On this occasion, Hermione (correctly) insinuates that Malfoy bought his way onto the team. Incensed, Malfoy calls her a Mudblood, and when Ron tries to curse Malfoy, Ron's broken wand backfires and he belches slugs all over the grass.

Near the pitch is a broomshed that houses school-owned brooms that students may borrow, including an old jerky Shooting Star that Harry uses after his Nimbus Two Thousand is destroyed by the Whomping Willow. Harry keeps his Nimbus here during his first year at the school.

Teams change into their Quidditch robes and prepare for practices and matches in the locker rooms on the edge of the field. As Gryffindor Quidditch Captain, Oliver Wood tends to keep his team in the locker rooms for quite some time in order to give players impassioned pep talks and long-winded explanations of strategy. There are also showers for the players to use—in one notable circumstance, when Gryffindor loses to Hufflepuff during Harry's third year (owing to the presence of Dementors on the pitch, which cause Harry to fall from his broom), Fred suspects Oliver may be trying to drown himself in one of them. A cupboard in the changing rooms holds a set of Quidditch balls to use for practice, and an office is reserved for the captain.

During the 1994–1995 academic year, the Quidditch pitch hosts the third task of the Triwizard Tournament and is transformed into a 20-foot-high hedge maze. The champions meet Ludo Bagman there one month before the task at 9 p.m., when the hedges look like long, low walls twisting and criss-crossing through the grass. According to Bagman, Hagrid is responsible for their growth.

Many years after Harry leaves Hogwarts, Delphi takes Harry's son Albus and Scorpius Malfoy to the Quidditch pitch in order to travel back to the third task of the Triwizard Tournament. She tortures Scorpius to force Albus to change the past with her, and when prefect Craig Bowker, Jr. comes looking for them, Delphi kills him.

Outdoor Classrooms

Not all of the courses offered at Hogwarts are taught indoors. Some subjects require students to leave the castle, where they can immerse themselves in the material while taking in the open air.

HERBOLOGY GREENHOUSES

Herbology classes are held in greenhouses located behind the castle near a vegetable patch. These greenhouses are numbered based on the complexity of the plants found within them. For example, first-years have class only in greenhouse one, but as Harry finds out during the 1992–1993 academic year, second-years work with mandrakes—a dangerous plant known for its screaming—in greenhouse three. As the resident Herbology professor, Pomona Sprout possesses the key to the locked greenhouses. Inside, these rooms smell of damp earth, fertilizer and the strange plants that grow there. In greenhouse three, the air is perfumed by flowers the size of umbrellas that hang from the ceiling. A trestle bench sits in the center of each greenhouse. In March, the adolescent mandrakes throw a wild party in greenhouse three—an indication that they are maturing. During Harry's fourth year, he and his fellow students work in greenhouse three again, this time with Bubotubers, and during the following school year, fifth years have class there as well. Students have been known to leave the greenhouses smelling strongly of dragon dung, Professor Sprout's preferred fertilizer.

CARE OF MAGICAL CREATURES CLASSES

Care of Magical Creatures classes take place outdoors, usually near Hagrid's hut and along the edge of the Forbidden Forest. During Harry's third year at Hogwarts, his class has its first Care of Magical Creatures class in a paddock where Hagrid introduces them to hippogriffs. The paddock is a fenced area around the edge of the

Forbidden Forest, about a five-minute walk from Hagrid's house. The following year, during the Triwizard Tournament, a separate makeshift paddock is set up near Hagrid's hut to house the flying horses that pull the Beauxbatons carriages. That year, students work with Blast-Ended Skrewts in the pumpkin patch behind the hut. Later, Hagrid digs a fresh patch of dirt in front of his cabin and hides leprechaun gold for the students to find using Nifflers. Under the influence of Veritaserum, Barty Crouch, Jr., confesses to Transfiguring his dead father into a bone and burying him there. During the 1995–1996 academic year, Hagrid takes the fifth years into the Forest to observe Thestrals. The area is a 10-minute walk from his cabin, where the trees are so densely packed that no snow and very little sunlight can penetrate the canopy.

FLYING LESSONS

First-year students take flying lessons with Madam Hooch on a smooth, flat lawn on the opposite side of the grounds from the Forbidden Forest. During Harry's first lesson, Neville Longbottom falls off his broom and breaks his wrist. While Madam Hooch takes Neville to the hospital wing, Malfoy threatens to hide Neville's fallen Remembrall in a tree and flies away with it; luckily for Neville, Harry gives chase. McGonagall witnesses Harry flying and catching the Remembrall—shortly after, she comes onto the lawn to make him the Gryffindor Quidditch team's new Seeker.

Hagrid's Hut

As Keeper of Keys and Grounds at Hogwarts, Rubeus Hagrid lives in a small wooden house on school grounds at the edge of the Forbidden Forest (see page 134) with his pet boarhound, Fang. The hut features a huge bed with a patchwork quilt in the corner, as well as a wardrobe, a chest of drawers and cupboards large enough to hold bucket-sized mugs. There is a large wooden dinette set in the middle of the one-room hut. Hagrid often boils water in a copper kettle and cooks in a cauldron over an open fireplace, and various hams and pheasants can be found hanging from the ceiling. Fang sleeps in a basket on the floor. The back door opens onto a small vegetable patch where Hagrid grows pumpkins for the Halloween feast (see page 33). With the aid of binoculars, Hagrid can see the Quidditch pitch from his house.

The first time Harry visits, he spots a pair of galoshes and a crossbow sitting outside the front door. Hagrid frequently invites the trio to his hut, where he serves tea and fruitcake, stoat sandwiches, beef casserole, rock cakes that are hard enough to break a tooth and treacle toffee that is likely to cement one's jaw shut. Harry often uses the Invisibility Cloak to visit Hagrid when school rules prohibit it.

In the spring of Harry's first year, Hagrid hatches a dragon egg in his hut and names the baby Norwegian Ridgeback Norbert. Soon, the room is littered with brandy bottles and chicken feathers as Hagrid attempts to care for the rapidly growing animal. Eventually, the trio convince Hagrid to let Charlie Weasley's friends take Norbert(a) before the dragon becomes impossible to keep hidden.

The following school year, when Ron's attack on Malfoy backfires and Ron begins belching slugs, the trio visits Hagrid, who provides a copper basin in which to let it all out. Hagrid mentions that he met Ginny nearby the previous day and thinks she was hoping to run into Harry at his house. Later in the school year, after Hermione is Petrified, Harry and Ron go to Hagrid's to question him about the last time the Chamber of Secrets was opened, but their visit is interrupted by Albus Dumbledore and Minister of Magic Cornelius Fudge, the latter of whom wants to take Hagrid to Azkaban due to his connection with the Chamber. Soon after, Lucius Malfoy arrives with an Order of Suspension signed by the school governors removing Dumbledore as headmaster.

During the 1993–1994 academic year, Hagrid keeps Buckbeak the hippogriff in his hut after the creature is sentenced to death. On the day of the planned execution, Hermione discovers Scabbers hiding in one of Hagrid's milk jugs. Dumbledore, Fudge, a member of the Committee for the Disposal of Dangerous Creatures and Macnair, the executioner, go into Hagrid's cabin to read the official notice of execution; meanwhile, with the help of a Time-Turner, Harry and Hermione manage to take Buckbeak to safety. Later, the friends hide in Hagrid's empty hut to avoid Lupin in werewolf form.

During Harry's fourth year at the school, a number of students take refuge in Hagrid's hut from the Blast-Ended Skrewts they're supposed to be working with for Care of Magical Creatures class. After Rita Skeeter exposes Hagrid's half-giant background, an incident which causes him a great deal of shame, he refuses to leave his quarters. When Harry, Ron and Hermione bang on his door, they encounter Dumbledore speaking to Hagrid and join the headmaster in convincing Hagrid not to resign.

For the first few months of Harry's fifth year at Hogwarts, Hagrid's hut is empty. Just as he returns, the trio rushes to see him, but Dolores Umbridge swoops in to interrogate Hagrid about his whereabouts. Later, during the practical portion of the Astronomy O.W.L., the test-takers witness Umbridge going to Hagrid's cabin with five Aurors—Hagrid fights them off and escapes with Fang in tow.

The following year, Hagrid keeps a barrel of giant grubs in his cabin to give to his aged Acromantula, Aragog. Following Aragog's death,

Hagrid holds a funeral for his beloved pet, whom he buries just beyond the pumpkin patch. Hagrid, Harry and Horace Slughorn toast Aragog's memory inside the hut. Later that night, Harry, with a little help from the Felix Felicis potion, persuades Slughorn to share the unaltered memory of his conversation with Tom Riddle about Horcruxes that took place many decades prior.

While fleeing the school after Dumbledore's murder, Death Eater Thorfinn Rowle sets Hagrid's hut on fire. Hagrid runs inside to rescue Fang, and Harry helps him extinguish the flames. During the 1997-1998 academic year, Hagrid hosts a "Support Harry Potter" party in his cabin, for which he manages to escape arrest.

THE GREEN MAN

According to the author, Hagrid was inspired by the Green Man, a medieval figure symbolizing nature and rebirth. The location of Hagrid's hut reflects his characterization as somewhere between civilization and the wilderness. He is the only Hogwarts staff member who does not live within the castle, residing instead on the very edge of the grounds, next to the Forest, making him part of the school and yet simultaneously separate from it. Hagrid's half-giant heritage likewise reflects this duality—he is a member of wizarding society, but due to his mother having been a giant, Hagrid has a stronger connection to the creatures that inhabit the Forest than most humans do. The hut serves as a threshold or boundary that lies squarely between the rules and order of the school and the dark mysteries of the Forest, the place Harry crosses to learn about and meet centaurs, Acromantulas and dragons.

Forbidden Forest

The Forbidden Forest is located on the grounds of Hogwarts and acts as a boundary for the school. Due to the fact that it is home to many dangerous creatures, the Forest is out of bounds to all students except during Care of Magical Creatures lessons (and the occasional detention). The Forest comprises beech, oak, pine, sycamore and yew trees, with an undergrowth of knotgrass and thorns— all of which become more dense the deeper a person ventures. Even capable students are likely to lose their bearings should they wander, and the area is especially difficult to navigate at night. Fred and George Weasley are known to have repeatedly tried to enter the Forest as young students.

In the winter of 1992, after Gryffindor wins a Quidditch match against Hufflepuff, Snape sneaks into the Forbidden Forest during dinner. Harry, spotting the cloaked professor entering the Forest, flies over on his broomstick to eavesdrop on his conversation with Professor Quirrell.

In May of the same year, Harry, Hermione, Neville Longbottom and Draco Malfoy serve detention in the Forest for having been caught out of bed late at night. Their punishment is to go into the Forest with Hagrid to search for an injured unicorn in two groups: Harry, Hermione and Hagrid in one and Malfoy, Neville and Fang in the other. While in the Forest, Harry, Hermione and Hagrid encounter centaurs Ronan and Bane, who tell them about the Forest's dangers, especially for Harry. Following an altercation between Malfoy and Neville, Harry swaps places with Neville and joins Malfoy and Fang. To their horror, Harry and Malfoy discover a hooded figure in the shadows crawling across the ground, drinking the blood of a dead unicorn. Fang and Malfoy flee in terror. The centaur Firenze comes to Harry's rescue.

In May of 1993, Harry and Ron enter the Forest with Fang to learn more about the Chamber of Secrets. By following the spiders fleeing Hogwarts into the Forest, they encounter Aragog, the Acromantula patriarch, who tells them about Hagrid's expulsion and the monster that lives within the school. Aragog's information eventually helps Harry and Ron discover Moaning Myrtle's connection to the Chamber of Secrets, though acquiring it nearly gets the boys killed by Aragog's many children.

At the end of the 1993–1994 academic year, after the trio encounters Snape, Remus Lupin, Sirius Black and the recently revealed Peter Pettigrew (a.k.a. Scabbers) in the Shrieking Shack, the group proceeds out of the tunnel and into the moonlight when Lupin suddenly realizes he hasn't taken his Wolfsbane Potion. With the full moon in view, he transforms into a werewolf. Panic ensues—Pettigrew transforms into his Animagus rat form and escapes, while Sirius transforms into his Animagus dog form and goes head-to-head with Lupin to protect the trio. Soon after, Lupin bolts into the Forest. After this incident, Harry and Hermione use a Time-Turner to rescue Buckbeak from execution, hiding the hippogriff in the Forest.

During Harry's fourth year, the dragons that will later be used in the Triwizard Tournament's first task are kept around the edge of the Forest away from prying eyes. To increase Harry's chances of survival, Hagrid takes Harry around the Forest to show him the creature he will soon encounter. Later that same academic year, Harry and Durmstrang champion Viktor Krum are walking near the Forest when they come across Barty Crouch, Sr., who looks visibly confused. Harry rushes up to the school for help, but when he returns with Dumbledore, Crouch is gone, and Krum is out cold.

During the 1995–1996 academic year, Hagrid leads his fifth-year Care of Magical Creatures students (including Harry) into the Forbidden Forest to meet Hogwarts's herd of Thestrals. Later, Hagrid takes Harry and Hermione into the Forest to meet his half-brother, Grawp. Not long after, the two friends lead Professor Dolores Umbridge into the Forest in the hopes of scaring her with the centaur herd. Umbridge insults the centaurs—due to her prejudices, she sees them as "half-breeds"—and they retaliate by carrying her deeper into the Forest.

During the Battle of Hogwarts, Lord Voldemort and his Death Eaters make their base camp in Aragog's old clearing. Two giants stand guard in the clearing. While the battle briefly pauses in order for both sides to treat their injured and collect the dead, Harry dons his Invisibility Cloak and heads to Voldemort's camp to sacrifice himself. Along the way, Harry figures out how to open the Golden Snitch he caught during his first Quidditch match and is able to access the Resurrection Stone. He turns it and sees his mother, father, Sirius and Remus standing around him in the Forest, neither ghost-like nor truly flesh. They encourage him and provide him a degree of comfort before accompanying him to the camp, where Harry removes his Invisibility Cloak and allows Voldemort to draw his wand, seemingly killing Harry but actually sending him to a limbo that looks remarkably like King's Cross station. Shortly after, he regains consciousness. When Narcissa Malfoy checks to see whether or not Harry is dead, he informs her Draco is still alive, and Narcissa lies to Voldemort, telling him Harry is dead. Voldemort tasks Hagrid with carrying Harry back to the school.

Decades later, Harry's son Albus Potter, Scorpius Malfoy and Delphi begin their adventures with a stolen Time-Turner by practicing the *Expelliarmus* spell at the edge of the Forbidden Forest, preparing (or at least intending) to save Cedric Diggory from dying in the final task of the Triwizard Tournament. Once Harry becomes aware of his son's plan, he and Ron hurry to the Forest in an attempt to prevent the students from traveling back in time. They search the Forest, only to run into the centaur Bane, who tells Harry he has seen his son in the stars with a black cloud surrounding him, and that if Albus is not found, Harry could lose him forever. With Ron closing in on Albus and Scorpius at the edge of the Forest, Albus uses the Time-Turner, sending himself, Scorpius and Delphi back to the first task of the 1994 Triwizard Tournament, where they disguise themselves as Durmstrang students. After disarming Cedric, Albus and Scorpius are sent back to the present-day Hogwarts on the edge of the Forbidden Forest, only to be found by Ron.

Later that year, Scorpius returns to the first task with an alternate timeline's versions of Hermione, Ron and Snape. This Hermione blocks Albus's Disarming Charm in order to return the timeline to what it was. They are ultimately successful, but in the process, they find themselves at the edge of the Forest, surrounded by Dementors, and the alternate Ron and Hermione sacrifice themselves to give Scorpius and Snape a chance to finish their mission.

CREATURES OF THE FORBIDDEN FOREST

ACROMANTULAS

Among the most dangerous creatures in the Forest is a family of more than 100 Acromantulas who have resided there since the first opening of the Chamber of Secrets in 1943. Aragog and his mate, Mosag, live with their progeny in a dome-shaped nest in the heart of the Forest.

CENTAURS

At least 50 centaurs live in the Forest, most of which avoid humans and do not involve themselves in human affairs, keeping tabs on them through astrological divination and communicating cryptically when interacting with them. The centaurs have a civil relationship with Hagrid—he knows many of them by name—until he brings Grawp into the Forest in 1995. One of the centaurs, Firenze, accepts a job as a Divination professor in 1996, at which time he is banished from the herd. The centaurs, apart from Firenze, do not fight in the first wave of the Battle of Hogwarts on May 2, 1998. After Voldemort casts the Killing Curse at Harry in the Forest, Hagrid criticizes the centaurs for not defending Hogwarts, and the herd watches from the tree line while Voldemort announces his victory. They are among the first to attack the remaining Death Eaters in the second wave of the battle. Following Harry's triumph over Voldemort, Firenze is accepted back into the herd.

THESTRALS

Hogwarts's Forest is home to the largest domestic herd of Thestrals, consisting of at least 100 creatures. These skeletal animals can only be seen by those who've witnessed death and are first covered in Care of Magical Creatures in the fifth year. At the end of the 1995–1996 academic year, Harry, Ron, Hermione, Ginny, Neville and Luna mount the Thestrals to travel to London, hoping to save Sirius Black at the Ministry of Magic.

UNICORNS

A herd of unicorns live in the Forest and are known to shed hair. Hagrid collects and uses this hair to bind bandages for injured animals due to the material's unique strength.

OTHER RESIDENTS

FORD ANGLIA

After its flight from London to Hogwarts on September 1, 1992, Arthur Weasley's flying Ford Anglia escapes into the Forest, where it eventually turns somewhat feral. It later saves Harry, Ron and Fang from being devoured by Aragog's family.

GRAWP

Grawp, Hagrid's half-brother, resides in the Forbidden Forest during Harry's fifth year after Hagrid returns from visiting a tribe of giants with Olympe Maxime. During the Battle of Hogwarts, Grawp fights Voldemort's giants and helps defend the school. He survives the battle and is seen laughing as students throw food into his mouth.

Hogsmeade

F ounded in the Middle Ages sometime after Hogwarts, Hogsmeade is the only village in Britain built by and for wizards. Its founder, Hengist of Woodcroft, had sought a place of refuge from Muggle persecution. Known for its thatched cottages and bevy of intriguing shops, Hogsmeade caters to Hogwarts students and staff, and its close proximity to the school makes it an ideal day trip destination.

Students in their third year and above are permitted to visit Hogsmeade on certain weekends throughout the school year with permission from a parent or guardian. The summer before Harry's third year at Hogwarts, the Dursleys refuse to sign his permission slip, but it doesn't deter him from donning his Invisibility Cloak and making the trip anyway. It is possible for students to lose Hogsmeade privileges, as Neville Longbottom discovers during the 1993–1994 school year when he loses the list of Gryffindor Tower passwords later found by Sirius Black. Harry also loses his Hogsmeade privileges during part of the 1995-1996 school year, but they are reinstated when Dolores Umbridge is removed from the school.

Hogsmeade has several restaurants, shops and landmarks, including:

- Dervish and Banges
- Gladrags Wizardwear
- The Hog's Head
- Honeydukes
- The post office
- Madam Puddifoot's Tea Shop
- Scrivenshaft's Quill Shop
- The Shrieking Shack
- The Three Broomsticks
- Zonko's Joke Shop

Harry and his friends visit all of these businesses throughout their time at Hogwarts, but a few of them are not described in detail.

One of these relatively unseen shops is Dervish and Banges, a wizarding equipment shop near the end of the High Street that sells and repairs "magical instruments" like Sneakoscopes. In the 1994-1995 academic year, Harry meets Sirius Black—disguised in his Animagus form—on "a path beyond Dervish and Banges" that leads to a cave somewhere above the village. The next year, a poster with pictures of escaped Death Eaters appears in the window of the store.

Another relatively unseen shop in the village is Gladrags Wizardwear, which also has locations in London and Paris. In 1995, Harry buys some "lurid" socks for Dobby from Gladrags.

One more Hogsmeade shop of which little is seen is Scrivenshaft's Quill Shop, which specializes in upscale and unique writing instruments. In October of 1995, Hermione buys a black-and-gold pheasant-feather quill from Scrivenshaft's after she and Harry hold the first meeting to gauge interest in Dumbledore's Army. Later, when Ron is practicing Apparition, his intended destination is Madam Puddifoot's Tea Shop. He ends up outside Scrivenshaft's instead.

There is also a post office (sometimes referred to as an "owl office") that has at least 300 owls available to carry messages and parcels. Owls sit on color-coded shelves that group them based on speed.

HOGSMEADE STATION

According to a map drawn by the author, Hogsmeade station is located on the opposite side of the castle from the village itself. Built at the same time as platform nine and three-quarters specifically to accommodate the Hogwarts Express, the platform is described as tiny and dark. From the station, students arriving on the Hogwarts Express are brought the short distance to Hogwarts by various means.

Many years after Harry and his friends leave Hogwarts, a middle-aged Ron is in Hogsmeade getting drinks with Neville when he spots Harry's son Albus with Delphi. This information later comes in handy when Delphi kidnaps Albus and Scorpius Malfoy.

THE HOG'S HEAD INN

The Hog's Head Inn serves so-called "interesting clientele." Aberforth Dumbledore—Albus Dumbledore's brother—has been its barkeep for at least 20 years. Located one or two streets back from the High Street, the inn advertises itself with a large wooden sign over the door depicting a severed boar's head spilling blood on a white cloth.

The bar is small and dirty. The windows are "nearly opaque" and the floor can barely be seen under the grime. Customers, when there are any, are rung up on an "ancient wooden till" behind the sawdust-covered bar. Harry notes even the cleaning rags behind the bar are filthy; he observes that as Aberforth wipes down a glass, it seems to get dirtier. He's hardly alone; Professor Flitwick suggests to Hermione that she and her friends should bring their own glasses if they plan on going there.

Behind the bar, a wooden staircase leads to a sitting room featuring a curtained window overlooking the street below and a framed portrait of Ariana Dumbledore over the fireplace. A secret passage to the Room of Requirement (see page 92) appears behind this portrait in the spring of 1998. The guest rooms, which can be found on the second floor, are just as filthy as the rest of the place. Once, Professor Trelawney warns Harry of bedbugs.

Compared to the Three Broomsticks (see page 144), the Hog's Head is known for its low prices, though it is described as being empty most of the time. This emptiness, however, attracts clandestine meetings and conversations.

In early 1980, Sybill Trelawney (not yet a Hogwarts professor) made a prophecy to Albus Dumbledore in the Hog's Head about Lord Voldemort and an unborn child. She was overheard by Severus Snape, an event which eventually led to the death of Lily and James Potter; the marking of their child, Harry, as the Chosen One; and the first downfall of Voldemort.

In the spring of 1992, Rubeus Hagrid wins a dragon's egg from a disguised wizard in the Hog's Head. This wizard is later revealed to be Quirinus Quirrell, who successfully dupes Hagrid into revealing information about the hidden Sorcerer's Stone.

In the fall of 1995, Harry and Hermione invite any student interested in learning to defend themselves to meet them in the Hog's Head, where they form Dumbledore's Army.

In May of 1998, Aberforth provides a hiding place in the Hog's Head for Harry, Ron and Hermione after they Apparate into Hogsmeade and the Death Eaters are alerted to their presence via a Caterwauling Charm. The trio is then able to use the secret passageway behind Ariana's portrait to enter Hogwarts and facilitate the movement of students and Order of the Phoenix members prior to the Battle of Hogwarts (see page 42).

TIES TO THE GOBLIN REBELLION OF 1612

It is theorized that a 1612 goblin rebellion was likely based in either the Hog's Head or the Three Broomsticks. According to Hermione, this rebellion was based out of "the inn" in Hogsmeade, and these two places are the only inns shown to be in the village. Because the Hog's Head draws a questionable crowd, it is likely the goblins would have chosen it as their headquarters to more easily avoid prying eyes.

KNOWN SHADY CLIENTELE

• **DOLOHOV** Death Eater and powerful wizard; convicted of the murders of Fabian and Gideon Prewett (Molly Weasley's brothers); fought in the First Wizarding War; sentenced to life in Azkaban; escapes Azkaban; participates in the Second Wizarding War; defeated in the Battle of Hogwarts by Filius Flitwick
• **MULCIBER** One of the earliest Death Eaters; fought in the First Wizarding War
• **MUNDUNGUS FLETCHER** A conman and a thief (banned for life from the Hog's Head but still enters in disguise)
• **NOTT** One of the earliest Death Eaters; fights in the First and Second Wizarding Wars
• **ROSIER** One of the earliest Death Eaters; fought in the First Wizarding War
• **WILLY WIDDERSHINS** A British wizard who engages in Muggle-baiting pranks

HONEYDUKES

Nestled with the other shops along Hogsmeade's High Street is Honeydukes, a beloved candy shop stocked with a dazzling assortment of enchanted treats. The store is owned by Ambrosius Flume and his wife, who keep the shelves filled with "the most succulent-looking sweets imaginable."

Ambrosius's name is likely derived from the word "ambrosia," the food and drink of the gods in Greek mythology. During his time at Hogwarts, Ambrosius was one of Horace Slughorn's favorite students, which may or may not insinuate that potion skills factor into creating practically irresistible magical sweets.

The candy shop is incredibly popular during the weekends when Hogwarts students visit the village. Even Percy Weasley, known for being incredibly patronizing, admits that Honeydukes is "rather good."

A SECRET PASSAGEWAY BEHIND GUNHILDA OF GORSEMOOR

Located among boxes and crates in Honeydukes's cellar is a door that leads to a secret passage to Hogwarts (see page 118). The Hogwarts end of the passage is concealed by a statue of Gunhilda of Gorsemoor, a one-eyed, humpbacked Healer who invented the cure for dragon pox. Coincidentally, Gunhilda can be found on Famous Wizard cards inside Chocolate Frog sweets.

THE THREE BROOMSTICKS

The Three Broomsticks is a popular inn at Hogsmeade that attracts Hogwarts students and teachers, goblins, Hogsmeade residents, and possibly even ogres. The pub is laid out with a bar, tables and a fireplace and serves drinks such as butterbeer, firewhisky, gillywater, mulled mead, red currant rum, oak-matured mead and a cherry syrup and soda with ice and umbrella.

The Three Broomsticks is run by Madam Rosmerta. Ron develops an immediate crush on the curvy and attractive barkeep and often tries to catch her eye or make her laugh at his jokes. She is well acquainted with Cornelius Fudge and the Hogwarts faculty and joins them in their conversation about Sirius Black's role as James and Lily Potter's Secret-Keeper. During the 1996–1997 academic year, Draco Malfoy capitalizes on her access to Hogwarts students and Imperiuses her, forcing her to pass on a cursed necklace to Katie Bell in the girls' bathroom and poison a bottle of mead. He communicates with her throughout the year using enchanted coins, and she informs him when Dumbledore has left the castle. The night of Dumbledore's death, Rosmerta tells Dumbledore and Harry about the Dark Mark over the castle and provides two brooms for them to return to Hogwarts.

Harry and his friends regularly enjoy visiting the Three Broomsticks, but on two occasions, Harry needs to be hidden while doing so. The first time, he is in Hogsmeade without permission and McGonagall, Flitwick, Hagrid and Cornelius Fudge enter the pub. He hides under the table and listens to their conversation while watching through the branches of a large Christmas tree. Here he learns that Sirius Black was believed to have betrayed Harry's parents. The second time, he uses the Invisibility Cloak to avoid unwelcome attention from being a Triwizard champion. Moody sees him, however, and Hagrid tells Harry to come down at night to see the dragons.

The Three Broomsticks is a convenient place to run into people and overhear conversations, which may be why Rita Skeeter spends a significant amount of time there during her year covering the Triwizard Tournament at Hogwarts (1994–1995). Harry barely avoids running into her there before the first task, and she later conducts a lengthy interview at the pub with

Hagrid. After the interview goes to press, the trio run into her again at the Three Broomsticks, where she is trying to gather dirt on Ludo Bagman. Harry and Hermione confront her about her treatment of Hagrid. The following year, Hermione blackmails the disheveled Rita into returning to the Three Broomsticks to conduct an interview with Harry about Voldemort's return.

Hagrid is also a regular patron of the Three Broomsticks, but Harry cannot find him there after Rita exposes Hagrid's giant parentage. The next year, Harry sees him at the pub drinking alone, covered in injuries from Grawp and discussing the importance of blood and family. Hagrid also visits the pub with several professors on various occasions over the years.

Every Hogsmeade weekend, the pub fills up with Hogwarts students— Harry spots Ernie Macmillan and Hannah Abbott trading Chocolate Frog cards and wearing *Support Cedric Diggory* badges; Cho Chang and her Ravenclaw friends; Fred and George attempting to waylay Ludo Bagman; Katie Bell and her friend Leanne; Luna Lovegood; Blaise Zabini; and Lee Jordan. Ludo Bagman offers to help Harry with the second task of the tournament after the two run into each other here. Harry confronts Mundungus Fletcher outside the pub for selling Black family heirlooms to Aberforth.

On occasion, Dumbledore pretends to get a drink at the Three Broomsticks to cover for the fact that he is leaving the school to look for Horcruxes. In order to avoid trouble with Umbridge, Hermione claims to have been searching for Dumbledore in various places, including the Three Broomsticks, though Umbridge is quick to point out Dumbledore is unlikely to be waiting around in a pub while the entire Ministry is looking for him.

After Voldemort takes over Hogwarts, the Three Broomsticks is regularly filled with Death Eaters keeping a lookout. When Harry, Ron and Hermione set off the Caterwauling Charm by Apparating into the village, a dozen Death Eaters exit the inn to search for them.

MADAM PUDDIFOOT'S TEA SHOP

Described ruefully by Harry as "that haunt of happy couples," Madam Puddifoot's Tea Shop is a cozy (if not crowded) store full of steaming kettles and steamy make-out sessions. Madam Puddifoot herself, a short woman with dark hair swept up in a bun, appears to be the main server at the shop, which is located on a side street past Scrivenshaft's (see page 140). Like Dolores Umbridge's office, the store is decorated with frills and bows. It also boasts a painted ceiling, a door that tinkles upon opening, and a slew of small round tables (just big enough for two), which are arranged within a foot and a half of each other.

For Valentine's Day, Madam Puddifoot decorates the shop with golden cherubs that hover over each table, tossing pink confetti over customers as they try to drink their tea or coffee. Mainly, this festive confetti seems to get in the eyes and coffee of the customers (at least, the ones who aren't too preoccupied to notice). On Valentine's Day in 1996, the shop is packed to the brim with couples holding hands, including (as Harry Potter notices) Roger Davies and his blonde date. Harry and Cho Chang, seated at the table next to them, have a disastrous date by the window of the store. Oblivious to Cho's emotional sensitivities in the wake of her boyfriend Cedric Diggory's murder, Harry tactlessly mentions needing to see Hermione. Cho bursts into tears and rushes out, leaving Harry to pay the bill.

Cho and Cedric, it turns out, once came to this tea shop on a Hogsmeade weekend. Harry bitterly suspects (without any real evidence) that Ginny Weasley and Dean Thomas spend time there together, too. Harry possesses a strong dislike for both the shop's saccharine aesthetic and the expectation of public displays of affection he feels it pressures him into.

Later, for Ron's extra Apparition lessons in Hogsmeade, he is expected to Apparate outside of Madam Puddifoot's. Even though he turns up near Scrivenshaft's, Ron takes a great deal of pride in this first successful attempt at Apparating.

ZONKO'S JOKE SHOP

Zonko's Joke Shop, a popular destination for Hogwarts students looking for tricks and diversions, specializes in such items as Dungbombs, Hiccup Sweets, Frog Spawn Soap, Stink Pellets and Nose-Biting Teacups. It can be found on the main street of Hogsmeade.

In his third year at Hogwarts, Harry is not allowed to go to Hogsmeade but slips into Zonko's while wearing his Invisibility Cloak. He finds it difficult to navigate the large crowds of customers and covertly passes gold to Ron to buy him things. These Zonko's products get Harry in trouble, however, when he is forced to rush back to Hogwarts after accidentally revealing himself to Draco Malfoy. When Snape brings Harry to his office and demands to see the contents of his pockets, Harry claims (and Ron later attempts to corroborate) that the Zonko's products he is holding were given to him by Ron after the previous Hogsmeade visit. Lupin also comes to Harry's defense with the claim that the Marauder's Map is simply a joke product from Zonko's as well.

Zonko's is described as having "jokes and tricks to fulfill even Fred's and George's wildest dreams." (Eventually, this pair of regular customers surpass Zonko's offerings with their own joke shop.) Fred, George and Lee Jordan bring bags of Zonko's products to the first meeting of Dumbledore's Army in the Hog's Head, one of which they use to threaten Zacharias Smith, a student who contents himself with challenging Harry's claims. The twins produce a long metal instrument from the shop that they claim will clean out Smith's ears (or, as they put it, any other part of him they stick it in).

For unknown reasons, Zonko's closes down in 1996, and Fred and George consider buying the location for an extension of Weasleys' Wizard Wheezes. They are less enthusiastic about this idea, however, after realizing that Hogwarts students have been banned from going to Hogsmeade for safety reasons.

THE SHRIEKING SHACK

Lauded as "the most haunted dwelling in Britain," the Shrieking Shack has gained this ghastly reputation from years of shrieks, howls and cries that the residents of Hogsmeade have concluded must come from violent ghosts. Dumbledore encouraged this rumor in an effort to conceal the more dangerous truth—that the Shack was used to hide Remus Lupin when he transformed into a werewolf each month during his time as a student at the school. The Shrieking Shack is connected to the castle grounds through an underground passageway accessible via the base of the Whomping Willow, and Lupin used this passage to escape to the Shack before his monthly transformations.

The passageway from the Whomping Willow opens up into a room with boarded up windows and broken furniture, a product of Lupin's violence in werewolf form. The second floor features a room with a large four-poster bed draped with dusty hangings.

During Lupin's years at Hogwarts, Madam Pomfrey took him to the Shrieking Shack every month to transform. He was then locked inside, biting and attacking himself and the house until he became human again. Lupin's friends James Potter, Sirius Black and Peter Pettigrew taught themselves to become Animagi in order to accompany Lupin during his transformations, discovering that he was calmer when joined by other creatures. Upon assuming his wolf form, he left the Shack with them and prowled the grounds of the castle and Hogsmeade at night. One day, Sirius decided to play a dangerous (if not potentially lethal) trick on Severus Snape by encouraging him to travel through the secret passageway to the Shrieking Shack while Lupin was transforming. James managed to pull Snape back before he reached the Shack, but not before Snape glimpsed Lupin in the room at the end of the tunnel.

During Harry's time at Hogwarts, the Shack is seen as a tourist destination for curious Hogwarts students. It is located at a higher elevation than the rest of Hogsmeade, and its long-overgrown gardens and boarded up windows add to its creepy appearance. Fred and George have attempted to enter the Shack, but the entrances have all been sealed (presumably by magic).

Harry and Ron go to see the house on a Hogsmeade visit, where Harry takes the opportunity to scare Draco Malfoy, Vincent Crabbe and Gregory Goyle by pretending to be a ghost while using his Invisibility Cloak. Harry throws mud at them and tosses a stick for laughs, but when he attempts to trip Crabbe, the frightened Slytherin student accidentally pulls Harry's cloak down, revealing Harry's head.

Later that year, Sirius (in dog form) drags Ron and Peter Pettigrew up to the second floor of the Shrieking Shack. Harry and Hermione follow and are soon joined by Lupin and Snape. Here, Harry learns Peter Pettigrew, who has spent the last thirteen or so years disguised as the Weasley family pet rat, is the one who betrayed his parents.

During the Battle of Hogwarts (see page 42), Voldemort hides away in the Shrieking Shack and watches the battle from afar, keeping his snake Nagini out of danger by way of a protective enchanted sphere. Lucius Malfoy is with him briefly until Voldemort sends Malfoy to fetch Snape. Harry, Ron and Hermione use the secret passageway to reach the Shrieking Shack and watch through an old crate as Nagini kills Snape at Voldemort's behest. After Voldemort leaves, they enter the room and siphon Snape's memories.

CHAPTER 4

STUDENT LIFE

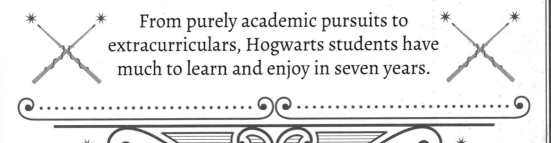

From purely academic pursuits to extracurriculars, Hogwarts students have much to learn and enjoy in seven years.

Academics

Hogwarts timetables are set for students by their head of House on September 2 each year, taking into consideration any electives they are entitled to take.

Students take part in formal instruction on each subject one to three times a week, although double periods are common. Until N.E.W.T. level, each class is composed only of pupils from one or two of the four Houses as a way of sorting students into two groups to keep class numbers under control. Students have a short break time between morning classes, then stop for lunch in the Great Hall around midday before resuming lessons in the afternoon. N.E.W.T.-level students enjoy the privilege of free periods, which most use as an opportunity for R&R, though some more ambitious students (like Hermione) use it to study.

Calendar

FALL

September 1 - At 11 a.m. the Hogwarts Express departs platform nine and three-quarters for Hogwarts, where the annual Sorting ceremony for new students is carried out and followed by a feast.

September 2 - Classes commence. Interestingly, this should fall on a Saturday during Harry's fifth year (1995), but the day is explicitly referred to as being a Monday.

Early September - Quidditch trials commence. Though not every House team holds trials every year and they're not always in the second week (as

they are in *Sorcerer's Stone*), they're usually held early in the school year.
October 31 - Halloween feast. Often interrupted in Harry's years by dramatic events.
November - Quidditch season begins. Harry's first-ever Quidditch match, where Gryffindor beats Slytherin 170–60, takes place on November 9.
October–November - About midway through the first term, the first Hogsmeade weekend of the year is held. In Harry's fourth year, it falls on the Saturday before the first task of the Triwizard Tournament (November 19, 1994).

WINTER

Late December - Christmas holidays commence. Most students go home.
December 25 - Christmas dinner is served to any staff or students remaining at school.
Early January - Christmas holidays end.
February 14 - Valentine's Day. In Harry's fifth year, this falls on the second Hogsmeade weekend, though that weekend can occur as early as December.

SPRING

March/April - Easter holidays commence and finish. Students can either go home or opt to stay.
May - Inter-House Quidditch Cup Final

SUMMER

June - End-of-year exams for all years, including O.W.L.s and N.E.W.T.s
c. June - Last Hogsmeade weekend of the year. In Harry's third year, this is the Saturday after Sirius Black escapes on Buckbeak.
Late June - End-of-year feast at which the House Cup is awarded
Late June - Hogwarts Express departs Hogsmeade for King's Cross, London on the day after the end-of-year feast.
July/August - Summer holidays. All students return home.

School Supplies

The summer before the beginning of each school year, students receive a letter from Hogwarts detailing the supplies they will need for the coming year that is written and distributed by the deputy headmaster/headmistress (Professor McGonagall during Harry's time at the school). Aside from books, the required school supplies are items of clothing and equipment needed by students to complete both their Hogwarts uniform and their Hogwarts education.

Most professors seem to prefer to use the same equipment and reference books year after year, so school supply lists from the second year onward are generally composed of textbooks, including an age-appropriate entry of Miranda Goshawk's *Standard Book of Spells*. Following Tom Riddle's failed job interview for the role of Defense Against the Dark Arts professor (an event that many believe caused the position to be cursed), the subject's book list likely reflects the changing tastes of every subsequent new professor. For more information on the textbooks used at Hogwarts, see page 164.

UNIFORMS

The Hogwarts uniform consists of plain black "work" robes and a plain black pointed hat. Where necessary, protective gloves (made out of dragon hide or a similar material) and a black winter cloak with silver fastenings can be worn.

Fourth-year students and older, who are allowed to attend the Yule Ball, have fancier dress robes on their school list in 1994 (and presumably in other years when Hogwarts has hosted the Triwizard Tournament).

Students are only asked to bring three sets of robes, suggesting keeping up with laundry for a castle full of students is quite a task for the Hogwarts house-elves. It's no wonder, then, that everyone is told to attach name tags to their clothes.

Coursework by Year

Coursework is only known for the years Harry, Ron and Hermione attend Hogwarts, beginning in 1991. Since Defense Against the Dark Arts is taught by a new professor each year, it is unclear what lessons count as standard. Students add at least two electives in their third year and drop courses they fail or don't wish to continue following their O.W.L.s. Certain courses are required at the N.E.W.T. level to pursue certain careers.

First Year

ASTRONOMY Students study the night sky through telescopes and learn the names of celestial bodies and the movements of the planets.
Known Homework: Complete star charts
CHARMS Students learn the swish and flick wrist movement of the Levitation Charm (*Wingardium Leviosa*) and cast the spell on feathers.
DEFENSE AGAINST THE DARK ARTS Coursework includes the Curse of the Bogies and ways to treat werewolf bites.
FLYING Students learn how to ride broomsticks.
HERBOLOGY Students learn about magical plants and fungi, such as Devil's Snare; their uses; and how to care for them.
HISTORY OF MAGIC This class teaches the history of the magical world, including politics, conflicts and other magical races in addition to wizards.
POTIONS This course covers basic potions including a cure for boils.
TRANSFIGURATION First years learn Switching Spells and how to turn matches into needles.

Second Year

First-year courses are continued in second year, with the exception of flying. Specific coursework is only known for some subjects.

DEFENSE AGAINST THE DARK ARTS Gilderoy Lockhart has students wrangle Cornish pixies and reenact passages from his books, including his supposed feats of turning a werewolf back into a human with a Homorphus Charm and curing a villager of a Babbling Curse.

Known Homework: Write a poem about Lockhart's defeat of the Wagga Wagga Werewolf (best one wins signed copies of *Magical Me*)

HERBOLOGY Students get their hands dirty repotting mandrakes and pruning Abyssinian Shrivelfigs.

HISTORY OF MAGIC Professor Binns lectures on the International Warlock Convention of 1289.

Known Homework: Three-foot-long essay on "The Medieval Assembly of European Wizards"

POTIONS Students brew Swelling Solution and Hair-Raising Potion.

TRANSFIGURATION Students turn beetles into buttons and rabbits into slippers.

THIRD YEAR

Students continue all core subjects from second year plus at least two electives.

ASTRONOMY

Known Homework: Complete star charts

CHARMS Pairs of students practice Cheering Charms on each other.

DEFENSE AGAINST THE DARK ARTS Professor Lupin teaches the *Riddikulus* charm and has students confront a boggart and banish it with laughter. Other Dark creatures covered include grindylows, hinkypunks, kappas, red caps, vampires and werewolves.

Known Homework: Read and summarize the chapter on boggarts

HERBOLOGY Students harvest Puffapods for their beans.

HISTORY OF MAGIC

Known Summer Homework: Essay on "Witch Burning in the Fourteenth Century Was Completely Pointless—discuss"

POTIONS Students brew Shrinking Solution.

Known Homework: Essay on Undetectable Poisons
TRANSFIGURATION Students learn about Animagi.

ELECTIVES

ANCIENT RUNES This subject teaches students how to translate an archaic system of magical writing.
ARITHMANCY This class involves numbers and their magical properties, veering into numerology. Number charts are used. (Arithmancy uses numbers to predict the future, making it an ironic choice for Hermione, who dislikes Divination.)
CARE OF MAGICAL CREATURES Students learn how to approach hippogriffs by making eye contact, bowing and waiting for them to bow back, as well as how to look after Flobberworms by feeding them lettuce. They also tend a bonfire full of salamanders.
DIVINATION The first term focuses on reading tea leaves. In the second term, the class moves onto palmistry, crystal gazing and fire omens.
MUGGLE STUDIES Students learn about non-magical society.
Known Homework: Essay on "Explain Why Muggles Need Electricity"

FOURTH YEAR

Students continue the same previous core subjects and electives they began in their third year. (Hermione, having taken more than the required amount, drops Divination and Muggle Studies.)

CARE OF MAGICAL CREATURES Hagrid breeds Blast-Ended Skrewts by combining Fire Crabs with manticores. Students feed them various foods to discover what they eat, take notes on their behavior, walk them on leashes and lead them into boxes with pillows and blankets to see if they hibernate (they do not). Substituting for Hagrid, Professor Grubbly-Plank introduces the students to adult unicorns. When Hagrid returns, he brings unicorn foals to class. In the spring, students use Nifflers to find leprechaun gold hidden in the dirt.
CHARMS Students practice the Summoning Charm (*Accio*) and the

Banishing Charm (*Depulso*), which they cast on cushions.

DEFENSE AGAINST THE DARK ARTS Professor Moody (really Barty Crouch, Jr., in disguise) teaches students about Unforgivable Curses and demonstrates the Imperius Curse, Cruciatus Curse and Killing Curse on spiders. He also casts the Imperius Curse on students to show them what it feels like and how to resist it.

DIVINATION Students learn astrology and complete a chart with the position of the planets at the time of their birth, which requires consulting timetables and calculating angles.

Known Homework: A detailed analysis of how planetary movements in the next month will affect you, based on your personal star chart

HERBOLOGY Students collect Bubotuber pus for use as an acne remedy, wearing dragon-hide gloves as protection due to the harmful effects of undiluted pus on the skin. They also prune Flutterby Bushes and repot Bouncing Bulbs.

HISTORY OF MAGIC

Known Homework: Weekly essays on 18th-century goblin rebellions

POTIONS Students brew antidotes and Wit-Sharpening Potion.

Known Homework: Researching antidotes

TRANSFIGURATION Students turn hedgehogs into pincushions and guinea fowl into guinea pigs.

Known Homework: Describe, using examples, how Transforming Spells must be adapted for Cross-Species Switches

Fifth Year

Students continue the same core subjects and electives (presumably) and prepare for their Ordinary Wizarding Levels (O.W.L.s).

ASTRONOMY

Known Homework: Essay on Jupiter's moons; complete star charts

CARE OF MAGICAL CREATURES The class sketches Bowtruckles and labels their anatomy. Later in the year, they work with Crups and Thestrals. Knarls, Kneazles, and Porlocks are also standard at this level.

CHARMS Students review Summoning Charms, cast Silencing Charms (*Silencio*) on animals such as bullfrogs and ravens, and charm teacups to grow legs.
Known Homework: Work out a countercharm
DEFENSE AGAINST THE DARK ARTS
Professor Dolores Umbridge only allows her students to read theory from the textbook and forbids any actual wandwork.
DIVINATION Professor Trelawney teaches dream interpretation until she is removed from her post by Professor Umbridge during the 1995–1996 school year.
Known Homework: Keep a dream diary for a month
Firenze, Trelawney's replacement, emphasizes the imprecision and futility of human divination in connecting tiny personal occurrences to planetary movements. Students burn sage and mallowsweet and look for shapes and symbols in the fumes.
HERBOLOGY Students work with Screechsnap seedlings.
Known Homework: Essay on Self-Fertilizing Shrubs
HISTORY OF MAGIC Professor Binns lectures about giant wars.
Known Homework: Foot-and-a-half-long essay on giant wars
POTIONS Students brew Draught of Peace and Strengthening Solution.
Known Homework: Foot-long essay on the use of moonstones; researching Confusing and Befuddlement Draughts; essay on various varieties of venom antidotes
TRANSFIGURATION Students practice Vanishing Spells on animals of increasing complexity, starting with snails and moving to mice and kittens.
Known Homework: Essay on the Inanimatus Conjurus spell

SIXTH YEAR
Students choose which courses they wish to continue after their O.W.L.s and need to have achieved certain scores in their O.W.L.s to take some N.E.W.T.-level classes, at the professor's discretion. Additional, specialized subjects, such as Alchemy, may be offered in sixth and seventh year if there is sufficient demand.

CHARMS Students turn vinegar to wine and learn the Water-Making Spell (*Aguamenti*). Nonverbal magic is expected.

DEFENSE AGAINST THE DARK ARTS Students learn nonverbal spells and attempt to silently jinx each other and repel the jinxes.

Known Homework: Essays on the best way to tackle Dementors and resisting the Imperius Curse

HERBOLOGY Students retrieve pods from inside Snargaluff stumps, wearing gloves, goggles and gum shields for protection, and puncture the pods with a sharp object to reveal the tubers inside.

POTIONS Horace Slughorn shows his class Veritaserum, Polyjuice Potion, Amortentia and Felix Felicis. Students brew the Draught of Living Death, and the best brewer wins a vial of Felix Felicis. Antidotes and Golpalott's Third Law (the antidote to a blended poison is more than the sum of the antidotes for the separate components) are also covered.

Known Homework: Research Everlasting Elixirs

TRANSFIGURATION Students learn to conjure birds (*Avis*) and perform human Transfiguration by changing the color of their eyebrows. Nonverbal magic is expected.

Known Homework: Essay on "The Principles of Rematerialization" (most likely for Transfiguration)

SEVENTH YEAR

Since Harry, Ron and Hermione do not return to Hogwarts for their final year while the school is under Death Eater control, little is known.

DEFENSE AGAINST THE DARK ARTS In the 1997–1998 school year, Amycus Carrow requires students to practice the Cruciatus Curse on those who have detention.

MUGGLE STUDIES Alecto Carrow takes over this now mandatory (previously elective) course in the 1997–1998 academic year and teaches anti-Muggle propaganda.

Exams

At the end of each academic school year, students must pass all of their classes to be able to continue into the following year. Each class has a written exam, and some also include a practical. Anti-Cheating Charms are applied to the exam papers and Auto-Answer Quills, Remembralls, Detachable Cribbing Cuffs and Self-Correcting Ink are banned. The grading system for first to fourth years is numerical values or percentages; Hermione has shown that students can score higher than 100 percent on an exam. In comparison, the O.W.L.s and N.E.W.T.s in the fifth and seventh years use a letter system.

FIRST-YEAR EXAMS
Charms: Students make a pineapple tap-dance across a desk.
History of Magic: Tests the student's knowledge about the invention of the Self-Stirring Cauldron by Gaspard Shingleton.
Potions: Students must brew the Forgetfulness Potion from memory.
Transfiguration: Students must turn a mouse into a snuffbox. Extra points are given for how pretty the box is and points are deducted if the snuffbox still has whiskers.

SECOND-YEAR EXAMS
During the 1992–1993 academic year, the end-of-year exams are canceled due to the reopening of the Chamber of Secrets and various students being Petrified.

THIRD-YEAR EXAMS
Care of Magical Creatures: Students are required to keep a Flobberworm alive for an hour.
Charms: Students perform a series of charms on their partners, including Cheering Charms.

Defense Against the Dark Arts: Students complete an obstacle course that includes wading across a deep pool containing a grindylow and across a series of potholes full of red caps, ignoring the misleading directions from a hinkypunk and finally battling a boggart.

Divination: Students look into a crystal ball and distinguish what can be seen.

History of Magic: Tests the student's knowledge of medieval witch-hunts.

Muggle Studies: This is a written exam, and Hermione scores a 320%.

Potions: Students must brew a Confusing Concoction from memory.

Transfiguration: Students must complete a series of tasks, including turning a teapot into a tortoise.

Fourth-Year Exams

Not much is known about the fourth-year exams at the end of the 1994–1995 school year. Harry does not have to take his exams, as he is a school champion in the Triwizard Tournament.

Fifth-Year O.W.L. Exams

The examination period is spread out over two weeks, with the theory exams in the morning and the practical in the afternoon. Both fifth and seventh years have their exams at the same time in the Great Hall. The four House tables are removed and replaced with desks facing the staff table.

Ancient Runes: Students are required to translate runes into English.

Astronomy: The theory exam tests students' knowledge of Jupiter's moons. For the practical, students observe the night sky and fill in a star chart.

Care of Magical Creatures: Students must correctly identify a Knarl among a group of hedgehogs.

Charms: The theory exam includes a question on the Levitation Charm. The practical exam requires students to make an egg cup cartwheel, along with levitating and color-changing an object.

Defense Against the Dark Arts: The 1976 O.W.L. written exam requires students to name the five signs that identify the werewolf. The 1996 practical exam tests students on banishing a boggart, and Harry receives a bonus point for producing a Patronus.

Herbology: The students must handle a Fanged Geranium.

History of Magic: Tests students' knowledge of the warlocks of Liechtenstein and the International Confederation of Wizards. During the exam, Harry has a vision of Sirius Black being tortured in the Department of Mysteries, which causes him to leave early.

Potions: The theory exam tests students' knowledge of the Polyjuice Potion.

Transfiguration: The theory exam includes a question about the definition of a Switching Spell. The practical exam has students vanish an animal.

SIXTH-YEAR EXAMS

Classes are only available to the students who achieve the required minimum O.W.L. score set by the professors to advance to their respective N.E.W.T. classes. During the 1996–1997 academic year, all exams are postponed due to the death of Dumbledore.

SEVENTH-YEAR EXAMS

These are the most critical exams given at Hogwarts in that they determine what a student can do as a career. A student's exams are in the subjects they have been studying since the sixth year, and the majority of exams have a theory and practical component.

O.W.L. AND N.E.W.T. GRADING SYSTEM

PASS GRADES	FAIL GRADES
Outstanding (O)	Poor (P)
Exceeds Expectations (E)	Dreadful (D)
Acceptable (A)	Troll (T)

Textbooks

Each academic year, Hogwarts students receive a supply and book list by owl post. Professors assign books according to their lesson plans (which is why the required book for Defense Against the Dark Arts changes from year to year).

ADVANCED POTION-MAKING by Libatius Borage was published around 1946 and is a N.E.W.T.-level textbook for Potions. It was used for N.E.W.T. Potions from as early as 1976, as during Harry's sixth year, he uses a copy of the book with handwritten instructions later revealed to be inscribed by Severus Snape.

ADVANCED RUNE TRANSLATION is used by N.E.W.T.-level students.

A BEGINNER'S GUIDE TO TRANSFIGURATION by Emeric Switch is a required textbook for first- and second-year students. During the 1992 summer holidays, Lucius Malfoy slips Tom Riddle's diary into Ginny's secondhand copy.

BREAK WITH A BANSHEE, GADDING WITH GHOULS, HOLIDAYS WITH HAGS, TRAVELS WITH TROLLS, VOYAGES WITH VAMPIRES, WANDERINGS WITH WEREWOLVES, YEAR WITH THE YETI by Gilderoy Lockhart are required textbooks for Defense Against the Dark Arts during the 1992–1993 academic year. The books contain personal accounts from the author about dealing with various dangerous creatures, which are later revealed to be fraudulent fabrications based on others' experiences.

CONFRONTING THE FACELESS is the Defense Against the Dark Arts N.E.W.T.-level textbook during the 1996–1997 academic year taught by Severus Snape.

THE DARK FORCES: A GUIDE TO SELF-PROTECTION by Quentin Trimble is the 1991–1992 Defense Against the Dark Arts textbook when Professor Quirrell teaches the subject.

DEFENSIVE MAGICAL THEORY by Wilbert Slinkhard is Hogwarts's Defense Against the Dark Arts textbook for the 1995–1996 academic year.

Chapters include "Basics for Beginners," "Common Defensive Theories and their Derivations," "The Case for Non-Offensive Responses to Magical Attack" and "Non-Retaliation and Negotiation."

THE DREAM ORACLE by Inigo Imago is a textbook used in Professor Trelawney's fifth-year Divination class and explores dream interpretation.

FANTASTIC BEASTS AND WHERE TO FIND THEM by Newt Scamander was published in 1927 by Obscurus Books. The book goes into detail about magical creatures, their Ministry of Magic classifications and the field of Magizoology. Required for first years.

FLESH-EATING TREES OF THE WORLD is a book for sixth-year students studying N.E.W.T.-level Herbology.

A GUIDE TO ADVANCED TRANSFIGURATION is a N.E.W.T.-level textbook used by students studying Transfiguration.

A HISTORY OF MAGIC by Bathilda Bagshot is one of the most famous books in the wizarding world. The book covers everything on magic up to the 19th century. Before Harry Potter first attends Hogwarts, he finds inspiration in the book to name his snowy owl Hedwig.

HOME LIFE AND SOCIAL HABITS OF BRITISH MUGGLES by Wilhelm Wigworthy was published in 1987 by Little Red Books and is the required textbook for third-year students taking Muggle Studies as an elective.

INTERMEDIATE TRANSFIGURATION is a required textbook for third- to fifth-year students.

MAGICAL DRAFTS AND POTIONS by Arsenius Jigger is used by first-year Potions students.

MAGICAL HIEROGLYPHS AND LOGOGRAMS is presumably a fifth-year Ancients Runes textbook. Hermione references the book one evening in the Gryffindor common room in March of 1996.

MAGICAL THEORY by Adalbert Waffling is for first-year students. The book covers the Fundamental Laws of Magic.

THE MONSTER BOOK OF MONSTERS is the third-year Care of Magical Creatures textbook in 1993. The textbook is unique in that the book tends to try to bite the reader's fingers off and can only be opened by stroking its spine.

NUMEROLOGY AND GRAMMATICA is the textbook used by third years studying Arithmancy as an elective.

ONE THOUSAND MAGICAL HERBS AND FUNGI is required for first years in Potions.

SPELLMAN'S SYLLABARY is a required textbook for students in the fifth and sixth years who have chosen Ancients Runes as an elective.

THE STANDARD BOOK OF SPELLS, GRADES 1-7 by Miranda Goshawk. Each academic year, the next grade in the series is required for Hogwarts students.

UNFOGGING THE FUTURE by celebrated Seer Cassandra Vablatsky. Covers palmistry, crystal balls and bird entrails. Required textbook for third years taking Divination.

Library Books

With thousands of shelves, there is an almost endless number of books in the Hogwarts library. Only a handful are pulled at integral events throughout Harry's time at Hogwarts.

KNOWN LIBRARY BOOKS AND WHO USES THEM

When Harry, Ron and Hermione are researching Nicolas Flamel, they search the following tomes (none of which, to their chagrin, contain any information about Flamel):

- A STUDY OF RECENT DEVELOPMENTS IN WIZARDRY
- GREAT WIZARDS OF THE TWENTIETH CENTURY
- IMPORTANT MODERN MAGICAL DISCOVERIES
- NOTABLE MAGICAL NAMES OF OUR TIME

Hagrid utilizes the following resources on dragon rearing while trying to learn how to care for Norbert(a) the Norwegian Ridgeback:

- DRAGON BREEDING FOR PLEASURE AND PROFIT
  Sections include: Essential Equipment, Recognizing Dragon Eggs, Dragons of the World (map) and A-Z of Ailments
- DRAGON SPECIES OF GREAT BRITAIN AND IRELAND
- FROM EGG TO INFERNO, A DRAGON KEEPER'S GUIDE

Hermione finds tips for flying in:

- QUIDDITCH THROUGH THE AGES by Kennilworthy Whisp, published in 1952 by Whizz Hard Books. It contains information about the history of broom sports and Quidditch over the last 1,000 years and explores Quidditch playing positions, balls, gear, fouls and teams.

Ron searches for evidence to protect Buckbeak in:

- FOWL OR FOUL? A STUDY OF HIPPOGRIFF BRUTALITY a historical survey of

incidents involving hippogriffs
- THE HANDBOOK OF HIPPOGRIFF PSYCHOLOGY a guide to hippogriffs

Harry and Hermione look for spells to defeat a dragon in:
- BASIC HEXES FOR THE BUSY AND VEXED a spellbook
- MEN WHO LOVE DRAGONS TOO MUCH a psychological study of dragon experts

Harry and his friends try to find ways to breathe underwater in:
- AN ANTHOLOGY OF EIGHTEENTH-CENTURY CHARMS a Charms reference book
- A GUIDE TO MEDIEVAL SORCERY a historical reference
- DREADFUL DENIZENS OF THE DEEP a guide to sea creatures
- MADCAP MAGIC FOR WACKY WARLOCKS a spellbook
- OLDE AND FORGOTTEN BEWITCHMENTS AND CHARMES a spellbook
- POWERS YOU NEVER KNEW YOU HAD AND WHAT TO DO WITH THEM NOW YOU'VE WISED UP a spellbook
- SAUCY TRICKS FOR TRICKY SORTS a spellbook
- WEIRD WIZARDING DILEMMAS AND THEIR SOLUTIONS a guide (includes a spell to grow nose hair into ringlets)
- WHERE THERE'S A WAND, THERE'S A WAY a spellbook

In the Restricted Section, Hermione finds:
- MAGICK MOSTE EVILE a Dark Arts reference book written in the Middle Ages by Godelot. It's the only book in the entire Hogwarts library—including those in the Restricted Section—that mentions Horcruxes, but doesn't go into detail and only refers to them as "the wickedest of magical inventions." This book emits a "ghostly wail" when slammed shut. Later, when Hermione is Minister of Magic, she keeps a copy of this book in her office.
- MOSTE POTENTE POTIONS an illustrated guide to advanced potions that contains instructions for making Polyjuice Potion

Harry studies for Potions class:
• ASIATIC ANTI-VENOMS by Libatius Borage, a book on healing potions

HOGWARTS: A HISTORY

A favorite of Hermione's, *Hogwarts: A History* is a 1,000-page book about the 1,000 years of history surrounding Hogwarts. Information in the book includes details on:
• The enchanted ceiling of the Great Hall
• How Hogwarts is hidden from Muggles. If a Muggle were to happen by the area, all they would see is ruins and a sign saying, "DANGER, DO NOT ENTER, UNSAFE"
• Rules of Apparating in and out of Hogwarts (mostly the fact that one cannot do so)
• The fact that Muggle electronics will not work at Hogwarts
Notably, the book does not mention the Hogwarts house-elves.

Rules

As a school filled with young witches and wizards coming into their magical powers, Hogwarts relies on rules to maintain an admittedly fragile sense of order. Some apply to all students, whereas others are based on age or events in the outside world. Harry breaks every single one of the known school rules during his time at Hogwarts.

RULES APPLICABLE TO ALL STUDENTS

CURFEW

Strictly enforced yet most commonly broken, curfew requires that students not be outside their dormitories at nighttime. Filch appears to barely sleep because of how seriously he takes his job of patrolling the corridors at night. The time that curfew starts for students in their fifth year seems to change to 9 p.m., and it's not clear what time it is before that point. Students seem to be discouraged (if not specifically forbidden) from leaving the castle after sundown no matter the time of night, especially as the danger increases in the outside world. Despite this rule, Harry uses his Invisibility Cloak to break curfew at least 15 times over his years at Hogwarts. Remarkably, he is only caught once by a teacher who cares, but the punishment is particularly severe—Minerva McGonagall docks a whopping 150 points from Gryffindor and gives Harry, Hermione and Neville detention.

THE FORBIDDEN FOREST

The name says it all. Students are only allowed to go into the Forest with Hogwarts professors or staff for Care of Magical Creatures classes or detention.

MAGIC IN THE CORRIDORS

Magic is forbidden in the corridors, most likely to prevent duels from occurring when students are unsupervised. Filch specifically reminds Dumbledore to include this in his start-of-term announcements multiple times, claiming in the fall of 1995 that he has made this reminder 462 times.

FIGHTING
As is the case in most schools, fighting is against Hogwarts school rules. This does not seem to deter many students, who often send curses at each other in the corridors or out on the grounds. Muggle-style fighting seems to be particularly frowned upon.

BANNED ITEMS
Filch seems to be solely responsible for the creation of an extensive list of items that are banned from school property. After the Weasley twins officially launch Weasleys' Wizard Wheezes, Filch institutes a blanket ban on all products from their store. Also included on this list are Fanged Frisbees and, presumably, Dungbombs. Filch asks Dumbledore to make these reminders at multiple start-of-term feasts, which Dumbledore does without much enthusiasm, referring curious students to the long list on Filch's office door. Filch seems to be given a large amount of leeway to ban things at random, including the song "Weasley Is Our King" in school corridors after Gryffindor loses a Quidditch game in early 1996. During the 1996–1997 school year, all students' belongings and mail are searched to make sure they are not bringing anything dangerous into the school. Filch uses Secrecy Sensors to search the students, and included in the confiscated items is a shrunken head.

LIBRARY RULES
For more information about library book usage, see the Library (see page 68).

RULES BASED ON AGE

BROOMSTICKS

First-year students are not allowed to bring their own broomsticks to campus, a rule broken in Harry's first year to provide him with a broomstick so that he can play on the House team.

HOGSMEADE PERMISSION FORMS

Beginning in their third year, students are required to have permission forms signed by their parents or guardians to visit Hogsmeade, leading Harry to sneak into Hogsmeade in 1993.

MAGIC OUTSIDE OF SCHOOL

Wizarding children under 17 are not allowed to use magic outside of school. All magical children have a spell on them known as the Trace that detects any magic occurring in the area where the child is present. This spell is fairly inaccurate, however, as it does not determine whether or not the child in question was the one who cast the spell.

RULES ONLY ENFORCED IN CERTAIN SCHOOL YEARS

THIRD-FLOOR CORRIDOR

During the 1991–1992 school year, the third-floor corridor on the right-hand side is out of bounds to "everyone who does not wish to die a very painful death." Despite the fact that the corridor itself can be opened with a simple *Alohomora* charm, this threat is assumed to be enough of a deterrent to keep people away.

STRICTER CURFEW

After the Chamber of Secrets is opened in the 1992–1993 school year and Hermione and Penelope Clearwater are Petrified in a double attack, the school implements a stricter curfew and more supervision. Students are required to be in their common rooms by 6 p.m. and are escorted in between classes and to the bathrooms by teachers. Quidditch matches, practices and other evening activities are canceled.

EDUCATIONAL DECREES

During Dolores Umbridge's reign at Hogwarts in the 1995–1996 school year, the Ministry of Magic adds a series of educational decrees to limit Dumbledore's control over the school. The first 21 decrees are unknown, but beginning on August 30, **Educational Decree Number 22** states that "in the event of the current headmaster being unable to provide a candidate for a teaching post, the Ministry should select an appropriate person." In September, Umbridge's position as High Inquisitor at Hogwarts is defined with **Educational Decree Number 23**, which allows her to inspect the lessons of other professors and remove them or put them on probation. After Dumbledore's Army's first meeting in the Hog's Head, **Educational Decree Number 24** is passed, which states, "No student Organization, Society, Team, Group or Club may exist without the knowledge and approval of the High Inquisitor." This not only makes participation in the D.A. worthy of expulsion but also forces the Quidditch teams to request permission to re-form as well.

Educational Decree Number 25 gives Umbridge the permission to change the punishments set by other teachers, allowing her to ban Harry, Fred and George from playing Quidditch for life. After 10 Death Eaters escape from Azkaban, **Educational Decree Number 26** establishes that "Teachers are hereby banned from giving students any information that is not strictly related to the subjects they are paid to teach." This is followed by the ban on students reading *The Quibbler* in **Educational Decree Number 27**, which only makes more students want to read Harry's interview. When Dumbledore takes the fall for the D.A., Umbridge is appointed headmistress via **Educational Decree Number 28**. Filch threatens Harry with the upcoming **Educational Decree Number 29**, which will allow him to string students up by the ankles in his office.

MANDATORY ATTENDANCE

After the Death Eaters take over Hogwarts in the 1997–1998 school year, attendance at Hogwarts is considered mandatory. This is used as a tool to control all magical children and weed out Muggle-borns.

Punishments

Just like at any school, Hogwarts students inevitably break the rules. Depending on the transgression, punishments range from House points deducted to detention or even expulsion.

HOUSE POINTS

Docking House points is common, and students who lose significant numbers of House points often invoke the ire of their classmates. This system is biased, however, since particular heads of Houses (Snape, most notably) tend to take more points away from other Houses than they do their own. In our knowledge of Harry's time at Hogwarts, for example, Snape takes 267 points from Gryffindor and none from Slytherin.

DETENTION

When the offenses are significant enough, many teachers will hand out detentions. Some detentions are disgusting, like cleaning out bedpans in the hospital wing, disemboweling a barrel of horned toads, pickling rats' brains and sorting through rotten Flobberworms (all set by Snape, unsurprisingly), while others are boring, like writing lines, recopying Filch's files, polishing silver and answering Gilderoy Lockhart's fan mail. Still others are dangerous, like searching the Forbidden Forest for a unicorn killer at night. Detentions are handed out for everything from petty misdemeanors, like cheek, not handing in homework and being out of bed after hours, to more outlandish crimes, like flying a car to school, pretending to be a Dementor, turning a corridor into a swamp, using forbidden jinxes and losing a list of passwords that allows a convicted murderer into a House common room.

   Overall, Minerva McGonagall, Severus Snape and Dolores Umbridge assign the most known detentions. Snape and Umbridge are particularly likely to assign lengthy detentions that include especially unpleasant tasks.

EXPULSION

Expulsion is commonly used as a threat but is infrequently followed through on by Hogwarts staff. Expelled students have their wands snapped in half, which forces them to the outskirts of wizarding society. The horror of this shameful outcome is enough to make Hermione believe she would rather die than be expelled.

Only two known students have been expelled from Hogwarts. Around 1914, Newt Scamander was kicked out for endangering students with an illegal magical creature. Dumbledore argued strongly against his expulsion, and it appears he was allowed to keep his wand. In 1943, Rubeus Hagrid was expelled for allegedly opening the Chamber of Secrets. Dumbledore convinced Headmaster Armando Dippet to keep Hagrid on as gamekeeper, but Hagrid's wand was still snapped in two.

Expulsion seems to be enforced when a student endangers the lives of others or breaks magical law. Using magic outside of school is a serious violation of the Statute of Secrecy, and students who break this rule twice will be expelled unless they can prove they were acting in self-defense.

CRUEL AND UNUSUAL PUNISHMENTS

During Dolores Umbridge's tenure at Hogwarts, punishments are pushed to the extreme. In her detentions, Umbridge forces students (notably Harry) to write lines using a quill she invented that writes in blood, etching the words written into the back of the student's hand. Umbridge also bans Harry, Fred and George from playing Quidditch ever again after they fight Draco Malfoy at the end of a match. She even gives Filch permission to whip the twins, but they escape before Filch can catch them.

After the Death Eaters take over in the fall of 1997, Amycus and Alecto Carrow require students to perform the Cruciatus Curse on those who have been given detention. Those who refuse or give cheek in class are physically wounded. The Carrows keep students in chains and torture anyone who tries to protect them.

Extracurriculars

Days at Hogwarts are so packed with practicing magic, searching for classrooms and digging into delicious feasts that free time can be hard to come by. While there aren't many known groups and societies at Hogwarts, students still manage to have plenty of fun.

On weekends or during holidays, students can be found playing Exploding Snap, Gobstones or wizard chess in their common rooms. Gobstones and Charms are both available as clubs as well.

Students who are interested in activism can try the Society for the Promotion of Elfish Welfare, which costs two Sickles to join.

Quidditch is a beloved sport at Hogwarts, and talented students may be able to join their House team. Other students are allowed to go down to the Quidditch pitch and practice their flying whenever the pitch is not in use. People who prefer keeping their feet firmly on the ground can still enjoy cheering on their House team from the safety of the stands.

Even more exclusive than the Quidditch team is the Slug Club, Professor Slughorn's elite society for well-connected and talented students. Slughorn hosts a Christmas party for members of this club, and Harry attends one such gathering in 1996.

Third-year students and above enjoy visiting the village of Hogsmeade on preapproved weekends (or, if they know the secret passageways, whenever they like). Here, they stock up on candy, pranks, school supplies and butterbeer to last them until the next Hogsmeade weekend.

During the 1992–1993 academic year, Professor Snape and Professor Lockhart host a Dueling Club, but this unlikely partnership only lasts for one fateful lesson.

Sixth-year students looking to learn how to Apparate can take the class with Wilkie Twycross.

Notices regarding available clubs, groups, teams and events at Hogwarts can be found on common room notice boards.

Quidditch

Beloved by many in the wizarding world, Quidditch is a popular pastime at Hogwarts. Almost the entire school (including several teachers) comes out to watch the matches and cheer on their House teams. In the lead-up to Quidditch matches, Quidditch players are sometimes jinxed in the hallways by members of opposing teams, and heads of Houses become noticeably more partisan than usual. After the games, winning players are treated like royalty, and huge common room parties are often thrown in their honor. Losing players, on the other hand, have been known to hide in shame from other members of their House.

Only seven players from each House are chosen to be on the Quidditch team. First years are allowed to try out, but since they aren't allowed to bring their own broomsticks, they rarely make the team. Harry Potter proves to be an exception to the rule, however, owing to Gryffindor's desperate need for a new Seeker during his first year at the school. This in turn makes him the youngest Seeker in a century.

The Quidditch captain is given ultimate discretion with regard to what types of tryouts are held and when. A captain who is happy with their team may choose not to hold tryouts in a given year; alternatively, they may hold tryouts for only one position they are looking to fill. It may come as a surprise to know the captain is not required to choose the person who did best in tryouts, either. Angelina Johnson, for example, passes over selecting Vicky Frobisher and Geoffrey Hooper in favor of Ron Weasley, knowing that Vicky is involved in too many other extracurriculars and that Geoffrey, for his part, is a whiner. Harry is spared from being put in this position by Hermione's Confundus Charm, which causes Cormac McLaggen to perform worse than Ron in the tryouts.

Unlike most Muggle sports teams, Quidditch teams do not appear to have non-starting players who practice with the team and are ready to join if a starting player is injured. When one of their starting players is out of commission, the captain frequently chooses someone else who did well in tryouts to replace them. When a captain does not have an alternative from tryouts—such as in Harry's first year, when he sustains an injury before the final Quidditch game—they are simply out of luck and have to continue with the game down a player. This strategy does not serve the teams particularly well, as Quidditch is a violent sport that consistently leads to players getting injured.

The result of these rules and conditions means that Quidditch is an exclusive sport at Hogwarts. Only seven players per House, drawn from all seven years, are allowed to participate, and other than the basic flying lessons given to first years, there doesn't appear to be much space for other students to practice their skills. Students from wizarding families, therefore, are at a strong advantage in trying out for their House teams, having grown up learning and practicing the sport and often owning their own brooms. It is doubly impressive, therefore, that Harry makes the team at such a young age, given that he was raised by the Dursleys. Another noteworthy player raised by Muggles is Dean Thomas, who is taken on as a reserve Chaser during his sixth year.

QUIDDITCH PRACTICE

Quidditch teams tend to practice three times a week, and before big matches, some captains might require practices as often as every evening. House teams book the Quidditch pitch for their practices, but these reservations can be overwritten by other teams if they can produce a signed note from their head of House. Students who aren't on the House teams are allowed to watch practices, but it isn't always a reassuring sight—captains are occasionally suspicious that members of other Houses may be spying on them.

The captain of each Quidditch team acts as a de facto coach, in charge of running team drills and imposing new strategies. Oliver Wood in particular takes this job seriously (some might say far too seriously) and treats his team to long-winded lectures at early hours of the morning and even in the corridors between classes.

QUIDDITCH MATCHES

Before Quidditch matches, players change into their Quidditch robes in the changing rooms and are given a pregame pep talk by their captain. The players then go out onto the field, and the captains of each team shake hands. At the referee's whistle, all players and the referee mount their brooms and kick off from the ground, beginning the game.

Quidditch matches are refereed most often by Madam Hooch. She tends to be a fair and impartial arbiter of the rules, although she has been known to get angry about flagrant fouls. In one game during Harry's first year, Snape referees instead. While a fairly blatant Slytherin partisan, in this case Snape has taken the job in order to watch over Harry and protect him from Quirinus Quirrell.

Each Quidditch match also has a student commentator who speaks into a magical megaphone. During Harry's first five years at Hogwarts, Lee Jordan is in charge of commentating. He is a dynamic and engaging host but often shows bias toward Gryffindor and includes personal tidbits about the players he knows and what he thinks about their brooms. After Lee graduates, Zacharias Smith is the first to take on the mantle. He is no less partisan and is particularly nasty toward the Gryffindor team. Luna Lovegood comes next, and although she cares very little about the game, she certainly adds her own amusing commentary and observations. Professor McGonagall takes on the job of monitoring the commentator, which often involves scolding them for biased language or unnecessary tangents.

Quidditch matches appear to influence House points to a certain extent. In Harry's first year, it's mentioned that Gryffindor gains a lead in the House Cup based on the points Harry wins through Quidditch. In 1992, Percy Weasley also congratulates Harry on winning Gryffindor 50 points through a Quidditch victory. It is unclear what factors in the game contribute to how many points the House wins. The only other time this is mentioned is in Harry's third year, when it's noted Gryffindor won the House Cup based on their performance in the Quidditch Cup match.

QUIDDITCH SEASONS

The Inter-House Quidditch Cup is played in a series of games where every House plays each other House once. This means each House plays three matches over the course of the year and watches three. The scoring for the Quidditch Cup seems to use a system where the House that wins the most individual matches wins the Cup. If two Houses tie with regard to their number of wins, then the outcome of the Cup appears to depend on some system of comparative scores. The evidence here, however, is contradictory between books, so it's possible there is some other point system being used (though a more likely explanation is that it's a mistake on the author's part, given her admitted difficulty with arithmetic).

Quidditch seasons have a structure that is fairly consistent each year. Matches always occur on Saturday mornings after breakfast. The first Quidditch match of the season occurs in early November and is usually between Gryffindor and Slytherin. The second match, between Ravenclaw and Hufflepuff, appears to be in late November or early December. There is a break for winter holidays, and then matches resume with a Slytherin vs. Ravenclaw game in the middle of January. Gryffindor and Hufflepuff play in the end of February or early March, and then the fifth match of the season is at the end of March or early April between Slytherin and Hufflepuff. This match may change in timing based on when Easter break falls. The sixth and final match of the season is between Gryffindor and Ravenclaw. It falls either in late May or early June, before or after the end-of-term exams.

This schedule is not entirely set in stone. In Harry's third year, the Gryffindor vs. Slytherin match is switched to Gryffindor vs. Hufflepuff due to Draco Malfoy's supposed injury, but there are plenty of other times when players are injured and games are not rescheduled. Some of this may be dependent on the timing—Harry is injured in the final game of his first season, so there cannot be a simple swap of teams because everyone else has already played. It also may be related to influence—Snape may be more likely as head of Slytherin House to make a fuss in order to get special treatment for his team.

The schedule itself is also not completely unbiased. Quidditch games are played in all kinds of weather, and winter in Scotland is not a pleasant time to be flying through the air. Gryffindor plays two of its three matches during the times of the year with the best weather, which might heighten their chances of scoring more points. Gryffindor and Ravenclaw also have the advantage of usually being the last teams to play, which means they know exactly how many points they need to win by in order to gain the Quidditch Cup and can therefore strategize accordingly.

CHEERS AND CELEBRATIONS

On game days, almost everyone at the school comes out to the pitch, wearing their House colors or the colors of the House they would rather see win. For example, Luna Lovegood wears her gigantic roaring lion hat to a Gryffindor vs. Slytherin game. Students from opposing Houses often place surreptitious wagers with each other over the match. Friends of the players may wave flags, rosettes and banners or enchant encouraging signs to flash colors. Fights sometimes break out in the stands between members of different Houses. Draco Malfoy perhaps orchestrates the most coordinated type of cheering seen at Hogwarts with his song "Weasley Is Our King," which highlights the ways in which Ron's mistakes help the Slytherin team. Malfoy even creates matching crown-shaped badges. This song is later co-opted by the Gryffindor team, however, when Ron manages to turn around his playing.

THE MATCH MUST GO ON...

Even at the intramural level played at Hogwarts, Quidditch matches are treated with the utmost seriousness. When players are injured or in danger, neither the professors nor the referees halt or call off the match while the danger is assessed. It is up to the captains in charge to decide whether to call off the match, and if they do so, they automatically forfeit. Many players are not willing to do this. Harry, for example, plays while riding a jinxed broom, being pursued by a rogue Bludger and being attacked by Dementors.

KNOWN QUIDDITCH PLAYERS THROUGH THE AGES

GRYFFINDOR

Minerva McGonagall (Position unknown, approximately 1954)

James Potter (*Chaser*, at least 1975–1976)

Charlie Weasley (*Seeker*, c. 1986–1990, *Captain* for at least one year)

Oliver Wood (*Keeper*, c. 1988–1994, *Captain*, at least 1990–1994)

Angelina Johnson (*Chaser*, c. 1990–1996, *Captain*, 1995–1996)

Katie Bell (*Chaser*, 1991–1997) → replaced by **Dean Thomas** (first two games of 1996–1997 season)

Alicia Spinnet (*Chaser*, 1991–1996, reserves in 1990–1991 season)

Fred Weasley (*Beater*, 1990–1996) → replaced by **Andrew Kirke** (second half of 1995–1996 season)

George Weasley (*Beater*, 1990–1996) → replaced by **Jack Sloper** (second half of 1995–1996 season)

Harry Potter (*Seeker*, 1991–1997, *Captain* 1996–1997) → replaced by **Ginny Weasley** (second half of 1995–1996 season, last game of 1996–1997 season)

Ron Weasley (*Keeper*, 1995–1997) → replaced by **Cormac McLaggen** (one game in 1996–1997 season)

Ginny Weasley (*Chaser*, at least 1996–1997) → replaced by **Dean Thomas** (last game of 1996–1997 season)

Demelza Robins (*Chaser*, at least 1996–1997)
Jimmy Peakes (*Beater*, at least 1996–1997)
Ritchie Coote (*Beater*, at least 1996–1997)

RAVENCLAW
Roger Davies (*Chaser* and *Captain*, at least 1993–1996)
Cho Chang (*Seeker*, at least 1993–1997)
Bradley (*Chaser*, at least 1995–1996)
Chambers (*Chaser*, at least 1995–1996)

HUFFLEPUFF
Cedric Diggory (*Seeker* and *Captain*, at least 1993–1994)
Zacharias Smith (*Chaser*, at least 1995–1997)
Summerby (*Seeker*, at least 1995–1996)
Cadwallader (*Chaser*, at least 1996–1997)

SLYTHERIN
Regulus Black (*Seeker*, approximately 1975)
Marcus Flint (*Chaser* and *Captain*, at least 1991–1994)
Terence Higgs (*Seeker*, at least 1991–1992)
Miles Bletchley (*Keeper*, at least 1991–1996)
Adrian Pucey (*Chaser,* at least 1991–1996)
Draco Malfoy (*Seeker*, at least 1992–1997)→ replaced by **Harper**
  (1996–1997, at least one game)
Bole (*Beater*, at least 1993–1994)
Derrick (*Beater*, at least 1993–1994)
Warrington (*Chaser*, at least 1993–1996)
Montague (*Chaser*, at least 1993–1996, *Captain* 1995–1996)
Vincent Crabbe (*Beater*, at least 1995–1996)
Gregory Goyle (*Beater*, at least 1995–1996)
Urquhart (*Chaser* and *Captain*, at least 1996–1997)
Vaisey (*Chaser*, at least 1996–1997)
Scorpius Malfoy (*Seeker*, in an alternative timeline, c. 2020)

Apparition Lessons

I t's a known rule that students and teachers cannot Apparate (magically disappear from one location and reappear in another) into, within or out of Hogwarts. For Apparition lessons, however, Dumbledore temporarily lowers the enchantment that prohibits Apparition at Hogwarts, but only for the duration of the lesson and within the lesson space, rather than the entire castle and grounds.

In Harry's sixth year, the course lasts 12 weeks, is held on Saturdays outside of lesson time and costs 12 galleons. It is only open to those who would be at least 17 years old on August 31, 1997, since 17 is the age at which you can take your Apparition test and obtain a license (and also the age at which Muggles can drive in the United Kingdom).

Though these lessons were originally intended to be held outside in the grounds, bad February weather forces the first lesson to be moved inside, into the Great Hall (see page 56), where every student is given an old-fashioned wooden hoop. Standing behind this hoop, each of them is encouraged to attempt to Apparate into their hoop by Wilkie Twycross, Ministry Apparition instructor.

Apparition is not a wholly safe method of travel, as Susan Bones proves in the first lesson when she splinches herself (leaves part of herself behind) while Apparating. Fortunately, the importance of the lessons warrants the supervision of all the heads of Houses at the event, and she is soon reunited with her detached leg.

As students discover, Apparition is difficult, and enthusiasm at the prospect of learning to do it soon gives way to frustration at Twycross and his favored slogan for what is necessary to achieve Apparition— the three D's: Destination, Determination and Deliberation!

Dueling Club

In December 1992, following Colin Creevey's Petrification by the monster from the Chamber of Secrets, a Dueling Club is formed at Hogwarts. Scared by the recent attacks, nearly the entire school shows up at the first meeting in the Great Hall, eager to defend themselves. Headmaster Albus Dumbledore gives Professor Gilderoy Lockhart permission to form the club for this purpose, but Lockhart is there more to take advantage of an audience than out of any concern for student safety. He is assisted by Snape, who is likely just as interested in hexing or cursing Lockhart as he is in safety.

The meeting begins with a dueling demonstration by the professors, where Harry first observes a spell he comes to use a great deal in the future: *Expelliarmus*. Next, attendees are split into pairs to practice Disarming Charms on each other. The scene descends into chaos—Harry and Malfoy quickly switch to offensive spells and Millicent Bulstrode grabs Hermione Granger in a headlock.

Lockhart attempts to use Malfoy and Harry in a demonstration, but with only Lockhart's poor advice on blocking charms to work with, Harry finds himself facing a snake conjured by Malfoy and has no idea how to stop it; instinctively, he attempts to communicate with it, revealing he can speak Parseltongue. Although this causes suspicion from his classmates (Parselmouths are often associated with the Dark Arts), it proves significant and useful to Harry throughout the series.

There is no other record of the Dueling Club, and it seems unlikely there was a second meeting after the first ended so disastrously. Though competitive dueling is a known activity in the wizarding world (Professor Flitwick is rumored to have been a dueling champion in his youth), there is no other record of a similar club or group existing at Hogwarts at any other time, with the exception of the far more successful Dumbledore's Army.

Exploding Snap

It's probably safe to assume Exploding Snap is a slightly more incendiary version of the Muggle card game and that it has nothing to do with detonating a certain Potions professor, as the original German versions of the books suggested when the game was mistranslated as "Snape Explodiert" or "Snape Explodes" (this was corrected in later versions).

Though it seems disingenuous to say that Exploding Snap is a non-competitive game (as anyone who has played Muggle Snap can attest), there is no record of any Hogwarts teams or championships for it.

Instead, it's an entertaining way to pass the time. Harry plays it on three train journeys from Hogwarts to London, and Ron memorably builds an Exploding Snap card tower, much to the detriment of his eyebrows.

Gobstones

Gobstones is a game like marbles, where each player has 15 Gobstones and must capture their opponent's to win. After each capture, a stone squirts a malodorous liquid in the loser's eye.

Gobstones are usually made of stone, but some, like the solid gold set Harry eyes in Diagon Alley, are made of precious metals.

Students at Hogwarts are known to play friendly games by the lake, but Gobstones is by no means a casual affair for enthusiasts. There is an office for the Official Gobstones Club at the Ministry of Magic. It is played competitively by adults and at a scholastic level. Eileen Prince (Snape's mother) was Captain of the Hogwarts Gobstones Team.

The Slug Club

The Slug Club is an exclusive group of students handpicked by Potions professor Horace Slughorn based on their connections, talent or other indicator of potential. Slughorn enjoys maintaining close relationships with such students, who usually go on to become successful and provide him with gifts, information and a sense of self-importance. Slug Club members are invited to dinner parties and other gatherings where they can make connections and meet esteemed alumni, including Quidditch players, authors and government officials. Slughorn revives the Club when he returns to Hogwarts in 1996.

KNOWN MEMBERS (1996–1997)
Marcus Belby*
Melinda Bobbin
Hermione Granger
Neville Longbottom*
Cormac McLaggen
Harry Potter
Ginny Weasley
Blaise Zabini

KNOWN ALUMNI
Avery (contemporary of Voldemort)
Dirk Cresswell (Head of the Goblin Liaison Office)
Barnabas Cuffe (editor of the *Daily Prophet*)
Lily Evans

Ambrosius Flume (owner of Honeydukes)
Gwenog Jones (Captain of the Holyhead Harpies)
Lestrange (contemporary of Voldemort)
Tom Riddle (Voldemort)
Eldred Worple (author of *Blood Brothers: My Life Amongst the Vampires*)
Marcus Belby's uncle Damocles (inventor of the Wolfsbane Potion; received the Order of Merlin)
Cormac McLaggen's uncle Tiberius (friends with Minister of Magic Rufus Scrimgeour)

*only present at the first meeting on the Hogwarts Express

Wizard Chess

Wizard chess is a popular game similar to Muggle chess, except the pieces move on their own when commanded by the players. Ron is the best chess player of the trio. He uses an old set inherited from his grandfather, so the pieces trust him.

During the 1991–1992 academic year, Professor McGonagall Transfigures a wizard chess set as a means of protecting the Sorcerer's Stone. The chessboard is large enough to fill a room and the pieces are taller than the trio. Challengers play as black and must defeat the white side to pass. When a piece is taken, its opponent violently smashes it and drags it off the board. Playing as a knight, Ron directs Harry as a bishop and Hermione as a castle, or rook. He skillfully moves around the board, taking white pieces and keeping his friends out of harm's way. In order to allow Harry to take the king, Ron sacrifices himself to the queen, who knocks him out cold—the king throws its crown at Harry's feet and the chessmen bow and let Harry and Hermione pass. Dumbledore awards Ron 50 points for playing the best game of chess at Hogwarts in many years, helping Gryffindor clinch the House Cup.

MEDIEVAL MAGICAL CHESS

Magical chess games appear in several Arthurian romances, including the Dutch *Roman van Walewein*, in which Gawain encounters a flying chessboard; the *Perceval Continuation*, in which Perceval loses chess to pieces that move by themselves; and the *Lancelot-Grail*, or *Vulgate Cycle*, in which Lancelot defeats an unbeatable chessboard.

Pets

Students are permitted to bring one pet with them to Hogwarts and can choose a cat, owl or toad. This rule does not appear to be enforced, however, since some students bring other animals. Most pets appear to live with students in their dormitories, but owls may reside in the school owlery (see page 83). Some staff members also have pets, several of which Harry comes to know while at Hogwarts.

KNOWN PETS

Milicent Bulstrode - cat
Albus Dumbledore - Fawkes (phoenix)
Argus Filch - Mrs. Norris (cat)
Hagrid - Fang (boarhound), Fluffy (three-headed dog), Norbert(a) (Norwegian Ridgeback dragon), Buckbeak (hippogriff), Aragog (Acromantula)
Hermione Granger - Crookshanks (cat/Kneazle)
Lee Jordan - tarantula (unclear if kept as a pet or used for other purposes)
Neville Longbottom - Trevor (toad)
Draco Malfoy - eagle owl
Harry Potter - Hedwig (snowy owl)
Ginny Weasley - Arnold (Pygmy Puff)
Percy Weasley - Hermes (screech owl)
Ron Weasley - Scabbers (rat/Animagus), Pigwidgeon (scops owl)

Weekends at Hogsmeade

Over the course of the academic year, third years and above can go down to the local village of Hogsmeade (see page 139) on specific weekends. To access the village, students need a signed permission slip from a parent or guardian. Even with a signed form, heads of House and the headmaster or headmistress can deny students access as punishment. Hogsmeade weekends can happen at any point but often coincide with holidays.

A day in Hogsmeade village starts with eligible students getting their names checked against a list of signed permission slips. Students can leave Hogwarts at any time during the day as long as they are back at the castle before dinner. Once in the village, students may go anywhere within the village limits and can visit several shops along the High Street, including the two most popular haunts: Honeydukes sweet shop and Zonko's Joke Shop. Students can also visit Dervish and Banges or Scrivenshaft's Quill Shop, the Three Broomsticks for a warm butterbeer or even Madam Puddifoot's Tea Shop just off the High Street for a romantic date. The brave may dare to visit the village's tourist attraction, the Shrieking Shack, before walking back to Hogwarts.

SIGNIFICANT EVENTS DURING HOGSMEADE WEEKENDS
1993–1994
Harry's unsigned permission form initially bars him from the trips, but Fred and George Weasley give him the Marauder's Map, which reveals secret passageways to Hogsmeade. One is through the one-eyed witch statue that leads straight into Honeydukes's cellar. Once Harry finds Ron and Hermione in Honeydukes, they go to the Three Broomsticks for a round of butterbeer.

During the final Hogsmeade visit of the year, Professor Lupin resigns as Defense Against the Dark Arts professor and packs up his office.

1994–1995

The first Hogsmeade weekend of the year takes place the weekend before the first Triwizard task. Harry uses his Invisibility Cloak to visit the village to avoid unwanted attention.

The second trip occurs after the Christmas break. While in the Three Broomsticks, the trio encounters Ludo Bagman, who offers to help Harry solve the golden egg clue. They also encounter Rita Skeeter and quickly escape her questions.

On the last known trip of the year, Harry buys Dobby new socks from Gladrags Wizardwear. The trio then makes their way to the outskirts of the village to meet up with Sirius Black face-to-face in a cave on the mountain.

1995–1996

During the first trip to Hogsmeade in 1995, Dumbledore's Army uses the Hog's Head pub to hold their first meeting. The next trip happens on Valentine's Day. Harry and Cho Chang go to the village together and have coffee at Madam Puddifoot's Tea Shop. The date ends with an argument between the two and Harry meeting up with Hermione in the Three Broomsticks. While there, he gives an interview to Rita Skeeter on his experience at the end of the previous year in the Little Hangleton graveyard. The interview is published in *The Quibbler* soon after, and Professor Umbridge bans Harry from going to the village for the rest of the year.

1996–1997

During the first Hogsmeade weekend, Katie Bell is cursed by an opal necklace while under the influence of an Imperiused Madam Rosmerta, which is Malfoy's doing. The events lead to the cancellation of future weekends and the Weasley twins' deciding against the possible purchase of Zonko's Joke Shop. One of the canceled weekends was due to happen on Ron's birthday.

Celebrations

Throughout the school year at Hogwarts, several celebrations occur regularly for holidays and important dates. Throughout Harry's time there, several less frequent celebrations are also held, like the festivities associated with the Triwizard Tournament (see page 38).

QUIDDITCH

Big Quidditch wins are often celebrated with a party in the common room. It is unclear how spontaneous these parties are. After an exciting win in their sixth year, Seamus Finnigan calls for Harry to join "a party up in the common room." However, once there, Harry mentions seeing a drinks table—a detail that seems as if it would need at least some planning to be properly set up.

These types of parties give the students an exciting environment in which to mingle. It is during the same party mentioned above that Ron and Lavender Brown are spotted kissing in a corner, which causes some drama within Harry's friend group.

At another of these post-match parties, Harry returns to the common room after having missed the entire match while serving detention with Professor Snape. When he arrives, the celebration comes to a halt when Ginny Weasley rushes to kiss him. Afterward, the pair ditch the party for some alone time on the grounds.

SLUG CLUB PARTIES

Slug Club gatherings are typically intimate affairs with about a dozen guests, hand picked by Professor Slughorn himself. During Harry's sixth year, however, the professor hosts a large Christmas party to which Harry brings Luna Lovegood as a guest. Slughorn decorates his office with "emerald, crimson and gold hangings" along the ceiling and walls so that the space resembles a tent. An ornate golden lamp dangling from the ceiling contains real fairies who emit light. Slughorn also arranges for musical entertainment—singing and mandolins—and utilizes the Hogwarts house-elves as waiters to serve an assortment of food and drink including pasties and mead. For more information on the Slug Club, see page 187.

YULE BALL

For more information on the Yule Ball, which takes place whenever Hogwarts hosts the Triwizard Tournament, see page 41.

DUMBLEDORE'S FUNERAL

A somber and unexpected form of observance comes during Albus Dumbledore's funeral, which takes place during Harry's sixth year. Classes and exams are canceled for the event, but several students are pulled from the school entirely by their concerned parents before the funeral takes place. Dozens of wizards and witches who had known Dumbledore are allowed to enter Hogwarts grounds for the funeral. Because there are no other formal funerals attended by Harry, it is unclear how typical the ceremony itself is of such events in the wizarding world.

The ceremony is held next to the lake. Hundreds of chairs are set in rows flanking a center aisle leading to a marble altar. The merfolk of the lake sing in their native language as Hagrid carries Dumbledore's body to the stone altar, and despite not being able to understand the language, Harry feels it speaks "very clearly of loss and of despair."

After the ceremony, white flames erupt around Dumbledore's body, and the smoke curls into strange shapes. When the fire clears, Harry sees that a white marble tomb has encased the body.

VOLDEMORT DAY

In one of the alternate universes of *Harry Potter and the Cursed Child*, Voldemort defeats Harry and takes over Hogwarts. In that grim timeline, Voldemort Day is celebrated with green banners hung all around the school that depict a snake.

CHAPTER 5

CASTLE INHABITANTS

A school of witchcraft and wizardry
is bound to have many colorful, eccentric
characters inhabiting its hallowed halls.

Headmasters & Headmistresses

Hogwarts has had quite a number of colorful leaders in its many years of existence. Harry gets to interact with or observe a few of them (or their portaits, at least) while studying at Hogwarts.

DILYS DERWENT *(active 18th century)*
Derwent began working for St. Mungo's Hospital for Magical Maladies and Injuries as a Healer in 1722. In 1741, she left St. Mungo's to serve as headmistress of Hogwarts until 1768. Later, her portrait was placed in the headmaster's office.

 A second portrait of Derwent hangs in St. Mungo's. This is convenient when Arthur Weasley is attacked by Voldemort's snake Nagini in 1995. Upon learning Arthur is injured, Headmaster Albus Dumbledore asks Derwent to go between the headmaster's office and her other portrait at St. Mungo's to keep him abreast of Arthur's condition.

 Following Voldemort's defeat in the Second Wizarding War, Derwent's portrait in the headmaster's office applauds Harry while sobbing (presumably with joy and relief).

EVERARD *(b. Unknown - d. Unknown)*
Much is left to speculation about when Everard, a man Dumbledore refers to as "one of the most celebrated heads," served as headmaster of Hogwarts. Everard has a second portrait at the Ministry of Magic, which Dumbledore instructs him to visit when Arthur Weasley is injured. Similarly, Everard uses his multiple portraits to warn Minerva McGonagall that Rufus Scrimgeour is on his way to Hogwarts from the Ministry of Magic after Dumbledore's death.

EUPRAXIA MOLE *(active 19th century)*
Mole served as headmistress of Hogwarts during the 1870s. She

became famous for the deal she made with Hogwarts poltergeist Peeves in 1876. During that year, caretaker Rancorous Carpe tried and failed to remove Peeves using an "elaborate trap," a plan that ended with disastrous results. The castle had to be evacuated for three days as Peeves ransacked it and threatened the students. To resolve this, Mole signed a contract with Peeves in which he agreed to stop causing havoc in exchange for a once-weekly swim in the boys' toilets, stale bread from the kitchen to throw and a custom-made hat from Madame Bonhabille (a French witch and hatmaker based in Paris).

DEXTER FORTESCUE (b. Unknown - d. Unknown)

Much is unknown about when Fortescue served as headmaster of Hogwarts. In his portrait, Fortescue can be found speaking loudly and using the same ear trumpet he used in life. His direct descendent, Florean Fortescue, runs Florean Fortescue's Ice Cream Parlor in Diagon Alley until his untimely death in 1996 at the hands of Voldemort's Death Eaters.

PHINEAS NIGELLUS BLACK (b. 1847 - d. 1925)

Black served as headmaster of Hogwarts from an unknown date until (presumably) his death in 1925. His great-great-grandson, Sirius Black, refers to him as the "least popular headmaster Hogwarts ever had." In his portrait, Black is described as a clever-looking wizard with black hair, dark eyes, a pointed beard and thin eyebrows. He is shown wearing the colors of his House, Slytherin.

He has two known portraits: one hanging in the headmaster's office and a second hanging in the Black family ancestral home, number twelve, Grimmauld Place. During the Second Wizarding War, Hermione Granger removes the Grimmauld Place portrait and brings it with her while hunting Horcruxes with Harry and Ron. Because of this, Black can lead Severus Snape to the trio and covertly provide them with assistance.

ARMANDO DIPPET *(active 20th century)*

Dippet served as headmaster of Hogwarts from at least the 1940s through the 1960s. During this time, the Chamber of Secrets—created by Hogwarts founder Salazar Slytherin—was opened by Tom Riddle, unleashing the basilisk within.

Not long after, the creature killed Hogwarts student Myrtle Warren in a bathroom. With the death of a student on his hands and a murderous monster on the loose, Dippet told Riddle that the Ministry was considering closing the school for the safety of the remaining students and staff. Riddle then manipulated Dippet into blaming the attacks on Rubeus Hagrid, leading to the latter's expulsion.

When Tom Riddle petitioned Dippet for a teaching position, the headmaster denied his request, suggesting Riddle reapply in a few years.

ALBUS DUMBLEDORE *(b. 1881 - d. 1997)*

Kind, calm and undoubtedly eccentric, Albus Dumbledore serves as headmaster of Hogwarts from the time of Armando Dippet's departure until his own death in 1997. Prior to taking on the role of headmaster, the legendary wizard taught Transfiguration at Hogwarts for many years (see page 204).

Shortly after becoming headmaster, Dumbledore was approached by Tom Riddle, who by then had started going by the alias Lord Voldemort and wanted to be hired as a teacher. Knowing that Voldemort truly desired the position not to educate young students but to recruit new Death Eaters, Dumbledore refused, and Voldemort jinxed the Defense Against the Dark Arts teaching position to prevent anyone from holding it for more than one year at a time.

Years later, as the First Wizarding War raged on, Dumbledore gathered together skilled witches and wizards he trusted and formed the Order of the Phoenix to combat Voldemort's growing forces. He sent two members, James and Lily Potter, into hiding after Sybill Trelawney, who had been hoping to be hired as a Divination professor, made a prophecy to him about the birth of a child who would defeat the Dark Lord. Death Eater Severus Snape overheard the prophecy and told Dumbledore that Voldemort believed it applied to the Potters' child. Despite having previously abandoned his desire to unite all three Deathly Hallows, Dumbledore borrowed one—the Invisibility Cloak—from James and still had it at the time of James and Lily's deaths. This was in addition to the Deathly Hallow he already possessed: the Elder Wand.

Now in charge of ensuring the safety of James and Lily's young son, Harry, Dumbledore hides the boy with his maternal aunt and uncle, Petunia and Vernon Dursley, until Harry is old enough to attend Hogwarts. Snape commits himself to working with Dumbledore as a double agent to ensure Harry is protected.

Ten years later, when Harry begins his wizarding education, Dumbledore and several trusted teachers establish multiple layers of security to hide the Sorcerer's Stone from Voldemort. Despite the fact that Harry is directly involved in Voldemort's attempts to steal the Stone, Dumbledore decides he is too young to know the truth surrounding his destiny. The following school year, when the Chamber of Secrets is reopened by Ginny Weasley under the influence of Tom Riddle's possessed diary, Harry's loyalty to Dumbledore brings Fawkes, Dumbledore's pet phoenix, to him in the Chamber of Secrets. Dumbledore comes to realize the magnitude of Voldemort's plan: to create several Horcruxes, all of which must be destroyed in order to vanquish the Dark Lord once and for all. In 1995, when Harry witnesses Voldemort's bodily resurrection, Dumbledore reassembles the Order of the Phoenix. Not wanting to accept the growing threat to the wizarding world, the Ministry of Magic discredits Dumbledore's claims in a smear campaign—he is stripped of his various titles, ridiculed in the media and eventually forced to flee Hogwarts.

In June 1996, Dumbledore confronts Voldemort and duels him at the Ministry of Magic, and the number of witnesses compels the Ministry to admit the truth about the Dark Lord's return. After Dumbledore is reinstated as headmaster, he finally reveals the prophecy to Harry and spends the summer searching for Horcruxes. Along the way, he falls victim to a curse that will kill him in less than a year. He arranges a plan for Snape to kill him in order to protect Snape's position as one of Voldemort's trusted followers. During the school year, the headmaster begins revealing more of the truth to Harry, giving him the knowledge he needs to hopefully defeat the Dark Lord in the short term—including information on Voldemort's past and the nature of Horcruxes. When Dumbledore discovers the location of another Horcrux, he allows Harry to accompany him to retrieve and destroy it. While they are away, Death Eaters successfully breach Hogwarts. Soon after, Dumbledore and Harry return to Hogwarts and head to the Astronomy Tower, where they meet Draco Malfoy and a number of Death Eaters. Snape casts the Killing Curse at Dumbledore, and he falls from the tower.

When Dumbledore's funeral (see page 193) is held in early summer 1997, it is attended by many who loved and respected him. His portrait later hangs in the headmaster's office, behind the desk.

DOLORES UMBRIDGE (active late 20th century)
Umbridge serves as headmistress of Hogwarts for a short period of time in 1996 after exposing Dumbledore's Army and being appointed by the Ministry through Educational Decree Number 28. She is widely despised by both students and faculty. The headmaster's office refuses to recognize her as the legitimate head and denies her entry by sealing itself shut to her. In a moment of desperation, Hermione tricks the headmistress into visiting the Forbidden Forest—during an encounter with centaurs, Umbridge insults them, and the enraged herd carries her away. She is removed from the school when the Ministry reinstates Dumbledore.

SEVERUS SNAPE (b. 1960 - d. 1998)
Snape serves as headmaster of Hogwarts during the 1997-1998 school year, when Death Eaters Alecto and Amycus Carrow are appointed

deputy heads. Since Snape's position as a double agent is still undiscovered at this time, he is able to use his power as headmaster to protect the remaining students as discreetly as possible. Dumbledore's portrait continues to give Snape instructions, including providing Harry with the sword of Gryffindor. When the trio return to Hogwarts to finish their quest, McGonagall duels Snape and he is forced to flee; this reveals that he can fly without a broomstick, a rare skill for which Voldemort himself is infamous. He dies during the Battle of Hogwarts when Voldemort orders Nagini to attack him. Snape's final act is giving Harry the memories necessary to understand Snape's complicated past. Harry ensures his teacher's portrait is hung in the headmaster's office.

MINERVA MCGONAGALL *(b. 1935 -)*

McGonagall serves as headmistress of Hogwarts from the conclusion of the Second Wizarding War until (presumably) present day. She undertakes the task of rebuilding the school and ensuring every student who was denied access by the Death Eaters is allowed to resume their studies. McGonagall eventually hires Neville Longbottom as Herbology professor and ushers in the next generation of witches and wizards when the children of Harry, Ron, Hermione and Draco begin their studies. Like their parents before them, the Potter and Malfoy children get up to outrageous and dangerous antics, the consequences of which McGonagall is forced to help rectify.

Professors

While there are an unknown number of professors at Hogwarts at any one time, there are at least 12 professors who handle the education of hundreds of students. The school hires human and non-human instructors, such as the ghostly Professor Binns and the centaur Firenze. Some professors take on multiple responsibilities, such as acting as the deputy to the headmaster or head of one of the four Hogwarts Houses.

Professors at Hogwarts have the power to award and deduct points from each House, assign detentions and expel students (although they likely consult with the headmaster first). Under Dumbledore's administration, they are forbidden to use any form of magical or physical force to punish a student. (At one point in time, professors were allowed to use corporal punishment.) They can also grant notes to students for a variety of reasons to allow them to leave class and grant permission for students to go to off-limits areas, such as the Restricted Section of the library, which Hermione uses in 1992 to access the recipe for the Polyjuice Potion.

Students are required to address their teachers either as "professor" followed by their surname, or, alternatively, Sir or Madam, depending on their gender. Rubeus Hagrid is a notable exception to the rule, however, as students usually refer to him by his surname.

KNOWN PROFESSORS

BATHSHEDA BABBLING
Little is known about the 1993 Study of Ancient Runes professor, as her name only appeared on the author's website on a list of Hogwarts professors. Her last name, Babbling, is befitting of her position as it is used to describe the act of speaking in obscure jargon.

HERBERT BEERY

Professor Beery taught Herbology during Armando Dippet's time as headmaster, though he left to teach at the Wizarding Academy of Dramatic Arts. His most memorable event while at Hogwarts was his attempt to adapt the "Fountain of Fair Fortune" tale into a stage show with himself as director, and the disastrous production nearly burned down the Great Hall.

CUTHBERT BINNS

Based on one of the author's university professors, Binns is the only ghost professor at Hogwarts and has been teaching History of Magic since before he died. He passed away in his sleep while taking a nap in the staffroom, woke up and went straight to work in his current form.

CHARITY BURBAGE

Professor Burbage presumably began teaching Muggle Studies at Hogwarts in 1990. To the public, she "resigns" from the position in 1997, but in reality, Death Eaters target her after she publishes an article in the *Daily Prophet* in defense of Muggle-borns. Voldemort kills her, and then she is eaten by Nagini at Malfoy Manor.

ALECTO CARROW

A Death Eater, Alecto invades Hogwarts at the end of the 1996–1997 academic year and becomes the Muggle Studies teacher (well, she teaches students to hate Muggles), replacing Charity Burbage. She and her brother, Amycus, serve as deputy headmasters to Severus Snape. Alecto is captured at the beginning of the Battle of Hogwarts in Ravenclaw Tower when Luna Lovegood Stuns her and is later bound and suspended in midair by Professor McGonagall.

AMYCUS CARROW

A squat wizard with a lopsided leer, Amycus, like his sister, invades Hogwarts in June 1997, where he urges Draco Malfoy to kill

Dumbledore. He joins the staff as the Defense Against the Dark Arts professor (really teaching Dark Arts) and also serves as a deputy headmaster to Severus Snape alongside his sister. Amycus and his sister torture students and encourage them to practice the Cruciatus Curse on their peers. Along with Alecto, he is captured just before the Battle of Hogwarts and held in Ravenclaw Tower.

BARTY CROUCH, JR.
After escaping from Winky the house-elf during the Quidditch World Cup in 1994, Barty captures Alastor Moody and impersonates him (with the help of Polyjuice Potion) to infiltrate Hogwarts. He sets Voldemort's plans for regenerating himself with Harry's blood into motion by manipulating the Triwizard Tournament. He is captured after the third task and is subject to a Dementor's Kiss when Minister of Magic Cornelius Fudge insists on bringing an Azkaban guard for "protection."

ALBUS DUMBLEDORE
A gifted, benevolent and decidedly eccentric wizard, Dumbledore teaches Defense Against the Dark Arts from at least the 1910s to 1927, when the Ministry of Magic forbids him from teaching the subject due to his refusal to fight the dark wizard Gellert Grindelwald. Later, he teaches Transfiguration from at least the 1940s until becoming headmaster, presumably. For more information on Dumbledore, see page 198.

FIRENZE
Prior to becoming the Hogwarts Divination professor, a position he takes over when Dolores Umbridge fires Sybill Trelawney in 1996, Firenze resides with the rest of his centaur herd in the Forbidden Forest. He has white-blond hair, blue eyes and a palomino body. Once he accepts the Divination position at the school, however, the other centaurs consider Firenze a traitor and banish him from the herd. The following academic year, Firenze shares the Divination role with Sybill

Trelawney. Firenze may have been based on a centaur from Greek mythology, Chiron, as both centaurs are considered outcasts from their herds due to their being more civil, friendly and willing to teach humans than others.

FILIUS FLITWICK
Filius Flitwick is the Charms professor and head of Ravenclaw House. A human with a dash of goblin ancestry, the vertically challenged professor is known to stand on a pile of books while teaching so he can see the entire class. Before the Battle of Hogwarts, Flitwick constructs a magical defense over Hogwarts and takes fighters up to one of the three tallest towers to defend the school. He is rumored to have been a dueling champion when he was younger. Flitwick enjoys drinking cherry syrup and soda with ice and an umbrella and loves decorating with live fairies. His most notable work is teaching *Wingardium Leviosa* to first-year students.

WILHELMINA GRUBBLY-PLANK
An elderly witch with gray hair and a prominent chin, Grubbly-Plank is known to smoke a pipe and use a monocle. She is the substitute professor for Care of Magical Creatures after the 1994 Christmas break, when Rita Skeeter indisposes Hagrid, and again at the start of the 1995 academic year when Hagrid is away negotiating with the giants. She nurses Hedwig back to health when the owl is attacked while delivering mail to Harry.

RUBEUS HAGRID
A half-giant with a wild tangled beard, Hagrid is a kind soul. While studying at Hogwarts in 1943, he was wrongfully accused of manipulating the creature that had been Petrifying students and expelled. Later, Hagrid became the Keeper of Keys and Grounds, and in 1993, he takes over the Care of Magical Creatures position following Professor Silvanus Kettleburn's retirement. During his first class, Hagrid

introduces the students to hippogriffs. Draco Malfoy, not heeding Hagrid's instruction on how to properly approach the creatures, soon gets injured, an event that results in his attacker, Buckbeak, being sentenced to death. Hagrid also teaches the students about Blast-Ended Skrewts and Flobberworms. He is briefly run out of the school in 1996 when Dolores Umbridge deems him an inept instructor.

SILVANUS KETTLEBURN
With most of his limbs missing, Silvanus had a reputation for reckless behavior and a love of dangerous creatures. His most infamous incident as a Hogwarts professor was when he provided an Ashwinder to stand in as the "giant worm" in Professor Beery's stage adaptation of "The Fountain of Fair Fortune." For more on that incident, see page 57.

GILDEROY LOCKHART
Famous throughout the wizarding world, Lockhart is known for his vast array of books on studying and defeating magical beasts. In 1992, Lockhart becomes Hogwarts's Defense Against the Dark Arts professor. Throughout the academic year, he proves totally inept at teaching students, and he accidentally blasts himself with a Memory Charm he had intended for Ron and Harry. Having received permanent spell damage, he currently resides in the Janus Thickey Ward at St. Mungo's Hospital.

NEVILLE LONGBOTTOM
Throughout his time at Hogwarts, Neville excels at Herbology. It's no surprise, then, that after finishing his schooling, he returns to Hogwarts to become its Herbology instructor.

REMUS LUPIN
A close friend of Harry's father, James, Hogwarts alumnus Remus Lupin takes over for Gilderoy Lockhart as the Defense Against the Dark Arts teacher in 1993. While on his way to the school aboard the Hogwarts

Express, he drives away a Dementor of Azkaban and provides students with chocolate to help them recover, earning him approval from Madam Pomfrey. Lupin takes care to prepare his students for encounters with Dark creatures and works on building their confidence with spell-casting. After Harry's second attack by Dementors, Lupin teaches him the Patronus Charm. At the end of the academic year, Professor Snape leaks to the school that Lupin is in fact a werewolf. This news, along with the fact that Lupin had forgotten to take his Wolfsbane Potion and had transformed on school grounds, prompts him to resign the next morning while students are at Hogsmeade.

MINERVA MCGONAGALL

Strict but fair, Minerva McGonagall is the head of Gryffindor House and teaches Transfiguration at Hogwarts from 1956 to 1998, when she becomes headmistress. A talented Animagus, she proves an encouraging and rigorous instructor. During the Battle of Hogwarts, McGonagall leads the school in fortifying the castle, and she even duels Voldemort herself. For more information on McGonagall, see page 201.

GALATEA MERRYTHOUGHT

Galatea Merrythought was a professor at Hogwarts from 1895 to 1945 and likely taught Defense Against the Dark Arts for most of that time. Before she retired, Tom Riddle asked to take over her Defense Against the Dark Arts position. Headmaster Dippet denied his request and told him to come back when he was older.

QUIRINUS QUIRRELL

Quirinus Quirrell may have been inspired by Edward Mordake, a figure from the late 19th century who, according to urban legend, had a menacing demon face on the back of his head. He was originally the Muggle Studies professor at Hogwarts before taking on the Defense Against the Dark Arts position for the 1991–1992 academic year. Prior to his time in the latter position, Quirrell took a year off to travel the world and gain experience in dealing with the Dark Arts, meeting Voldemort along the way. Upon his return to the school, Quirrell is now timid and delicate—Voldemort has taken up residence at the back of Quirrell's head, a fact the professor conceals by wearing a purple turban. Throughout the 1991-1992 academic year, Professor Quirrell attempts to steal the Sorcerer's Stone and bring Voldemort back to life. During his final attempt, Harry prevents him from obtaining the Stone through his interactions with the Mirror of Erised. Realizing the Mirror has given his student the object, Quirrell attacks Harry, but when he touches Harry's skin, terrible blisters form all over his body, and he dies.

AURORA SINISTRA

Originally named Aurelia Sinistra in early notes for *Harry Potter and the Prisoner of Azkaban*, Professor Sinistra is the Astronomy teacher at Hogwarts during the 1990s. First-year Gryffindors take her class on Wednesdays at midnight on the Astronomy Tower. In 1992, she helps carry Justin Finch-Fletchley's Petrified body up to the hospital wing, and during the Yule Ball of 1994, she dances a two-step with Alastor Moody—or rather, Barty Crouch, Jr. Her last name is reflective of her role at Hogwarts, as Sinistra is the name of a magnitude 3.5 star in the constellation Ophiuchus, a.k.a. Serpent Handler.

HORACE SLUGHORN

A charming and jovial man, Slughorn wears elegant, old-fashioned clothes, such as a waistcoat with golden buttons and a velvet jacket. He was the Potions professor and head of Slytherin House until 1981, when he retired. In 1996, Slughorn comes out of retirement to teach the subject again at the request of Albus Dumbledore. During the 1997-1998 academic year, he is the head of Slytherin House, taking over the role from Severus Snape. He prides himself on teaching students who will make their mark on the wizarding world and capitalizes on this by creating what is known as the Slug Club, an elite group of students for which he occasionally hosts exclusive gatherings.

SEVERUS SNAPE

Intense, brooding and brimming with sarcasm (especially toward Harry, whom he openly loathes), the greasy-haired, bat-like head of Slytherin House is Hogwarts's imposing Potions professor from 1981 until 1996. A bully who openly favors students of his own House, Snape teaches Defense Against the Dark Arts in the 1996–1997 academic year, a position he had wanted for many years, and leaves the position when he becomes headmaster of the school. For more information on Snape, see page 200.

POMONA SPROUT

A squat witch with gray hair covered by a patched hat, Sprout is Herbology professor during Harry's time at Hogwarts. Her fingernails and robes are often covered in dirt owing to her work in the school's greenhouses. In 1991, the head of Hufflepuff House helps protect the Sorcerer's Stone by installing Devil's Snare. In the 1992–1993 year, she tends to the Whomping Willow when Harry and Ron crash the Weasley family's flying Ford Anglia into the tree and grows the mandrakes that are used to cure the Petrified victims of the basilisk. During the Battle of Hogwarts, she and Neville lead students throughout the castle in attacking the invading horde of Death Eaters with vicious plants. "Pomona" comes from the Roman goddess of fruit trees, while "Sprout" is an English word for a young plant.

SYBILL TRELAWNEY

The great-great-granddaughter of famous Seer Cassandra Trelawney, Sybill Trelawney is the Hogwarts Divination professor. Her given name has ties to ancient oracles, as Sibyl is often a name held by people who can enter a trance state to communicate with the Greek and Roman gods and goddesses. Thin with large glasses and a spangled shawl, she wears chains and beads around her neck and an array of rings and bangles on her arms. During the 1995–1996 academic year, Umbridge puts her on probation and unsuccessfully attempts to evict her from the school. Trelawney continues teaching the following year, sharing her classes with Firenze, who took over for her when she had been fired. During the Battle of Hogwarts, Trelawney throws her crystal balls off the balcony above the entrance hall onto the heads of Death Eaters fighting below.

DOLORES UMBRIDGE
Sadistic, cruel and committed to making sure students don't practice defensive magic, Umbridge teaches Defense Against the Dark Arts at Hogwarts during the 1995-1996 academic year. She is sent by the Ministry to interfere at Hogwarts, where she is appointed as High Inquisitor and later becomes headmistress. For more information on Umbridge, see page 200.

SEPTIMA VECTOR
As the Arithmancy professor, Vector works with the magical properties of numbers. Her last name ties into mathematics, as a vector is a quantity with both magnitude and direction.

School Governors

Like most educational institutions, Hogwarts has a board of governors to oversee the goings-on at the school. But given how rarely they are mentioned throughout many of the dangerous and dramatic events that mark Harry's education, one could argue they are exceedingly laid-back or even negligent in their duties.

In the 1992–1993 year, Lucius Malfoy uses his position as a school governor to try to remove Dumbledore from Hogwarts. Lucius keeps a close eye on the unfolding consequences of his slipping Ginny Weasley Tom Riddle's diary and leverages the mounting number of attacks on students as a means of uniting the governors in voting to present Dumbledore with an Order of Suspension. Later, it's revealed Lucius secured some members' votes by threatening to curse their families.

Twelve people, Lucius included, are on the board at this time, but despite this, no other witch or wizard is ever named as being or having been a Hogwarts governor. The other members call for Dumbledore's reinstatement as headmaster as soon as Ginny is taken into the Chamber of Secrets, and Lucius is promptly sacked. After his dismissal, Lucius continues to exert his influence with the governors to ensure Buckbeak the hippogriff suffers repercussions for attacking Draco.

Until Educational Decree Number 28 makes Dolores Umbridge headmistress, only the board of governors can appoint or dismiss Hogwarts headmasters and headmistresses.

Procedure dictates that the school governors be involved in decisions about whether or not to close the school. Closure becomes a possibility during the two openings of the Chamber of Secrets, in light of the student injuries caused by Draco's attempts to assassinate Dumbledore (so Hagrid surmises) and after Dumbledore's murder, when the heads of Houses decide they should consult the governors.

Notable Staff

The Hogwarts professors are far from the only people who keep the school running. Even before mentioning the castle's house-elf contingent, there are a number of ancillary roles among the human (or part-human) Hogwarts staff worth knowing about.

CARETAKER

The Hogwarts caretaker is mainly responsible for keeping the castle in clean and working order but also performs an assortment of other tasks, from checking that the students visiting Hogsmeade have permission to do so to punting students across an enchanted swamp blocking a school corridor. During Harry's time at Hogwarts, the caretaker is Argus Filch, a vindictive Squib (a non-magical person born to at least one magical parent) who feuds with Peeves the poltergeist and hates all students. He longs for the "good old days" when he could use chains and whips on anyone who misbehaved and is quick to take advantage of Professors Umbridge and Carrow giving him the opportunity to do so. One of Filch's predecessors, Apollyon Pringle, also favored corporal punishment and left Arthur Weasley with scars after he broke curfew with Molly Prewett.

FLYING INSTRUCTOR

This position is the only member of the teaching staff at Hogwarts who is not a professor. Hogwarts employs a flying instructor to teach first-year students the basics of operating a broomstick and oversee the school's Quidditch program. In Harry's time, this is Madam Rolanda Hooch, and while she referees almost every Quidditch match at Hogwarts, she has little to no involvement in the House teams' practices, only overseeing Gryffindor training sessions when Harry's life is thought to be under threat from Sirius Black.

GAMEKEEPER

Also known as the Keeper of Keys and Grounds at Hogwarts, the gamekeeper looks after the grounds and everything that lives in them, from the pumpkins used to decorate the Halloween feast to the Thestral herd that pulls the school carriages to the fantastic beasts that live in the Forbidden Forest. The gamekeeper lives in their own cabin near the Forest and carries a large ring of keys to the school. When Molly Weasley was at Hogwarts, this position was filled by a man named Ogg. Gamekeeper Rubeus Hagrid is the first Hogwarts staff member Harry meets. For more on Hagrid, see page 205.

LIBRARIAN

The Hogwarts library is staffed by one librarian while Harry is at Hogwarts—a witch named Madam Irma Pince. Almost as distrustful of students as the caretaker Argus Filch (something they seem to bond over), Madam Pince fanatically protects her books from rule-breaking students who would graffiti them, eat over them or try and retrieve them from the Restricted Section without authorization. She is highly suspicious of anyone loitering in her library and is often found dusting and polishing her precious books.

NURSE

Madam Poppy Pomfrey is the nurse Harry regularly visits during his Hogwarts education. A skilled witch, she single-handedly presides over the school's hospital wing and tends to all but the most serious injuries and ailments that befall its students and staff. In the original British editions of the books, Madam Pomfrey is always referred to as the school's "matron," the traditional term for a woman in charge of domestic and medical arrangements at a boarding school in the U.K. This was changed to "nurse" for ease of understanding in the U.S. editions of the earlier books but like other similar substitutions, was left unchanged in the later books.

House-Elves

House-elves are a magical race with large eyes, bat-like ears and their own form of nonverbal magic that does not require a wand. This includes the ability to Apparate to places where there may be magic preventing witches and wizards from doing the same, such as Hogwarts. Though they traditionally belong to rich, old wizarding families for whom they cook, clean, etc., house-elves can be freed from their enslavement if their masters present them with an item of clothing. Due to this caveat, they are usually seen wearing household linen such as pillowcases.

Harry first encounters a house-elf when Dobby, the Malfoy family elf, tries to protect him from the opening of the Chamber of Secrets by throwing increasingly dangerous obstacles in his path to stop him from attending school. In 1993, Harry tricks Lucius Malfoy into freeing Dobby by giving him a sock.

The largest population of house-elves in Great Britain is found at Hogwarts, where all the elves wear tea towels with the school's crest until Dobby and Winky (an elf who is freed as a punishment by her master, Barty Crouch, Sr., after the Quidditch World Cup in 1994) arrive. Dobby enjoys outlandish outfit combinations and especially socks, which he believes should not match.

Dobby initially has trouble finding work as a free elf who wants compensation, but Dumbledore agrees to pay him wages, give him holidays and let him call the headmaster whatever he like (house-elves are usually not allowed to speak ill of their masters). Dobby is considered highly strange by the rest of the school elves, who believe being given clothes is a shameful thing, including Winky, who copes with her freedom by drinking large quantities of butterbeer.

The traditional mark of a good house-elf is that they remain unseen and unheard, so Harry usually only sees them around Hogwarts when Dobby or Kreacher (the Black family house-elf Harry inherits after Sirius Black's death) visit him, with the exception of Professor Slughorn's Christmas party. Where possible, the Hogwarts house-elves keep to the kitchens (see page 72), which lie directly beneath the Great Hall. The elves send up food to the tables above at mealtimes but are only too happy to provide food to visiting students for House parties and afternoon snacks.

This outdated notion of remaining professionally invisible to the other castle inhabitants is done away with by the school's house-elves during the Battle of Hogwarts (see page 42). Ron and Harry grapple with the ethical dilemma of asking the creatures to fight or telling them to flee for their safety, but the house-elves choose to act of their own volition before the friends find a solution. Kreacher leads the Hogwarts house-elves into the fray during the battle's final moments. Armed with the carving knives and cleavers used to make many a meal, they attack the Death Eaters and help turn the tide of the war.

A Note on the Origin and Legacy of S.P.E.W.

Hermione sets up the Society for Promotion of Elfish Welfare during her fourth year at Hogwarts after she discovers the widespread poor treatment of house-elves by wizards. Her initial name for the society—"Stop the Outrageous Abuse of Our Fellow Magical Creatures and Campaign for a Change in Their Legal Status"—is too long to fit on badges, so she instead makes it the heading for their manifesto. Hermione appoints Harry as secretary and makes Ron treasurer, but despite persuading a few other students to join, she remains the society's only enthusiastic member. Hermione's active promotion of her society peters off as the Second Wizarding War begins in earnest, but after the war, she carries the spirit of S.P.E.W. into her first job in the Department for the Regulation and Control of Magical Creatures at the Ministry of Magic, proving herself instrumental in greatly improving the lives of house-elves.

Notable Ghosts

The most haunted residence in Britain, Hogwarts is home to numerous spirits that roam the school, about 20 of which appear in the entrance hall before Harry's Sorting. For the most part, they are not particularly terrifying beings and even avoid the Shrieking Shack (see page 148) because it is rumored (inaccurately) to be the most haunted place in Britain and occupied by a rough crowd of ghosts. The Hogwarts ghosts mingle with the students and staff and even provide entertainment at the Halloween feast, performing a bit of formation gliding in 1993. Ghostly business is handled by holding a ghost's council. In 1994, the Hogwarts ghosts convene to debate whether or not to allow Peeves to attend the start-of-term feast in light of some of his recent shenanigans. Despite their House allegiances, according to Nearly Headless Nick, the Hogwarts ghosts generally get along with each other.

PROFESSOR BINNS
For more information on Professor Binns, see page 203.

THE BLOODY BARON
The Slytherin House ghost, the Bloody Baron is perhaps the most stereotypically creepy and frightening of the Hogwarts ghosts. Blank eyes stare out from his gaunt face, and he wears chains and robes caked with silver bloodstains, the origin of which he does not share. He is the only being that Peeves appears to fear or respect, making him the only one able to exert any control over the poltergeist. The threat of going to the Baron to report his antics is one of the few ways to put a stop to Peeves's troublemaking. Ron suspects Nearly Headless Nick is terrified by the Baron as well, although Nick denies this.

In life, the Baron was a hot-tempered man who grew violent when his unrequited love, Helena Ravenclaw, did not return his affection and refused to come home with him at the request of her dying mother, Hogwarts founder Rowena Ravenclaw. After slaying Helena, he killed himself out of remorse; as a ghost, he wears chains as a symbol of his penance. A miserable and foreboding presence, he is often found groaning and clanking his chains around the Astronomy Tower.

THE FAT FRIAR

The Hufflepuff ghost was executed for his use of magic. During his lifetime, the friar drew suspicion from his higher-ups in the church by curing people of the pox simply by poking them with a stick (this was presumably his wand). It didn't help that he also had a tendency to pull rabbits out of the communion cup. Typical of a Hufflepuff, the Fat Friar is quite friendly, forgiving and repeatedly willing to give Peeves another chance despite the poltergeist's constant troublemaking. He still holds a slight grudge, however, for not being made a cardinal during his lifetime.

THE GRAY LADY

Originally called the Whispering Lady in the author's earliest writings, this quiet spirit is actually Helena Ravenclaw, the slain daughter of Hogwarts founder Rowena Ravenclaw. She appears as a tall young woman with long hair, and her floor-length cloak hides a telling stab wound in her chest. Jealous of her mother in life, Helena stole Rowena's diadem and fled with it in the hope of making herself smarter and more important, a betrayal Rowena kept secret even from her fellow Hogwarts founders. Seriously ill and desperate to see her daughter once more before her death, Rowena sent a baron who was in love with Helena to locate her. When he found Helena hiding in an Albanian forest, she refused to return with him. In a moment of rage, he stabbed her. Before the baron arrived, Helena hid the diadem in a hollow tree. This is where Voldemort found it centuries later, after convincing the Gray Lady to reveal its location when he was a student.

NEARLY HEADLESS NICK

Sir Nicholas de Mimsy-Porpington is the dignified and congenial Gryffindor ghost, happy to welcome new students to his House, make conversation and give directions. He is, however, rather sensitive about the fact that his head was not properly separated from his body during his botched beheading, which took 45 strokes of a blunt ax. The first draft of *Chamber of Secrets* contained a scene in which Nick sings a song telling the story of his execution. The bit of skin keeping his head attached to his neck prevents him as a matter of practicality from joining the Headless Hunt, a group of fully decapitated ghosts who use their severed heads for games and entertainment. In life, Sir Nicholas spent his time in the court of King Henry VII until he tried to use magic to make a lady-in-waiting more beautiful but accidentally caused her to sprout tusks in the process. This terrible mistake resulted in his execution on October 31, 1492, the 500th anniversary of which he commemorates with a large deathday party in 1992. He is a bit snobbish and, as evidenced by his magical mishap, not quite as skilled a wizard as he believes himself to be.

Nick has long, curly hair and wears a plumed hat, tights, a doublet and a ruff that conceals the injury to his neck. He prefers to be called Sir Nicholas and not the moniker that refers to the state of his neck, although he does find some pleasure in the reactions to his head swinging off and wants other ghosts to believe he is considered frightening. He even reenacts his beheading for the 1993 Halloween feast. Nick does miss food and drink, though, and does not appreciate jokes about his lack of life. In 1992, Nick is Petrified by the basilisk, along with Hufflepuff student Justin Finch-Fletchley, who is spared the serpent's direct gaze by seeing it through Nick. Nick receives the full blast but can't die again, so his usually white transparent figure turns black and smoky, and he floats horizontally. He has to be wafted to the hospital wing with a fan and is revived by mandrake draught in the spring.

The friendly ghost is accustomed to being approached by students who have suffered a loss to ask about how people assume a spectral form. He admits to Harry that he became a ghost because he was afraid of death; sometimes he doubts whether it was the right decision.

MOANING MYRTLE

Myrtle Elizabeth Warren was a Muggle-born Ravenclaw student who attended Hogwarts in the early 1940s. She was killed in June 1943 when she made direct eye contact with the basilisk Tom Riddle released from the Chamber of Secrets. She had been crying in the second-floor girls' bathroom after another student, Olive Hornby, made fun of her glasses when she heard a boy's voice and emerged to tell him off, only to die after seeing a pair of large yellow eyes.

Moaning Myrtle, whom the author initially called Wailing Wanda, is a squat ghost with a sad face partially covered by limp hair and thick glasses. After becoming a ghost, Myrtle followed and tormented her school bully until Olive reported her to the Ministry of Magic, which sent Myrtle back to Hogwarts. Myrtle primarily lurks in the toilet where she died and tends to flood it when she gets upset, so most students avoid it. She can visit other parts of the castle and has been known to turn up in other lavatories, including boys' bathrooms. Forever a teenage girl, Myrtle maintains the hallmarks of adolescence, such as sensitivity and flirtatiousness. She has a soft spot for Harry and for Draco Malfoy in his sixth year, when he confides in her about the stress he is under. She spies on boys in the prefects' bathroom but only emerges to speak to Harry and help him figure out the mystery of the golden egg after seeing Cedric Diggory do so. Through the pipes, she can access the lake (sometimes accidentally if someone flushes the toilet), where Harry encounters her during the second task of the Triwizard Tournament. When Harry's son Albus attends Hogwarts, Myrtle points Albus and Draco's son, Scorpius, to a sink that empties into the lake where they can travel back in time to the second task.

Peeves

Adestructive and mischievous poltergeist, Peeves has existed since the beginning of Hogwarts. Due to the castle's high density of magical adolescents, Peeves is stronger than the average poltergeist and appears in a material form. One of his greatest joys is tormenting the resident Hogwarts caretaker, from the original Hankerton Humble all the way to Argus Filch.

For centuries, Hogwarts headmasters have attempted to get rid of Peeves without success. Rancorous Carpe, the caretaker in 1876, led the most recent attempt: He built a multi-step trap ending in an enchanted bell jar, which Peeves easily destroyed. Enraged, the poltergeist managed to get his hands on several pieces of weaponry in the process, and the entire castle needed to be evacuated. Hogwarts headmistress Eupraxia Mole ended a three-day standoff by signing a contract that gave Peeves a new custom-made hat, stale bread to throw and a weekly swim in the first-floor boys' bathroom. Since that time, no serious attempts to expel Peeves from the castle have been made (although Argus Filch continues to hope).

Peeves's chief motivation is to create chaos, which sometimes means helping professors. He'll tell on students who are out of bed at night, provide information about escaped convict Sirius Black or warn the castle about a basilisk attack. Other times, he will side with students—messing with Filch so that students can get away or dropping a Vanishing Cabinet above Filch's office to distract him from attempting punishment.

Among his vast repertoire of destructive activities, Peeves has been known to throw walking sticks at people, drop trash bins on their heads, pull rugs from underneath their feet, throw chalk at them, grab their noses from behind, write rude words on the chalkboard, play tennis against the wall, tease Moaning Myrtle, stuff keyholes with chewing gum, wake people up by blowing in their ears, drop water bombs on them, create chaos in the kitchens, overturn a vase on a passerby, throw chairs at people, drop a bust of Paracelsus on them, blow ink pellets, attempt to strangle people with tinsel, upend tables, shut Mrs. Norris in suits of armor, smash lanterns, juggle torches, throw parchment in the fire or out windows, pull all the taps off the bathroom sinks, drop tarantulas in the Great Hall, blow raspberries when people speak, drop a chandelier, spread rumors about students and refuse to let people pass through a door unless they set fire to their pants.

Peeves also amuses himself by writing song lyrics to which he sometimes choreographs dance routines, using these musical talents to get on Harry's nerves or spread rumors about him. The poltergeist loves climbing into enchanted suits of armor; at Christmastime, he fills in their Christmas carols with his own rude lyrics.

Despite Peeves's destructive nature, he is occasionally useful for protecting the school from unwanted intruders. During Umbridge's reign as headmistress, Fred and George recruit Peeves's help in making her life difficult. He takes this task seriously and throws the castle into more chaos than usual, occasionally with the help of Hogwarts teachers. Umbridge claims to Filch that she is going to rid the castle of Peeves, but—luckily for her—she does not attempt it.

During the Battle of Hogwarts, Professor McGonagall calls upon Peeves to create chaos for the Death Eaters, which he does by dropping Snargaluff pods on their heads. This suggests Peeves has a small amount of loyalty, either toward the castle or toward certain students and professors. Peeves shows a certain level of respect toward the teachers and Dumbledore in that he will not disrupt their lessons or offices. He is deeply frightened of the Bloody Baron, who is the only one who can exert any amount of control over him. The ghosts are forced to form a council in 1994 to decide on how to deal with Peeves's desire to attend the start-of-term feast. The Fat Friar urges forgiveness, but the Bloody Baron refuses Peeves's request, much to the relief of everyone in attendance.

About the Authors

MuggleNet.com, the #1 Wizarding World Resource Since 1999, is dedicated to honoring the magic of the wizarding world by providing reliable, fun, informative content to our readers. The site is run by wizarding world afficionados who are passionate about making MuggleNet the best it can be. We take pride in our diverse group of 100+ global volunteers, ranging in age from 19 to 52.

A special acknowledgement to Felicia Grady and Kat Miller, directors of *MuggleNet.com*, for providing support, insight and feedback, as well as for planning and coordinating this project with the publisher and the incredible MuggleNet staff.

LAURIE BECKOFF is a Gryffindor, Campaign Coordinator at MuggleNet, and producer of its academic podcast, *Potterversity*. She received her bachelor's in English from the University of Chicago and master's in Medieval Literatures and Cultures from the University of Edinburgh, focusing on medievalism in *Harry Potter*.

JENNIFER CREEVY is a proud Hufflepuff from near London, U.K. She co-manages the MuggleNet Content Team and loves little more than metaphorically wandering the corridors of Hogwarts with a cup of tea in her hand.

LUCY DEMUTH is a Gryffindor and a Creative Media Manager at MuggleNet who was introduced to *Harry Potter* by her mum when she was 8. The films inspired her to pursue a career in the film and television industry, where she has received a bachelor's in Screen Production from Swinburne University of Technology in Melbourne.

SOPHIA JENKINS is a Hufflepuff and the Contributions Editor at MuggleNet. Like Luna Lovegood, she believes in the power of a strong imagination, which inspires both her MuggleNet editorials and her personal fantasy writing.

MARISSA OSMAN is a Ravenclaw who has been with MuggleNet since 2017. In her Muggle life, she is an author as well as an academic who researches literature, culture and pedagogy, representing both the intellectual and creative values of her House.

Media Lab Books
For inquiries, call 646-449-8614

Copyright 2022 Topix Media Lab

Published by Topix Media Lab
14 Wall Street, Suite 3C
New York, NY 10005

Printed in China

ISBN-13: 978-1-948174-95-4
ISBN-10: 1-948174-95-2

1C-C22-1